The Bloodline

The Ancient Ones Chronicles

Barbara Hinesley

The Bloodline

This book is a work of fiction. Any references to any events or real people are used fictitiously. Other names, characters and incidents are the product of the author's imagination, and any resemblance to actual events or persons, living or dead, is entirely coincidental.

Dedications

Dedicated to Tamara and Luanne who always believed in me even when I didn't believe in myself.   Thank you so much.

Tamara, you have inspired me on this journey and I hope you know how much I appreciate and love you for it.

Luanne you are the best beta-reader and friend. I could not ask for more. Thank you for all you have done for me and for being my kindred spirit. I love you.

"Never, I repeat, never fall in love with a human. In the end, it never works out the way you want it to. Trust me on that one." She spoke with conviction and certainty. So much so I almost couldn't question her about it. Almost.

Chapter 1

"Well, this is a fine mess you've gotten yourself into, Alyssa," I say as I wake in that dark, dank, moss-infested dungeon.

Thinking back, I try to contemplate how exactly I got myself in this predicament to begin with. I mean, I was always getting myself into trouble, into situations, but none in which I couldn't get myself out of. This one, on the other hand, could be different.

Katarina had warned me of other vampires, but she put particular emphasis on warnings about one named Dante Ortello. She warned he is a vampire who is strong and fierce. One who doesn't believe in the mixing of the races; human and vampires. Dante doesn't believe in allowing humans to know of our kind's existence. If he believes you have crossed the line, he becomes the hunter, and, in the end, the judge, jury, and executioner.

"Do not cross him, Alyssa." Katarina always cautioned me, but I never really put much stock in her warnings about him or the others as seriously as I am at this moment.

There was one problem, though. Katarina always warned me to be weary of Dante, but it wasn't Dante I needed to be worried about. It was the ones he answers to that I should have been warned of. It's The Ancient Ones that hold me here in this dungeon now. I was never told of their existence, and now, now it's too late.

"Why? Why didn't Kat tell me about them? Why?" I scream aloud as I bash my fist against one of the stone walls that traps me here. Little pea-sized gravel debris falls all around my feet as I slide down pulling myself into a ball in my arms. "But I didn't listen to her, did I? No, and now I'm stuck in this situation, and I can't see any way out of it or here. Good job, Alyssa. Good job." I sob.

I try to remember it all. Try to remember every little detail since the night my life changed, hoping it'll help me find the reason why this has happened to me. I know I haven't followed all the rules. Okay, I've broken most of them, but that can't be a good enough reason for me to deserve this, could it? No. I mean, it can't be. They're stupid rules to begin with. Idiotic things like don't fall in love with a human, don't make any human friends, and, basically, stay away from all humans period. They're ridiculous. No one could really fault me for breaking those, could they? Well, it appears someone has. What the hell have I done? A frustrated, guttural scream escapes me once more. *Think, Alyssa. Think. What did you do so horrible to land you here?*

A very short time I've had in this new life of mine. Not so long ago Katarina found me in that alleyway and saved my life. Or taken it, depending on how you look at it. I resented her for it then, but looking back now, I see I had a pretty damn good life. Well, truth be known, two pretty good lives. Too bad I took it all for granted. As I sort through it all, I allow my memories to take me away from this wretched, odor-filled room, even if only for a little while.

It was two days before my twenty-first birthday, and David and I made plans to go out for pizza. Things had become strained between the two of us, and the alone time was supposed to be a nice distraction from finals and all the craziness going on around school. It was supposed to be a turnaround point for us. It was anything but.

The warm night breeze whipped around us sending my hair into a swirling mess of little whips stinging my eyes with each and every blow. My soft cotton, yellow sundress, and Estee Lauder perfume used to be David's favorites, but that night he didn't seem to notice either of them.

With the worried knot in my stomach growing, I hadn't even noticed we walked right past our favorite pizza place and, instead, entered a more formal, upscale restaurant a few blocks away. I knew David. We have pictures of us in diapers together and had officially been together since we were sixteen. This was not going to be good.

Before being seated, David interlocked our hands and softly kissed my forehead. "We need to talk," he said as the waitress handed us menus.

"Okay. About what?" I asked hesitantly. Truth be told, I didn't want to hear the answer.

"After we eat. It's nothing really," he said, keeping his eyes diverted and head down pretending to look over the menu. He was stalling, and I hated it. Stalling from David wasn't good. Stalling from any man equals not good, but David abhorred wasting his precious time. He always has.

After ordering and finishing off the appetizers in complete and utter silence, he finally spoke up. "Alyssa, I think we should see other people." Barely taking a bite of my meal, I was impaled with that one sentence.

"You're dumping me?" I could barely choke out the question.

"It's not working anymore. I'm sorry. It's not you, it's me." Was he kidding me right now? This was his "nothing" we had to talk about? What was he thinking? How could he do this to me?

"We've been together almost five years and you're giving me the 'it's not you it's me' line? You are unbelievable, David. Un-freaking-believable."

"Please, Alyssa. Keep your voice down. You're causing a scene." His quick glances around revealed his true intentions on bringing me here.

"You thought by bringing me here I wouldn't cause a scene? Wow, David. You really don't know me at all, do you?" I had to shake my head at the thought. What a douche.

"Please, calm down. This isn't working anymore. We're not working anymore. Can't you just accept that? We're going off to different colleges anyway. Don't make a big deal about this." The stupid look of disbelief on his face made me want to smack it right off of him. I couldn't take it. I had to get out of there. With a shake of my head, I pushed back from the table, threw my napkin down, and stormed out.

He's damn right it's him and not me. He would regret this. He always did. He'll come crawling back just like he did all the other time she broke up with me except this time I won't take him back. Forcing the tears back and wanting to just get back to the sanctity of my room, I decided to take a shortcut. That turned out to be my fatal mistake.

My fuming thoughts were soon replaced by the sound of another pair of footsteps hitting the hard, gritty pavement behind me.

"Who's there?" I asked meekly, glancing around the darkness that surrounded me. God, I sounded like one of those idiot bimbos in a cheesy horror flick expecting the killer to say, 'Here I am. Over here.'

But what did I hear? Just like the bimbos, I heard nothing, and I saw no one. The footsteps had stopped, and I found myself questioning if they were ever really there in the first place. Wrapping myself in my arms, I continued on with more haste. With nothing but blackness to guide me, I took a wrong turn and found myself even more lost than I was before. The sound of foreign footsteps behind me returned and gained momentum. This time I didn't hesitate, I took off into a full blown sprint skidding into yet another darkened alleyway. The rusted dumpsters halfway down made for a great hiding place, or so I thought. The beating of my heart drummed so loud in my ears it drowned out all the other sounds. It pounded so hard and fast I felt it would explode in my chest from the sheer terror that enveloped me. After a minute or so I was able to slow my breathing only to find there were no footsteps to be heard, again. There was absolutely nothing but myself feeling utterly ridiculous.

"Wow, Alyssa. Paranoid much?" I asked aloud.

A few quick swipes and I was dusted off and bending down to pick up my purse when a hard, cold blow to the back of my head left me paralyzed. Crumbling to the ground in a heap, my vision blurred, and my body was useless. I couldn't move.

In a breathy whisper, my assailant said, "You and me, we're going to have some fun tonight, baby. Mmm. You smell good. I could just eat you up."

One violent heave and I was flipped on my back with the weight of his body crushing my own. It felt like an elephant was sitting on my chest. My breath labored and my heart pounded. His slimy tongue slithered up my neck and encircled my cheek causing my skin to crawl. His rotten, putrid breath cut off my air supply as his grimy hand wrapped around my neck attempting to choke the life out of me. With his jagged nails digging deep into my flesh, his knee plowed against my thighs forcing my legs apart. The sound of his zipper unzipping threw my mind into a tailspin. With one rip my panties were gone and my mind was thrown into full blown panic mode.

Holding back the vomit that rose in my throat, self-preservation kicked in. Using all the force I could muster up, I shoved violently against his flabby chest and added a hard, perfectly aimed kick right between his legs. It was a quick scramble to get back on my feet, but, before I could, a callous-ridden hand clamped down hard on my ankle, yanking me back and scraping me across the rocks and glass that filled the alleyway. My cry of pain delighted him and my tears amused him as he ripped and tore at my once beautiful dress. I couldn't believe this was happening to me. Why? This can't happen to me. My screams for help echoed off the buildings, and I said a prayer in my head that someone would come and save me. One more hard hit to the face, and I was finished. Darkness.

The insurmountable amount of pain radiating from the back of my head eventually woke me. Reaching back, I touched it gingerly finding my hair soaked and a quick glance at my hand revealed the culprit to be my own warm, wet, sticky blood. Deep down I knew in my heart I wouldn't make it out of that alleyway alive, but I refused to give in, to succumb so easily at the hands of that monster. I wanted that lowlife to pay for what he had done to me, and I wanted to be the one who made him.

Slowly, I scraped and clawed my way out of the darkness toward the main street, my legs dragging futilely behind me. Rocks and glass impaled my already tender, bruised flesh. At that point in time, I didn't care. I just wanted to reach somebody, anybody, who could help me. I hadn't made it more than thirty feet when my body refused to go any further relinquishing to the pain. After countless attempts, I finally managed to roll myself over onto my back so I could focus on the millions of beautiful, twinkling stars in the dark, midnight sky counting each individual one to stay conscious, to stay alive. I couldn't give in. I couldn't give up and let that monster win. I had to fight. I had to live. I had to make him pay.

Before my thoughts could go any further, a beautiful angel appeared over top of me. Oh, God. I was right. I wasn't going to make it. I was dying, or was I already dead?

Her soft beautiful voice broke through the quiet of the night, "I'm here to help you. Please believe that. I'll make the pain stop. Forgive me for what I'm about to do to you, but it must be done. It's imperative you understand that if I do not do this, you will not make it. You will die here tonight by the hands of that evil man who left you in this death hole to rot. Do you understand?"

A bloody, pain-ridden smile slid across my lips welcoming any help she could provide me. At that point, I didn't care what she did. Save me. Kill me. I just wanted the pain to stop. My beautiful angel bent down to my neck and a searing pain began to burn first in my neck then throughout my entire body. The scorching pain was so agonizing I couldn't focus on much of anything except this beautiful woman was no angel but perhaps a demon or even Satan himself. She was not my savior. She was not making the pain stop. She was making it worse. Before everything went black again, the "angel" placed her finger upon my lips to hush my pain-filled screams.

Whispering in my ear she said, "This pain is only temporary. I know right now you don't understand what has happened, but in time it will all make sense. I'll help you make sense of it all and figure out everything you need to know." Removing her finger from my lips, a sympathetic smile graced her beautiful face. A face I now wanted to claw off, and I would have if I had the strength to do so.

A veil of darkness slowly crept over me overtaking all of my senses one by one before completely incapacitating me. That is when Alyssa Nicole Saunders died.

Chapter 2

My death that night in that alley was nearly three years ago, and I still reach back and feel the spot on my head thinking about it. The pain of losing my human life still haunts and affects me in ways even I'm unaware of. The loss of that life drove me most of this new life and not always in a good way. Hanging on to that pain caused many of my heartaches and a lot of the troubles I found myself in this go round. I'm not trying to make excuses. I'm simply stating facts.

Waking up in that cramped, dreary metal box was my worst nightmare coming true. All I could do was panic. I'm extremely claustrophobic and hate small confined spaces. I couldn't breathe. All I could think about was finding a way out. Any way out. My small hands pounded and clawed frantically at the metal encasing me to no avail. Silver metal shavings fell all around me as my fingernails broke and split in my desperate attempt to free myself.

A soft, familiar voice caught my attention freezing me like a deer in headlights sending chills down my spine. Angelic and sweet sounding yet I knew it was dripping with betrayal as she proved earlier. It was the voice of the stranger from the alleyway.

"Come, Alyssa. It's time to get out now."

With full-blown panic controlling me, I couldn't focus. All I could do was scream, cry, and beg for her help. I didn't care who it was, I needed help. I needed out of the box that had me trapped like a rat in a cage.

"I'll help you this time, but you must learn that all you have to depend on in this world is yourself. That is your first lesson from me. If you can learn that now, you will save yourself a lot of heartache later. Now, let's get you out of there."

Something clicked, like a metal door handle being unlatched and lifted. Finally, after what seemed to be forever, I was able to free myself from that cold metal vault of a prison. Terror gripped me as I actually saw where I was and what I had climbed out of only moments ago. I was in a morgue and had been trapped in one of the drawers.

Why?

Why was I trapped in what they use to hold dead bodies in, and, more importantly, why was I in a morgue at all? I wasn't dead. This was obviously some sort of a mistake. *If I didn't need therapy before, I would definitely need it now*, I thought to myself.

"This isn't right. This cannot be real. It has to be a joke, right? I'm not dead. Why am I here? I'm not dead. I'm …"

Cut off mid-sentence by the stranger, she said, "I'll try my best to help it all make sense to you, Alyssa." Her voice was calm and tranquil.

"You're the woman from the alley, aren't you? I remember you. Who are you?" I asked, accusingly pointing my finger at her.

"Yes, I am, Alyssa," she stated with an ease to her voice, as if she was trying to relax me with her tone.

"Who are you? Satan? Or, let me guess, you're going to try to tell me that you're an angel sent here from God to help me? How are you going to help me when you're the one who did this to me? Whatever … this may be? You. And now you are going to stand there and try to pretend like you want to help me? Get away from me!" I screamed, trying to push past her.

Except … she didn't budge. My violent shove didn't move her even one inch. She simply smiled a gentle smile and said, "Your strength will come in time, Alyssa. To answer your question, no, I am not Satan, nor did God send me here. My name is Katarina, and I'm trying to help you. You were going to die, Alyssa, do you understand that? I couldn't let that happen to you. Not to you. I truly am sorry if you are confused and upset, but I really am here to help you. If you will let me, that is."

Her eyes held the disappointment and hurt she felt by my anger toward her, but I knew no other way to be. What exactly did she do to save me, and, a better question was, why was I in a morgue?

The fear and hostility inside me was mounting, and, before I knew it, all the anger boiled over. "Oh really, and why is that? You don't even know me." Again I tried to shove past her, except this time there was a different result.

This time I succeeded. I pushed her across the room until she crashed against the steel doors that lined the far wall. It didn't matter. She was back in front of me within a blink of an eye. Shock overtook me. Not only due to the fact of her being right back in my face so quickly but at the sheer strength I had to force her to fly halfway across the room.

She smiled at me again seemingly completely unimpressed with what had just transpired and said, "No, I don't know you per se, but you remind me of someone I knew a long, long time ago. She was very special and dear to me. So far, you even seem to be a spoiled, little brat like she was, as well." She chuckled.

"And how are you going to help me?" I questioned brazenly, yet still trying to compose myself inside.

"I'll teach you everything you need to know as to survive in our world. "What does that even mean? Survive in *our* world. *What the heck has this chick gotten me into,* I wondered.

That's when I looked at Katarina, really looked at her. She had gorgeous blonde, flowing hair with the slightest bit of wave to it that under the dim light appeared to glow like a halo surrounding her head. She looked like an angel. Her porcelain complexion was flawless. Her eyes were the color of espresso, very warm and inviting. Katarina was gorgeous, perfect, and in fact, flawless. The sound of her voice reassured me everything would be okay and slowly calmed me. The more she talked the more comforted and at ease I was.

Katarina explained what happened just before she stepped in that fateful night. I wasn't ready for it, but she continued anyway. So obviously she felt I was. "I was watching when that man attacked you in the darkened alleyway. I watched him hit you in the head with a lead pipe. It was planned, orchestrated even. All he needed was an innocent victim, and you were that victim. Even after watching all of that, I still wasn't going to interfere. I shook my head and turned away. It wasn't a new sight. I'd seen similar situations play out many, many times over the years. But then, as the man rolled you over and began ripping off your dress, something made me look down at your face. That is something I never do, Alyssa," Katarina explained. "However, this time something was different. I felt compelled to look as if some unseen force was pulling my attention down onto your face. When I saw you," Katarina said, "I was in awe. I could not believe what I was seeing. That face, that face that reminded me so much of a sister I lost so long ago. It wasn't something that could be ignored. I felt a compulsion to step in. A compulsion to intercede and intercede I did. The man is now dead and will never be found. You don't have to worry about him harming you or anyone else, for that matter, ever again."

"I want my mom and dad. I want to see them right now. I have to let them know everything's fine. I have to tell them I'm all right. Tell them I'm not dead." I knew they'd probably be worried sick and wondering where I was. I hated them always worrying about me as a child, but, at that moment, all I wanted to do was crawl into my mom's arms like a big, old baby and cry.

"I'm sorry, Alyssa, but you can't see them." That was the only response Katarina gave to me. I waited for more of an explanation but received none.

"And why not?" I glared at her, demanding to know. Who was she to tell me I couldn't see my parents'. Who the heck does she think she is? She's a nobody to me. Nothing. *What would make her possibly think I would actually listen to her,* I thought to myself.

"Because you're dead, for all intents and purposes anyway. Well, at least they all believe you're dead. You woke up in a morgue. That has to tell you something. Your family has already identified your body. They already made plans to have you cremated as, apparently, you told them you wanted. In fact, they'll be receiving your ashes in the morning. How would you explain this to them?"

"I don't know … I would … I …" I started to say before being cut off.

"Really, Alyssa? Really? How about this: hey Mom and Dad, guess what … I'm not dead. I am now, in fact, the undead. I'm a vampire. How well do you think that would go over, Alyssa?" The question flowed from her lips so breezily it was as if she had just asked me my favorite color.

"I'm a what?" Disbelief took over. I could not have just heard what I thought I heard. Right? Did she really just say vampire? She's insane.

"A vampire," Kat responded flatly. Her tone annoyed, as if my disbelief was anything but reasonable.

"That's impossible. Vampires don't exist. Not really. It's a made up story. Fiction," I stated matter-of-factly, completely flabbergasted. This woman was crazy. She honestly believed she's a vampire and has made me into one, as well? One word: nuts.

Instinctively, my eyes dart down to see if they had cut me open yet. Even though I didn't believe a word coming out of her mouth, to me, it was still a rational action. I was in a morgue, after all, as she so eloquently pointed out.

"Wait. Did you say they're going to receive my ashes tomorrow?" What game was this woman playing at? Whatever it was, it was sick and demented, and I wanted no part in it. First vampires, now my ashes. Crazy doesn't even begin to describe her or this messed up situation.

"Yes, your ashes. Well, they'll believe they're your ashes. It took a lot of persuasion on my part, but the medical examiner believes he did your autopsy and sent you on your way to the funeral home. The mortician believes he cremated you, and tomorrow he will hand deliver ashes to your parents informing them they are your remains."

"Why would he do that? They aren't me, so why say they are?" Shocked, my mind was unable wrap around the context of what she was saying.

"He's doing it because I told him to. As I said earlier, it took a lot of persuasion on my part for them to do this. The easiest way for me to explain it is, I tricked their minds to believe what I wanted them to believe. I tricked the medical examiner's mind to believe he did the autopsy on you, and I tricked the mortician's mind to believe those ashes he is distributing to your parents' are your remains. It was that or you would've been cut opened and autopsied. Draining you of all your blood would have killed you completely. There would be no coming back as you did after your attack. This was the only way I knew to save you. Now your parents' can have closure, and I can have peace knowing they'll never come looking for you." She acted as though none of this was a big deal, but it was. It was a huge deal.

"Why wouldn't I want them to come looking for me?" I asked defiantly.

"Well, that brings us to the second thing you need to know. The first was learning you only have yourself to depend on in this world. The second thing you need to know is that your family, your friends, none of them can know you're alive. And they definitely can't know what you are. Humans can't know we really exist, Alyssa. It would ruin all they believe in, and ultimately, ruin them and us. There is a delicate balance between our worlds right now. If that balance is upset or disturbed in the slightest, it would have devastating consequences for us all. It would become one big witch hunt, again. Except this time, it would be a hunt for vampires. If that happened, I would hate to think what some vampires would do to the humans. It would put us all in danger. Humans especially. You need to understand the gravity of this. Do you understand what I'm saying?" she said, boring her eyes into my own.

"Yeah. Fine. I get it. I'm alive, but I'm not. I can't have contact with anyone I know or love. Great." What was the point of still being alive if I couldn't be with the ones I love? No. I didn't understand what she was saying. Not even a little bit. I had the attitude of a two-year-old that didn't get her way, but I didn't care. I wanted my mommy.

"No, Alyssa, I don't believe you truly understand. There are rules, and if you don't follow these rules not only does it place you in danger but everyone you love and care about, as well. Your family, your friends—and even though you may not like me—it places me in danger also. As the one who turned you, I am responsible for you and ultimately all you do. I'm responsible for all your actions and the results of those actions. There are things in this world, in the vampire world, you know nothing about. Since I'm the one responsible for you, it's my job, my duty, to teach you. I'll do everything I can to help you. To keep you safe, but you have to let me. I'm very sorry, but everyone, everything, you knew and loved is now gone, much like your past life. This," Katarina waved her delicate hand around displaying the darkness, "is your new life."

All I could see, all I could smell, was death. Is that what my world consisted of now? Only death?

"You must learn the rules in order to survive. You have to accept it because there really is no other way for you now. This was the only choice I had to offer you. If I had not done this to you, for you, you would be dead right now. Would you've have preferred that? Would you have preferred death?" Her questioning eyes roamed over my entirety searching for my answer.

Is that not what this world consisted of already? I mean, I am in a morgue. I can't have any contact with my family. Do I have to slink around in the shadows, too? Maybe death would have been better. "Yes ... No ... I don't know, but I didn't get a choice though, did I?" My words barbed at the end. "I would have at least liked an opportunity to have a choice in the matter. It was my life. It should have been my choice. I should have had the right to decide if I wanted to die or live like this. Whatever this may be!" I shouted.

"I understand you're angry, and you have every right to be, but it's far too late for all of that now. You have to come with me and come with me right now. A guard is coming. He must've heard all the commotion. We don't have a lot of time, Alyssa."

Lost and confused, I could hear the footsteps clacking against the tile floor. The reality of the situation was I really saw no other choice but to follow behind this stranger as she slipped out of the morgue undetected and into the shadows of the night.

Chapter 3

Katarina's house was stunning, elegant in fact. Driving up the cobblestone drive sent my heart racing. The house was a warm glow amidst the darkened desert sky. Her face lit up as she ascended the limestone steps to welcome me into her home through the beautiful beveled glass French doors. Greeted by marble flooring and pillars, my attention was solely on the gold and crystal chandelier hanging from the ceiling in the foyer. The clanking sound of metal against glass jerked my attention toward where Katarina had thrown her keys. On top of the glossy cherry wood table sat a delicate brilliant cut glass pedestal bowl with pink and gold flashed edges now stuffed with her keys.

"You must be starving. Come this way."

I shadowed her steps but stopped to admire the dramatically decorated living room. Gold and plum colored curtains drew my attention up to the twenty-feet high ceilings lined with detailed crown molding. The stone fireplace looked warm and inviting as the fire roared peacefully unattended. Red and yellow flames flickered sending a warm glow cascading through the museum-like room. This was the sort of house most could only dream about and now, it seems, was my reality.

Realizing I lost her, I followed the sounds of clinking glass into the kitchen. I walked in just in time to catch her pouring a dark red liquid into two wine glasses. Pulling back one of the black leather bar stools out from the granite topped island caused a high-pitched screeching sound as the metal slid across the shiny polished floors.

"Sorry," I winced. The whining pulsated through my ears, and I shook my head like a dog trying to stop the ringing.

Stifling a laugh, Katarina slid one of the glasses toward me.

"What's this?" I scrunched up my nose at the sight of it as it sloshed against the sides of the glass. Watching the liquid run back down leaving a filmy residue behind did not make it appear any more appetizing to me.

When Katarina pushed it closer, the smell caught in my nostrils, and I snatched it to me without hesitation. That was my first taste of blood. The red goodness spilled down my throat, and I was happily surprised at how sweet and filling it was. When she offered the second glass, I seized it out of her grip. Embarrassment from my behavior and manners wasn't enough to keep me from drinking.

"It'll start to slow down."

Finishing off the glass, I wiped my mouth with the back of my hand and asked, "What will slow down?"

Scanning the room hoping for more of the delicious red goodness, Katarina caught my wondering eye and chuckled. "Your thirst, Alyssa. It will slow down. You won't have to eat as much or as often." She refilled my glass while still keeping her eyes on me.

I watched as she poured it out of a red wine box in the refrigerator, but it definitely wasn't wine I was drinking. It's a good idea, I suppose. You wouldn't have to try and explain what it was when you had company over. Little did I know at the time, Katarina never had people over. Ever.

"Right now you are at your weakest, Alyssa. Your most vulnerable. In time you will gain control and strength." Katarina tucked the box back into the refrigerator.

"My most vulnerable?" I was completely lost.

"Yes. Right now you're weak. You don't know how to properly use all you have been given yet, and some strengths will come to you later on. Your body is still changing. Speaking of, you look exhausted. You should rest. Come, I'll show you to your room."

Walking up the suspended staircase behind Katarina gave me a whole new view of the house. This was nothing like the house I grew up in, which was clear on the other side of town. My house was a small, red, stucco one level with three tiny bedrooms. This was the kind of house my mother could only dream of owning one day.

The double doors where she stopped swung open and a slow gasp slipped out of my mouth.

"I'm glad you like it."

"Like it? I love it. How could I not? It's beautiful. It's perfect."

Spinning around taking in every inch of the spectacular bedroom, I had a grin plastered on my face so wide my cheeks hurt.

The king-sized white poster bed had gold inlay flowers going all the way up all four posts. Like a child, I ran and jumped on the bed kicking and flailing my arms and legs giggling with delight. It wasn't until I caught a glimpse of myself in the oval shaped mirror that I noticed Katarina was no longer there. I looked to her for answers on what I was seeing, but all that could be found was a closed door.

Cautiously creeping toward the mirror, I was unsure of who the woman staring back at me was. It couldn't be me. It had to be a trick. The woman in the mirror was beautiful, perfect. I was awkward, nerdy even. The icy blue eyes that reflected back had a touch of me in them somewhere, but those eyes were intense, piercing, and soulless. Slowly touching my hands to my face, I watched as the woman in the mirror's actions mimicked my own. She was me. I was the beautiful woman looking back at me. Breath quickening, I couldn't help but stare. I reached out and touched the mirror in amazement as I smiled at my new appearance and nodded in approval.

Many of the vampire lore's humans are told aren't true. The first one I found to be a complete fallacy was about vampires not having reflections. Guess what. We have one.

It was hard to fall asleep that night. The impossible sounding things Katarina told me I would be able to do and my new look all swirled around in my head. On top of all that, my newly heightened senses were on full alert. I could hear a raccoon digging through a trashcan out back, an owl searching for prey in the distance, and a mouse scurrying by trying to go undetected from the owl. But it was the smell of the freshly bloomed Black-Eyed Susan's that eased my tensions and the red maple tree swaying in the light, airy breeze outside my window that finally lulled me to sleep.

Our first morning together was strangely normal. I traipsed downstairs with my hair pulled back and still in the bathrobe I found in the bathroom off of my bedroom. Katarina was in a pink silk kimono robe sitting at the island swirling the red drink in her ceramic coffee mug when I came strolling in.

"Good morning, Alyssa. I hope you slept well." She was perky. Too perky.

How could anyone be so pleasant that early in the morning and look that perfect, too? I shook my head in agreement, yawning. I was drained despite the best sleep I'd had in years.

As if she could read my mind, she said, "Your body is still recuperating and adjusting to the change. You will even out." Katarina slid a mug toward me as she stood up.

Once again I was astonished by how quick my reflexes were. I caught the mug and pulled it up to my lips without batting an eye.

Sauntering over to the windows, Katarina yanked the cord forcing the blinds open in one fluid motion. My eyes grew wide with fear. What was she thinking? Everyone knows vampires die in the sunlight. I was waiting for my body to burst into flames when …

when …

nothing.

Absolutely nothing, except now a splitting headache was pounding in my head. I pinched the bridge of my nose with one hand while rubbing my temple with the other. Neither helped.

"I'm sorry. I know it hurts, but, in time, you'll build up a tolerance to it." I tried to focus on the words coming out of her mouth, but the pain was too horrendous. It was a migraine at the worst level.

"I thought vampires died in the sunlight?" I barely managed to stammer out.

"Not us. Not the new ones, anyway. The first ones, yes. I guess. All the stories have some form of the truth to them, I suppose. The newer vampires, like us, have adapted. We've evolved as to ensure our survival. That's also why our hearts beat and why we breathe. Give it time. It will get better." After closing the curtains, she sat back down on the leather stool next to me. "Today you should feed and get some rest. Tomorrow we will get started on the lessons of our kind you must learn."

I didn't argue. I didn't even protest. I didn't have the mindset to ask any questions. I needed a quiet, dark room. The pain was getting worse, and I prayed that if I slept it would just go away. I grabbed the mug and went back to my room. Pulling all the drapes shut, I laid down and pulled the down-filled pillow over my head to block out the remaining light seeping in from the small slit between the drapes.

My dreams brought no peace to me that night. I was surrounded by darkness. Pictures of my family appeared around me everywhere as if they were framed on a wall. Just as quickly as they appeared, they vanished. A long, thin, white line materialized, and I was straddling it. On the right side were my mother, father and someone I couldn't quite make out. His face was a blur, and, all in all, he himself was hazy. There were others behind them, but this man was standing right beside my family. He was important. I could feel it. On my left side were Katarina and another man. Like the other, this one was blurry and hazy, as well. He too was important; I just couldn't figure out why. Others were behind them, and I could tell they were making a stand. A stand against my parents, against my family. There shouldn't have been a choice to make but there was, and I couldn't seem to make it.

Jolting up, my heart pounded as I gulped for air. Walking over to the window, I peered through the little open slit in the curtains. Seeing it was safe, I flung them open and allowed the full moon to light my room. The clock by the bed was glowing three a.m. I laid back down trying to force myself back to sleep but, after an hour of tossing and turning, I gave up and went downstairs. After pouring myself a glass of the red goodness, I waited as the hours slowly trickled by.

Eight a.m. came and so did Katarina. After all the pleasant formalities of the morning were out of the way, it was time to get to work learning how to live and survive in this new world that had been thrust upon me. I needed something to take my mind off the dream that kept me up all night, so I welcomed the distraction.

The training she subjected me to was excruciating, and Katarina seemed to make sure of that. It was if she enjoyed my pain, enjoyed tormenting me and enjoyed seeing agony and defeat pouring out of me. She said it was necessary to prepare me for my new life. I didn't see how me getting thrown into a wall repeatedly would show me how to survive, but she was the boss.

Trying to teach me to fight was probably hilarious to her considering I had never been in a fight in my entire life. She explained while yes, I am stronger than any human I would ever encounter, there are other vampires out there and not all of them are our friends. I wouldn't have a problem over-powering any one of the humans I came into contact with; it was the other vampires I needed to worry about. Learning to maneuver and defend myself was a crucial aspect to my survival.

After all the physical training of the day came my lessons of our kind. Lessons on everything from the true history vampires, as she knew it to be, to the rules and, above all, on all she knew the infamous Dante Ortello. Katarina informed me he was considered one of the most feared vampires. He was one of the surly vampires she had spoken of before. Dante was a self-proclaimed Savior of our kind. To him, it was his job, his duty, to make sure the humans never learned of our existence. If he felt someone was stepping over the line, leaving a trail, or possibly allowing our kind to be discovered, he interceded. He would decide the vampire's fate and, in all instances she knew of, it had been death. She obviously had an issue with this Dante, and apparently he was not one to be taken lightly was the basic lesson I took on that subject. Other than that, I never really put much stock or thought into him or the warnings of him Katarina gave to me.

That same routine went on for months. During that time, I was able to learn more and more of Katarina, as well. She refused to interject or interfere in human matters of any kind. In fact, she made sure she distanced herself as far from the human world as possible. She had been in her new life for over a century now, and, according to her, every day that passed only reiterated the fact that she didn't want any more to do with the human world. Katarina devised a plan that went so far to the extreme of not coming into contact with humans that she refused to even feed on them. She chose blood banks or, in the worst-case scenario, animals to get the blood she needed to sustain herself.

She said, "Just because we aren't human anymore doesn't mean we have to behave inhumanely either. I don't interfere either way. It's neither my place nor position to do so." I saw it as a contradiction. If you see an act of cruelty inflicted onto another, I see it as inhumane not to interfere. Katarina didn't agree. "We are not supposed to be here. Well, at least I'm not supposed to be here, and we have no business interfering."

I understood what she was trying to say, but I couldn't help but think it was something more than that. There was something deeper that she refused to divulge, even to herself.

Katarina also refused to make friends or build relationships with anyone. "Why should we? You have to leave before anyone can find out who and what you really are. You can never truly let anyone in. There really is no point, Alyssa."

I often wondered how many broken hearts she had to go through until she discovered that fact. How many heartaches she had until finally, one day, she said to herself enough was enough.

"Never, I repeat, never fall in love with a human. In the end, it never works out the way you want it to. Trust me on that one." She spoke with conviction and certainty. So much so I almost couldn't question her about it. Almost.

"But what if you meet *the one*?" I asked. I probably sounded childish to her, but I didn't care. I wanted to know. I needed to know. I still believed in all the fairytale stories my mother read to me as a child. I still believed in love and happily-ever-after's.

She shook her head in dismay. "There is no such thing for our kind, Alyssa." Katarina's face fell flat and unemotional but a flicker in her eyes gave her away.

With a scoff, she said, "Have you learned nothing from me so far? We are not human and no one, no human, can ever know what we are. And as far as finding someone within our own kind, well, those never work out either. None of us ever stay in one place for too long, and, well, forever is a long time, Alyssa. To our kind, forever means just that … forever. There is no *the one*, Alyssa, that is a childish, whimsical fairytale that's fed to us as children. It does not exist. The sooner you learn that, the better off you will be."

Katarina was very adamant about that fact. There was more behind what she was saying, but it was lost on me. I wasn't quite sure what to make of it. I nodded my head but still held the belief in my heart that it could happen. Maybe, just maybe, there is still love for us, for the damned ones. There has to be, right? We cannot be so forsaken that we don't even deserve love. We are not all bad. Take Katarina for instance, her heart seems to be in the right place. Doesn't she deserve love? Don't I? But with that, I dropped the subject.

25

In almost every way I found I was the complete opposite of Katarina. I still very much wanted to be a part of the human world, whereas she couldn't stand it. I craved it, she despised. I needed some form of a connection, she longed for solitude. I felt as though I deserve it, she was determined to disappear into anonymity. My life was ripped away from me when I still had so much left to do, so much I wanted to do. I was still so young, in both regards for that matter, vibrant and, in my eyes, still so full of life. I felt as though I had every right to behave as any other almost twenty-one-year-old would, regardless of my situation.

That was what I called it, my situation. I couldn't help it. I wanted it all. I wanted the friends, the complicated messes that came along with having them and all the connections that Katarina detested and avoided at all costs. I still tried to behave as though I was human, as though nothing in my life had changed. I was trying to pretend as if it were all a bad dream, one big nightmare if you will. Katarina was sickened by my reprehensible attitude toward my new life.

I started sneaking out to check on my family, as well. At first, it was just to make sure they were okay. When I saw the devastation and pain on my parent's faces, I was beside myself with guilt. Had I not been so stupid that night and decided to take that shortcut, I never would have been in that situation. I never would have been at the mercy of that monster that tragic night. I would still be trying to fit in and figure out what I wanted to become in life. But no, I didn't do that. Fate had other plans for me. Fate led me right into the hands of that monstrous man, and now I was stuck watching my family from afar.

That one time became a weekly ritual, which, in turn, became a daily ritual. I would watch my parents drudge through their day in a fog almost. It was as if they died right along with me that horrible night. There was no life, no happiness in their eyes. Only sorrow and pain. No smile graced their faces. Empty shells of their former selves were all that was left of them, and it was all my fault.

It was amazing what my new eyes could see and catch. They could pick up the slightest quiver or flinch. My ears could hear the tiniest waiver in a voice. Too bad when you're not paying attention they catch nothing. Had I been paying attention I would've heard someone sneaking up on me. I would've been able to defend myself, but I wasn't. And now I'm stuck here reliving the past looking back and analyzing all of my indiscretions wondering exactly which one landed me in this dungeon.

Katarina knew I had been sneaking out behind her back and checking in on my family. I'm not exactly sure how she knew, but she knew. The only reasonable explanation I could come up with was I wasn't as smooth as I thought I was.

"This is a dangerous game you're playing at, Alyssa," Katarina whispered in my ear. I about jumped out of my skin when I heard her.

"I'm just looking," I snorted before turning my attention back to my dad kneeling beside the memorial he and my mother built for me under my favorite tree in our backyard.

"Come, we must go. We have to leave here, or you're going to get yourself caught, if not worse. Either way, it won't have a pleasant ending for us."

Katarina decided right then, at that moment, we needed to move. I'm not sure how long she had known what I was up to, but it was pretty apparent it was long enough to know I wouldn't, I couldn't stop. I would eventually get caught. Whether it be by my family or worse, another vampire. She wanted a new town, a new city, a new start for us. That was what she called it, a new start. I guess she felt if we moved it would help me adjust more to my new life. Move on, for lack of better terms. All the threat did, in the end, was make me long to hold onto my human life even more. She was going to rip me away from the only home I'd ever known. Rip me away from the last link I had with my family. The last link I had to my life, my real-life. The last link to my humanity.

Six months into my new life and all I wanted was to be me again. The one thing I was always trying to change before was the one thing I long to be again. That was impossible, though, according to Katarina. I was still unable to go out into the sunlight. Not because it hurt or burned me alive as all the legends said, but because it drained me. It made me weak, tired and gave me an immense headache. An extreme butt-kicking migraine is the best way to describe it. Katarina said in time it would come, and I would be able to go out in the daylight and be fine.

While Kat was busy putting plans together for where and when we would move, I continued to sneak out to watch my dad and mom every evening at sunset visiting my memorial or lack thereof I should say considering it wasn't even my ashes they spread there. It hurt knowing I was that close but couldn't reach out and touch them, hug them, comfort them. I wanted to tell them I was alive and okay. But, unless I wanted them to suffer a worse fate than I did, that pipe dream was just that. A dream.

Every once in a while I would even see David visiting it. Seeing him there, hunched over sobbing, I knew he really did love me. That hurt me the most. Had he realized that sooner, maybe none of this would've ever happened. But seeing him like that, crying, made all my anger toward him disappear. Deep down that was when I knew Katarina was right. If I didn't get away, I would do something that could possibly put us both in danger. I didn't want to admit it to her at the time, but I knew moving was the right thing to do. If we stayed, I wouldn't be able to control myself much longer. Not knowing all the pain I was putting my family and David through. A move was needed, but it didn't mean I would like it.

Chapter 4

North Carolina seemed like a decent enough place to move. Katarina said Raleigh would be a better city to settle down in. It was right in the middle of the hustle and bustle of it all yet we'd be able to blend in and go unnoticed. She was right on that account. We did blend in and some might even say we were able to live undetected. For a while that is.

Katarina owned a house there, as well. Apparently living for a hundred years or so gives you time to acquire a few things, money being one of them. I, against Katarina's wishes I might add, still continue to live as though nothing in my life had changed. For me, it was easier that way. I was able to cope with or, should I say, avoid all the craziness that was my life. That was easier than facing the truth of my situation.

I was, by all accounts, a typical twenty-one-year-old. In my head, things were fantastic in North Carolina. I made a few new friends and kept up my normal lifestyle to the best of my abilities. Katarina made her disdain of my choice to have human companions well known, but I didn't care. They gave me something Katarina would never be able to, a connection to the old me. The me I so longed to be again. The me who had a family, friends, a life. The me Katarina would never understand even if she actually tried.

Meeting Marcy at the bookstore had been a godsend. We clicked instantly reveling in the fact we both loved Jane Austen. I let her take the last copy of Pride and Prejudice they had in the store and she introduced me to Ashley and Natalie. It was as if we had all known each other our entire lives. I refused to apologize to Katarina for having friends. In fact, I thought she should try it sometime.

I was still training with her, but I wasn't interested in learning self-preservation. I wanted to have fun. I had all of eternity to learn that stuff, didn't I? What were a few more days or years even for that matter? If only I had known then what I know now.

"Focus, Alyssa, focus." Katarina barked like a drill sergeant.

"I'm trying," I said. It wasn't true, though. To be honest, I was really concentrating on the plans I had with Ashley, Marcy, and

Natalie for later that night, and Katarina knew it. There wasn't much I could get by her, and I was learning to detest her even more for that.

"No, you aren't. Fine. You want to be done? You think you don't need to learn anymore defensive maneuvers, fine, you're done then." Katarina said dismissing me with a wave of her hand and a disconcerting glared.

In reality, I knew she didn't mean it, but I wasn't going to let a piddle little detail like that stand in my way. "Thanks, Kat. You're the best." And with that, I went racing up to my room taking the stairs two, some, three at a time.

It was too hard to concentrate on how amazing the night was going to go and my lessons all at the same time. The last thing I was worried about was learning more maneuvers and vampire laws. Who really needs them anyway, or so I thought.

"Alyssa." Bellows a voice, knocking me out of my fantasy of the past and back into the reality of the present.

I look around the dungeon of a room and see the stranger who holds me here for the first time. "Yes?" I jump up and timidly reply as I know what me being here means. It means my death. It means the end of all I know, and, unlike before, there is no coming back from this death.

"Do you know who I am?" His icy glare chills me to my bones.

"Yes, I do. You're one of the Ancient Ones."

"Very good. And do you know why you are here?" His eerily cool demeanor gives me another reason to shiver.

"Yes. I'm here to die. I know that." There's no reason to play coy. There's nothing I can do to save myself at this point. Maybe the truth can be my saving grace. I highly doubt it, but it doesn't matter now.

"Well then, on that note, you are way ahead of your predecessors, Alyssa." And with that, the enormous steel door slams shut and he's gone.

I am once again left alone with only my memories to keep me company. "What have I gotten myself into?" I slide down the wall crying quietly into my dirt-stained hands.

I drift back into the past again thinking about of all the things I could have changed, should have changed and all the things I would never have changed, no matter what the consequences were to me. The night I went out with the girls was definitely one I would've changed.

It was by all accounts a perfect night. The bright, full moon lit the midnight sky with a soft glow, a gentle summer breeze blew playfully through the trees, and, to top it off, I looked amazing. I picked a blood red, one shoulder, goddess style dress and, to accentuate it, a deep crimson red lipstick. I let my dark mocha hair cascade around my porcelain face. With my hair down, my icy-blue eyes stood out more. All that kept running through my mind was this is what life is about: good friends, good times, and great laughs.

The girls and I decided to be brave and head straight to the bouncer instead of getting in line. I had seen it work in the movies so why not give it a try? To our shock and surprise, it worked. He unhooked the rope and ushered us straight in. I'd never been to a club before and being let in V.I.P. style made it even more exhilarating.

The club was alive with not only people but with the beat of the music. It was exciting and my feet were moving the moment we stepped through the doors. Lights flashed and moved to the beat, dancing around the dance floor like they had a mind and soul of their own. Unable to hide my excitement, I grinned from ear to ear moving my body to the rhythm.

The girls immediately went up to get a drink, but I had no interest in that. It wouldn't have affected me anyway. So instead, I found a spot on the dance floor and made it my own. People were all around laughing and having a great time with their friends. I needed that. I needed another reminder of why I should hang on to my humanity.

The girls eventually found me, but they were already tipsy. God knows how many shots they took in my absence. We danced all night. We danced until we couldn't dance anymore. Guys danced with us then left as quickly as they came when it was apparent we were sticking together and wouldn't be leaving with them. We didn't care. We were having a blast. The time flew by, and before we knew it, the club was closing down.

All three girls piled into the cab, and I laughed at the site of them all crammed in like sardines in a can. "I will be fine, guys. Go," I said still laughing.

"Are you sure, Alyssa? We can make it work." Marcy's green eyes were bright but filled with worry. I knew what she was thinking, a girl walking alone at night wasn't safe, and she was right. It wouldn't have been safe for her or any one of them to do what I was about to do, but I wasn't any ordinary girl.

"I'll be fine. Go. I'll catch up with you guys tomorrow." Her concern was endearing but definitely not needed. Not for me anyway. I wanted to reassure her. What could happen to me? No human could hurt me, but I couldn't tell her that. So I simply waved them off.

"All right, but call me tomorrow," Marcy said. There was a reason I called her mama bear, she always worried about everyone. She reminded me of Katarina in that way.

"I will. Now go," I said still laughing.

I enjoyed the peace and quiet of the night. I often got lost in my own thoughts when I walked. So, when a man slipped out of the shadows of an alleyway and was in my face, I panicked. All the training I had learned was quickly forgotten. Turning and walking in the other direction revealed another man leaning up against the shadowed brick building. The sneer on his face was all too familiar, and I had an aching knot growing in the pit of my stomach.

I didn't have a good feeling about this at all. All that kept running through my mind was not again. This was not going to happen to me again. I refused to let it happen. Not again. The foul smell of stale beer and sweat poured off the first man so strong bile rose up in my throat. I literally threw up in my mouth a little. When the hard punch landed square on my jaw, something inside of me snapped. All of the self-control I'd been trying to have, per Kat's request, disappeared.

A sneer crept across my face this time as I said, "Thanks for that." That was all I needed. One hit. One reason to lose control, and he had given it to me.

A quick swing knocked out the first one, I snatched up the second by his neck and pinned him up against the building. My fangs grew by instinct, and I delighted in the pleasure of it. It was the first time they grew in anticipation of a feeding, and the raw, primal feel of it only fueled me more. This time, I was the one delighting in his tears of pain and screams of fear. This time, I refused to be the victim. His leathery skin was no match for my razor sharp canines as they ripped through it in one bite. Red goodness squirted in my mouth, and I laughed as he screamed in agony. I ripped and tore until his neck was nothing more than a mangled mess of shredded flesh.

His counterpart finally came to, shrieking in horror at seeing his friend's mutilated body lying next to him. I giggled hysterically as his fear only drove me to make his end more gruesome. He deserved no less for what he and his buddy planned on doing to me. With him, I took my time. A bite here. A rip there. I did it slowly, watching as every bit of blood drained from his putrid body.

By the time I finished with them, there was no life left in their limp bodies. Perhaps it was because of how close the attack reminded me of the one that stole my life, but I felt no remorse for what I had just done to those two men. If you could even call them men. In my head, the world was better off without them. Who would even miss them? That was how I rationalized it to myself. I was helping all the young girls and women of the city. I knew that wasn't the first time they had attacked an innocent woman, and I knew I wouldn't have been their last. I'm not sure exactly how I knew it, I just knew. I did the world a favor, I thought to myself.

When I came home that night my whole appearance was disheveled. Blood spattered my body, my hair was tangled and knotted, my lipstick smeared and one of my heels had broken off.

"What happened to you? What did you do, Alyssa?" It was really not a good time for Katarina to act like a mother to me right then. Her accusations only added fuel to my already enraged fire.

"What did I do? What did I do, you ask? How about you ask why I did it, or, better yet, what made me do it?" I said, glowering at her. My lip curled, my breath heavy. I stalked toward Katarina like a cheetah stalks its prey. I didn't even realize my fangs were visible until I had her backed into a corner. Katarina had never seen this side of me before, and I believe at that point, she was truly frightened of me.

"Easy. Okay, obviously something happened. Perhaps you would feel better if you told me about it," Katarina said waving her hands in truce trying to calm mesh always tried to calm me down, but this time, it wouldn't work.

I tried to explain to her what occurred earlier that night, but the more I told, the more I realized how much I wanted to bring them back to life just to make them pay even more. They deserved to suffer for what they did to all of those other women. It wasn't just me, there had been others. I saw it when I was drinking away their lives. They stole so many lives and didn't even care. The more I spoke, the angrier I became.

Kat tried to explain that was the reason she refused to have anything to do with humans or their world anymore. She said there were too many malicious people, and we were better off not being a part of it. I didn't want to hear any of it. All I wanted was revenge. That was the moment it all caught up to me. Every little bit of it. My life ripped away from me, my new life, and how, even unbeknown to me, I blamed Kat for the situation I now found myself in. Looking back, I see I was a very angry and unappreciative person at that point in time.

Chapter 5

Some periods of time are harder for me to recall than others. That period of my new life is one of the harder ones. I was dark. I was so full of anger, rage, and hate that I tried to block it out of my mind. But I couldn't. Katarina tried her best to pacify me, but at that point, there was nothing she could've done that would have worked. Nothing.

All I saw, all I wanted, was blood. That last attack brought back all the horrible memories of the first and everything it ripped away from me. The first one ended my life; this one just pissed me off. I was sick and tired of being scared, alone, and vulnerable. I was tired of being the one hunted, so I decided to turn the tables. I became the hunter. I hunted those who trolled the night in search of innocent victims, and I saved those victims who had no idea what terrors awaited them in the shadows. I policed the streets for those too weak to defend themselves and canvassed for deviants who were up to no good.

The one thing I will never forget, however, was my first hunt. Not the two men from the alley. They hunted me. I mean the first time I was the hunter. There was no moon that atramentous night. The ominous cloud coverage worked well to my advantage. I was quiet and quick without effort. The ease of it only fed my ego more. I shadowed the miscreant for five city blocks without him ever knowing. His beady eyes shifted around as his shaky hands fumbled with the lock he was attempting to pick. He overlooked me with each pass of his shifty eyes. That was why I chose to hunt him that night, his shady demeanor.

His attention switched from the lock to a frail, silver-haired woman stepping off a bus alone, and a serpentine smile slid across that grimy face of his. He trailed behind her watching as she shuffled down to the corner store and then a few blocks more. Her floral dress and taupe orthopedic shoes reminded me of my own grandmother. All she was missing was a big netted hat with an over-sized daisy right in the front. She slowly ascended the stairs up to her apartment with her pocketbook in tow. I could hear the sliding of the chain against the door, but my opponent's ears weren't that perceptive.

I smirked with the knowledge of how observant the woman was. She never acknowledged she was aware of the danger that pursued her, but the lock and chain confirmed she knew. When the door was stopped by the chain and mace sprayed into his eyes, I laughed out loud. Groaning in pain, the monster heaved his body angrily against the door. The wood split and cracked against the pressure of his boney shoulders ramming into it. The poor woman's heart was beating so erratically she was dangerously close to having a heart attack. A shrill scream escaped her tiny, frightened body, and that was it. That was the turning point. There was no going back now. I had to act and act fast. I snatched him away into the darkness of the shattered lights of the alleyway. After draining the life from him, I left his carcass to rot in a nearby, rusted dumpster. It was fitting, I thought. An appropriate place.

Unfortunately, it wasn't long before his body was found. It was the next day, actually, when the trash company came to empty the dumpsters. The police ruled it an accident. They claimed he fell into it in a drunken stooper and hit his head and blamed the bite marks on rats or some other animal attack. My confidence grew with that. I had taken a miscreant off the streets and gotten away with it. I felt untouchable.

My hunts weren't exclusive to men. I hunted equally, fairly and a lot. Each time I left the body to rot. They deserved nothing special. They did far less for the ones they had hurt. They never stopped to consider how their actions affected the innocent ones they degraded, so I saw no reason to extend any courtesy their way. Because I wasn't disposing of the bodies I left in my wake, the trail starting becoming noticeable and not just by the humans either but by the infamous Dante Ortello himself.

"That," Katarina said, "is never a good thing. We need to move, Alyssa, and move right now. Do you understand me?" There was such an urgency in her voice it was undeniable even to me.

"Yes, I understand," I sneered, unhappy at the prospect of having to move, yet again.

Katarina and I became more distant, and I was purposely pushing her away. Kat didn't like me hunting. According to her, I didn't have the right to judge others or their actions. It wasn't my place to interfere. What was the purpose of us being here then if not to do something? Anything? She chose to do nothing. I couldn't understand that. Why fight so hard to stay alive if all you do is run, hide and avoid all contact with everyone and everything? I didn't like her opinions, and she didn't like the path I was taking. We were at an impasse.

At that point in time I could care less what she thought. I could care less what anyone thought. It was as if I was daring someone to cross me, even the feared Mr. Dante Ortello. The more I think about it, the more I think maybe, just maybe, I wanted someone to put me out of my misery. Katarina had different plans for me, though. To her, I was the chance to help the little sister she was unable to save all those years ago. To her, I believe, I was the last chance at having some kind of an actual family, and there I was spitting in her face as she was trying to save me from myself.

Once again we had to move. We were in Phoenix a full six months after my change before we had to move. Now six months after moving to Raleigh, we had to move again. Why? I didn't want a new town, or city or start. I was bitter. I know now it was pain and heartache that drove me down the wrong path. No one could have saved me because I didn't want to be saved.

Katarina thought it was time for more training on my self-control and, if this was the path I chose to take, covering my tracks.

"In case you have forgotten, Alyssa, whatever you do, I am responsible for the outcome. If you want to die that is your choice, I can't stop you, but please, do not take me with you. I'm trying to be your friend. To be quite honest, you are the closest thing to a family I have, so why do you feel it so necessary to always place us in danger? Why?" Katarina asked, her eyes pleading for me to stop.

She tried. She really, really tried, but I shot her down at every turn. I still don't see how she could stomach me most of the time back then. I wouldn't have been able to. Katarina was an amazing friend, and I was lucky to have her on my side. The problem was I only realize things once it's too late. I didn't want to take her down with me, but I was in such a dark place I didn't see or think of anyone else's needs. I was selfish. I regret all of it now.

"I don't know." I huffed. "Then just stop being responsible for me."

"It's not that easy, Alyssa. I can't just stop being responsible for you. It doesn't work that way." She said with disappointment filling her eyes.

"Why? Why can't it just work that way? Why does your kind have to make everything so ... so ... so freaking difficult and complicated?" I asked, standing there, hand on hip, accusing her.

"My kind? In case you have forgotten, Alyssa, they are now your kind as well," she said, her arms folded against her chest.

"Not by choice," I said as I brushed past her and stormed out, slamming the door hard behind me.

New York City, now that's a city. Not only is it enormous but it's always so busy. There seemed to be something new to do everywhere we turned. Katarina owned a beautiful townhome in Manhattan's upper Eastside. The stunning three-level, five-bedroom home was completed with cherry hardwood floors and crown molding. This confirmed being around for a few centuries allowed you to acquire things, houses now being added to the list alongside money. I wondered if I would be so lucky.

Our first night there Katarina did something completely out of character for her; she walked the streets of New York with me all night long. I was like any typical first time tourist, taking pictures and jaw dropped as I spun around looking at the wondrous views and sites. To my own astonishment, Katarina threw her head back with such a boisterous laugh her whole body jiggled. That was the first time in a year, the first time since I met her, in which I heard her laugh. I mean really laugh. It was a beautiful sight and sound to my ears. Her secretive brown eyes lit up matching her warm, inviting smile. With this side of Katarina, I had a sense of friendship, a sense of togetherness. Which, apparently, unbeknown to me, was exactly what I needed. With dawn approaching, I was terrified I would never get to see this side of her again.

The next day I heeded her warnings about my trail of bodies and decided to listen to her on how to cover my indiscretions. I also decided to work on my self-control, which I must admit, was lax. It was hard to change and, to be honest, a lot of trial and error on my part. The easiest way for me, I found, was to burn the bodies. Kat said a bottle of lighter fluid and a match was all I needed. Both would fit perfectly in a purse. There would be no evidence of bite marks, and it would take the authorities longer to discover who it was and any possible motives. It made complete sense once I actually listened and let her talk.

Kat and I fell into a nightly ritual. For a few hours every night we would walk the busy streets of the city laughing, joking, and getting to know each other a little better each time. Of course, she was still not happy with my lifestyle choices, but she was more of the friend I needed instead of the authority figure I rebelled against. Katarina's a very sweet-natured person. She tends to enjoy the simpler things in life such as a sunrise coming up over a mountain or laying around lazily reading books by Shakespeare. Those were the things which eased her, and I was finally beginning to understand it.

I continued my hunting, and New York City was filled with prey for me. To me, they were the lowlifes, the scumbags that no one wanted or really had a need for. I felt like I was doing my civil duty. I was helping clean up the streets of that great city. Yes, I admit it now, I was very much delusional in those days. That was what occupied my nights, hunting the ones I felt were unworthy of life.

That's how I first ran into Antonio Moretti. I wasn't sure why he was at the warehouse that night lying face down on the concrete floor. I didn't care. I swept over the men like the shadows of the night just as Katarina had taught me. I dragged one away and drained him dry, then the next, and the last one I drained right there. There was nowhere for him to run, no one to hear him screams, except for the man who was tied up, and I doubted he would be of any assistance to the thug that held him captive. Then again, he must have done something unscrupulous to get mixed up with those kinds of animals, I thought to myself.

Slowly bending down, I untied the nylon rope that tightly bound his wrists and ankles. Mimicking his every move, I mirrored him as he stood. Sliding the gag out of his mouth, I narrowed my gaze while sizing him up. He was a decent enough looking man. If he wasn't intertwined with the characters he was, he would've been someone I could've found attractive. He was around my age, short dark brown hair with intense, dark brown eyes. He stood five foot ten with a lanky frame. We locked eyes for a brief second, and I was gone.

There was my good deed for the night, I thought. Yet, something gnawed at me, something wasn't right. I double backed and follow him. Did I make the wrong decision? Should I have killed him, too? He wasn't the typical scumbag I hunted, but I had to be sure. Kat warned me no human could know of our kind's existence, but who would believe him? I couldn't take a chance of being wrong about him, though. I couldn't make another mistake. I had to be sure.

He ran faster than I would've thought. I followed him on foot and watched as he flagged down a cab. The cab went to a posh neighborhood not far from mine and Kat's townhome. That in itself worried me. He leaped out, ran up the stairs and began beating on a dark oak door. The light glowing from inside illuminated the porch as the gold handle turned. He pushed his way in past a man inside. I made my way to the back and crouched down in the bed of freshly planted shrubs.

For once, I was grateful for not being normal. Grateful my ears allowed me to hear things human ears could not. "What the heck, Antonio?"

"Just listen. I was kidnapped, right and then there was this ... this woman. She came out of nowhere. She was the most beautiful girl I've ever seen, and she saved me. But I think she ate them or something. I don't know, man. I'm just ... my head really hurts." The couch deflated under the pressure of his body falling onto it.

"Uh huh," said the other man. "She ate them?"

"Yes. She like, just, ate them. Then she looked at me and was gone. She disappeared. She was beautiful and her eyes, I will never forget those eyes. They were like blue ice. I got chills just from looking into them. She was tiny. Small. Maybe a buck, buck ten, but she lifted them up and dragged them off like they were nothing. You don't believe me do you?" The long exhale contained frustration at the realization. I stifled a laugh at that. If someone had told me that story a year ago, I wouldn't have believed them either.

The other man tried to comfort him. "It's not that I don't believe you, baby bro. It's just ... I think maybe you hit your head or something."

"Really? Really? I hit my head? Does this look like I hit my head?" I peered into the window to see the man, now known as Antonio, holding up his rope burned wrists.

"What the heck is that from?" The taller, broader man asked as he grabbed Antonio's arm.

"Oh, apparently that's just me hitting my head. I told you. They kidnapped me, and then a woman came and saved me."

"Who kidnapped you, Antonio?" The man demanded in an almost parental tone.

"I don't know, Nick. Three guys. They forced my car over and knocked me out. The next thing I know, I'm waking up in a warehouse. I can take you there. They're dead, so they have to still be there, right?"

"Yeah. Let's go." Nick, whom I could only assume was Antonio's older brother, didn't sound too convinced but had to see for himself. The front door opened and shut again. When I heard the click from the door locking, I left. There was no reason to follow them. I knew what they would find. I'd already set the building on fire before I left.

After that night I checked in on Antonio regularly, just to be sure I had done the right thing. He laid low, staying in his brother's house for awhile. After a week, I left it alone. I never saw his brother but chalked it up to none of my business.

Katarina was on me about leaving witnesses. She didn't like me hunting humans, she didn't like me being anywhere near humans to be exact, but she really didn't like the fact that I left one knowing of our kinds existence even less.

"What was I supposed to do, Kat? Kill him? He didn't do anything wrong." I couldn't believe the words coming out of her mouth.

"No, obviously I'm not saying that, Alyssa. What I am saying is this is exactly why you shouldn't be doing what you are doing in the first place. Now we're in danger. Again."

"I get you don't like what I'm doing, but now you are demanding I kill someone that did absolutely nothing wrong. You make no sense. I finally did a good thing, a selfless thing, and you're complaining. There is no pleasing you." Shaking my head, I stalked out.

The summer sun perched high in the cloudless sky. I was so distracted by what Kat implied I didn't even notice the light wasn't affecting me as it usually did. I walked for hours listening to people talk, laugh and complain about inconsequential things that wouldn't matter to them in a week from now, all the while, completely unaware of the danger that lurked all around them. Unaware of how some of their worst nightmares were real. Movies, stories they thought were only for entertainment or to scare children into obedience were, in fact, true. How I drifted among them able to pluck whichever one of them I chose off at any given moment, if I so desired. They were oblivious to it all.

Sitting down on one of the wooden park benches, I kicked off my shoes. The warm, gritty sand exfoliated my feet as I shoved them down deep while I watched the children running around screaming and squealing in delight. They swung and dangled from the playground equipment without a care in the world. Free as a bird from any worry. Moms and dads watching, smiling, and laughing with their children and occasionally having to hug and kiss away cuts and scraped knees. I wanted that once; a family, children, normalcy. Now I would never have it. I had to forget about that dream, push it back into the dark recesses of my mind, and move on. That wasn't my life anymore. Now I'm a watcher of the night. I had to protect the innocent. I had to try to save them from a fate that I, myself, was not spared. Death. At the time, I thought I was doing the right thing.

That night started a chain of events not even I could have fathomed. I patrolled the streets like many other nights before when I came across a scent that caused my skin to crawl. The streetlight pouring in from the windows fell sharply across his angular face. Shadows twisted and distorted it into a monstrous site, while he stood hovering over a girl half his size. With her soft blue dress torn, she reached desperately to cover herself as tears streamed down. Her face was red from being hit repeatedly and her lip split open with blood flowing down.

"Now, tell your boyfriend I want the rest of my money."

Quiet sobs escaped her bruised and busted mouth as she cowered in the dark corner of the abandoned building. She shook her head in agreement as I retreated reluctantly with my lips snarled and fists clenched. He would be punished but not now. I couldn't leave anymore witnesses, and the street was crawling with them.

She came barreling out into the crowded street, stumbling and falling the whole way. Her swollen and bruised eyes darted around the crowd as the sheep of people gawked but continued on their way. Everyone stopped and stared but refused to help the poor girl. Blood glistened as it dripped down her lips onto her chin. I could do nothing more than watch as she disappeared around the corner. Creeping behind her in the shadows, I followed her until she was safely in her apartment. A metal fire escape leading to her bedroom window was easy to ascend but watching her cry herself to sleep was anything but easy.

Once back at the scene of the crime, I picked up the stench of the monster and followed it to a run-downed warehouse out by the docks. Perched on a roof across from the cement building, I watched as he high-fived his buddies bragging about all of the disgusting filth he had just done. Nausea rose up, and I swallowed hard, forcing it back down. Swooping in, I saved him for last, forcing him to watch as my teeth ripped through the flesh of his comrades. One hand held him in place while the other destroyed his partners. I laughed every time he winced in horror at what I was doing. As if I was the monster here. I slammed the atrocity against the wall and drained him slowly, painfully watching with my eyes as I let the last bit of life seep out of his body through the wound I purposely made.

The shuffling of footsteps coming up behind me did not go undetected, but I refused to turn and miss seeing his eyes turn empty and vacant. The cool metal of a gun barrel pressed into my head as Antonio asked, "Who are you? Better yet, what are you?"

I turned, letting the disgusting filth drop to the floor. With my eyes narrowed and mouth stained with blood, I laughed at him. "Do you think I'm afraid of you? Do you honestly believe you could hurt me?" I sneered. This was the thanks I got for saving his life? Maybe I should've just killed him where he laid.

"Do you know who I am?" He asked, forcing his voice to drop an octave, but the slight tremble in it along with his shaky hands gave him away.

"You ask as if you think you're important. Let me let you in on a little secret, you're not. Not to me." The bitterness and disdain in my words gave even me cause for concern.

"My name is Antonio Moretti, and, because of you, my own brother thinks I'm crazy. Everyone I know thinks I'm nuts, but I'm going to show them all that I'm not. I'm taking you to them, and then they'll see I'm not crazy. They'll see I'm right. You're coming with me. Come ..."

Before the utterance of the last word, I stood behind him with his own gun pressed against his temple. "You know, you were so much cuter hogtied and gagged." I whispered before pistol whipping him.

He fell limp into my arms. Carrying him out wasn't hard, me not strangling him, on the other hand, was extremely difficult. He was becoming a bigger nuisance then I had anticipated, and I had to wonder why he was constantly mixed up with scum.

Leaving a trail of fire behind me, I disappeared into the night.

Chapter 6

Kat suggested with the knowledge of our existence now known by a human, I should pull back. Lay low for awhile. Perhaps go back to eating her way. It was safer. Less conspicuous. There would be no way to find myself in a situation like I was in again. I was tired of fighting with her, tired of fighting period, so I decided to try it again. The evils I beheld with my own eyes were enough for a hundred person's lifetimes. I needed a break. The hatred those sights left inside me festered, leaving my heart decayed and hollow. I needed a change, and I hoped that would bring me the peace I desperately craved.

After a month of feeding her way, there was a noticeable change in my attitude. I was less angry with the world, with my situation and, most importantly, with myself. Kat and I started growing close again. We started talking. Really talking. We connected on a more personal level than we ever had before. We were becoming a real family. I desperately missed my own, and, after some of our conversations, I realized so did she.

We often talked of what life was like back when she was human, the differences between then and now, and occasionally of her sister. Her name was Beth, and she was seventeen years old. She was the baby of the family and, apparently, a lot like me. She had beautiful, long, dark brown hair as soft as silk with eyes bluer than the Texas sky and a heart of gold. She had her temper tantrums and often got her way, but Katarina didn't mind much. Or so she said.

"She was my baby sister, and it was my responsibility to take care of her. I practically raised her from an infant myself. That was how things were done back then. Everyone helped, and everyone had their own part to do. If we didn't do our part, we didn't eat or have warm clothes or heat. We all contributed in some way. We had to. We were a family. Every little chore mattered. It was the difference between having food or not. I was lucky. I was able to play with Beth all day. We were only five years apart; it was fun for me. We had other things to do, as well, but it wasn't a bother.

Children had more responsibilities, more expectations than they do now. I didn't resent it. I didn't think of it or see it as a job or a chore, it was my life, and I loved it. I loved her. I still do," Katarina explained.

Sometimes it was hard to hear about Katarina's past life. That's what we choose to call our lives before the change. Our past lives. Obviously she loved her family very much, and it pained her to lose them. Her eyes always filled with sadness and tears when she thought of them. She was heartbroken over losing all she knew and loved. Who could blame her? I was, too. Kat, as I often lovingly referred to her as, refused talk about what happened to her or her family. I wondered how she was turned but none of her family was. Could it be like my situation? From what little I did hear, I think it was a touch of both. Kat's past was one of the biggest mysteries that shrouded her from me. She told me everything. Everything except for that. That was the one thing she kept tucked away and hidden even from me.

"Well," I said, "let's go."

"Go where?" She asked skeptically.

"Out," I said excitedly.

"I don't go out," she snorted.

"Well … tonight you do. So, let's go." A sly smile slid onto my face right before I ran up the stairs to my closet.

I found the perfect outfit for her to wear. It suited her to a tee. It was a cute, simple white dress with a small slit on the side. I fixed her hair up with ringlets and curls swept off to the side. Her makeup was less simple, a smoky gray cat eye with lips of crimson.

"Gorgeous," I said.

She turned slowly to look into the gold framed mirror hanging on the bathroom wall. She didn't even recognize herself. She had never tried to make herself stand out before. Kat hid her beauty behind the four walls she used to entrap herself. When she did have to go out, she forced herself to dull down her beauty, blend in with the masses if you will. One simple makeover changed all of that. She was beautiful, gorgeous, exotic, and just plain incomparable. There was no possible way she could blend in looking like that.

"Wow," she whispered. "I had no idea I could look like this." She couldn't tear her eyes away from herself.

"You're beautiful," I replied. "Now, I'm going to go get ready. It won't take me long. Not that it will matter. No one will even notice me with you standing there."

"That isn't true, Alyssa," Kat said, stunned by my words. "You're beautiful."

"It was a joke, Kat. True, but a joke all the same. It's okay. Enjoy it. You need to have some fun." I smiled and ran back into my room.

I was excited that, for once, I was getting a chance to show her the world I knew and loved. A world full of life, not one only consumed with hate, greed, and destruction. I had spent all of this time in her world, living by her rules. Sort of. Now it was time to teach her how to cut loose, have fun and be just plain reckless. I wanted to show her it wouldn't kill her to act crazy every once in a while. I was thrilled to be able to teach her something. For once, I was introducing her to something she had no idea about or experience of. Tonight I was the teacher.

I didn't make myself up as much as I did her, but I still looked presentable. I pulled my mocha hair back and my eyes were done in a smoky black cat eye style. And my lips, well, red has so many purposes.

I bounced up to Katarina in my black heels and said, "All right, let's go knock 'em dead." I laughed out loud at my own joke.

"That's not funny, Alyssa," she scolded.

"No? Not even a little bit?" I asked gesturing with my fingers.

"No," she said firmly with eyes wide. We both erupted into laughter as we scurried down the front steps.

The cool night breeze whirled around us and the moon acted as our own personal spotlight as we strolled toward our destination. We weren't even half way to Club Fallen and the men were already hitting on Kat left and right. Batting her eyes and acting coy, she flirted back in her own innocent way. Not wanting to stand in front of the pizzeria all night, I dragged her away from her would-be suitors.

When we turned the corner to the club Katarina's whole demeanor changed. Her posture straightened, her eyes turned playful and a seductive smile slid across her cupid shaped lips. Kat swayed up to the front and whispered sweet little nothings into the bouncer's ear. He unhooked the purple velvet rope and gestured for her to enter. Kat reached back, grabbed my hand and led me into the packed room. Groans from the people waiting in line were quickly drowned out by the roaring music inside. Maybe Kat knew more about this world than I gave her credit for. That was a side I never knew she had in her.

Club Fallen was amazing. Music blaring, people dancing and the vibe was pure energy. I shrugged off the temptress Kat had become a few short moments ago and dragged her off into the dance floor. Any fears about Kat's abilities to dance were discarded instantly. Her hips swayed with the music and every man around us focused their undivided attention on her and that radiant smile that lit up the room. Eyes closed and lost in the music, she was oblivious to all the stares aimed toward her. She had broken out of her shell, and I found myself getting lost in her hypnotic sways and movements like everyone else. I found it easy to get swept away and forget all the troubles that plagued me just a few short hours ago.

Everything was going perfectly. We were smiling and laughing when, out of the corner of my eye, the sexiest man I had ever seen in either lives caught my attention. The black button up shirt hugged his muscular chest and arms just enough to show off how well he was built. It hung untucked from the dark wash denim jeans he wore. There was something about him that exuded authority. His eyes locked onto mine, and I couldn't fight it. I didn't want to. I needed to know him, but the moment I started his way, he vanished into the crowd and was gone.

"Dang it," I said frustrated.

"What?" Katarina asked curiously.

"Nothing," I grumbled. "It's just I saw a really hot guy, and now he's gone. That's all. Nothing big."

"Oh." She giggled, seeming to slip back into the shy quiet girl I had come to know and love.

Grabbing her by the hand, I screamed over the music, "Come on. Let's go powder our noses," as I dragged her toward the bathroom.

Walking toward the line that stretched outside the bathroom door, Kat gushed about how much fun she was having. I was happy to see a smile on her face. After all I had put her through it was the least I could do for her. I nodded and smiled as she rambled on and on. We made our way through the line at a snail's pace. One comes out. One goes in. Move. Stop. Move. Stop. Glancing over at the men's restroom, I wondered why they never had a line.

Finally, it was our turn and Kat dragged me out mere seconds after we entered. She found a spot on the dance floor and owned it within seconds. Dancing, spinning around and swaying to and fro with the music. I watched in amazement as she commanded the attention of everyone around her without trying, without even knowing what she was doing.

A different pair of sultry eyes caught my attention from across the dance floor. He moved effortlessly toward me, locking my eyes with his. His full lips graze my ear as he leaned in close and asked me to dance. Chills ran through my body and my stomach fluttered. A guy like him would have never shown me attention before I was turned.

"Sure," I replied. "What's your name?" I hollered over the music. I could hear him just fine, but his mere human ears would have trouble.

"Nicholas," he yelled back, "but you can call me Nick. And you?" The neon strobe lights flashed in his dark eyes.

"Alyssa," I replied. "Nice to meet you." I tried to be cool, calm and collected, but I couldn't stop the smile that kept creeping up on my lips.

"You too." He said, a sexy, devilish smile crossing his well-defined face.

A few dances later, and I was finally able to pull myself together. "Thanks, but I have to check on my friend."

"All right. I'll catch up with you later then," he said with a smile that reached all the way to his dark mysterious eyes.

I looked around and found Katarina dancing with a tall, blonde man around her age. His casual style of a t-shirt, light washed denim jeans and sneakers appeared to fit his easy going personality. She was smiling and laughing with her stranger so I saw no need to interrupt them.

Pulling out one of the hard, brown, wooden stools from the bar, I sat where I could still watch her. Nick followed shortly after and slid in next to me. Acting very nonchalant, he leaned over and whispered, "Can I buy you a drink?" It was adorable, but I couldn't let myself get distracted. Even if he was gorgeous.

"No thanks," I replied cheerfully. Kat was happy which made me even happier.

"Hmm, well then, would you perhaps like to dance some more?" he asked, one brow raised.

"Sure," I shrugged. I couldn't see any reason not to. My eyes shifted over to where Kat was still talking with her mystery man, who I would have to grill her about later. He grabbed my hand and we were lost out on the dance floor again.

He was mesmerizing, and I was getting dangerously lost in the moment. Not a smart move. He smelled alluring. It was Armani and, on him, it was intoxicating. As the hours flew by I was losing control of the situation, and he was gaining it. That is never a good thing.

The night came to an end and the club was closing down. The lights flickered on one by one which was when I could really see him and his entrancing eyes. They were so dark they were almost black. I caught the smile tugging at my lips that was trying to give me away.

Licking the corner of them instead I said, "I have to go. I need to find my friend."

"Well, I'll wait right here, and after you find your friend maybe we can all go and get a bite to eat." That smile of his was going to get me into trouble if I wasn't careful.

I had no time to think, "I don't know," was all I could reply. I looked around eventually finding Katarina waiting for me by the door. I skipped up to her and said, "Well 'Ms. I Don't Go Out', did you have fun?"

"Yes. Yes, I really did, Alyssa. Thank you," she replied, a huge, undeniable smile on that perfect face of hers.

"Well, I'm glad to hear it. I guess we should get going then," I said. I had the sneaking suspicion if we didn't leave right then and there I would be in a world of trouble with Nick.

"Looks like you have an admirer." She nodded her head toward Nick. "Just remember what I said about getting close with humans. I'm going home. Have fun, and, just remember, don't get too close. Okay?" She cautioned, whispering so low it was audible only by me.

50

She knew I couldn't be like her and avoid humans. She'd given in on trying to convince me and now simply warned me to be mindful of how close I let myself get.

"All right," I said, lips pressed together as I nodded in acknowledgement.

She kissed my cheek and walked out as brazened as she walked in. What was that about, I thought to myself as I waved goodbye to her.

Nick was still waiting for me by the bar, leaned against it, looking in my direction and smiling that seductive little grin of his. There was something about him, some reason, I just couldn't abstain from. He oozed mystery, danger and trouble. He was hiding something, but I wasn't quite sure what it was. He had all the qualities of that typical bad boy persona your parents warn you to stay away from but, for some reason, you just can't seem to resist. His eyes were hypnotizing, and that smile was entrancing. He was reeling me in hook, line and sinker and there was nothing I could do about it. I got the distinct feeling that was how my prey felt right before I would strike. Yet, knowing all of this, I still couldn't stay away from him or what he was about to start.

As we walked out Nick nodded his head in acknowledgement toward the doorman and asked me, "Do you want to go get a bite to eat?"

"No. I'm good but thanks, though," I said meekly.

"All right. Well then, what do you want to do?" His midnight eyes made it impossible to concentrate on anything else.

"I don't know. Do you want to just walk around?" Seriously? That was the best I could come up with? This incredibly sexy man was flirting with me and that was the best I could do? Had I been with David for so long I didn't know how to flirt or be with anyone else? Actually, David was the only boy I was ever with. He had been my boyfriend since I was sixteen years old but the only boy I'd ever been interested in my whole life. He was all I knew.

"Sure," he said, his brows furrowed in confusion.

He played along and walked for an hour or so with me talking about nothing really at all. He was charming but very reserved. I guess, in the same respect, so was I so I couldn't complain. I had to look up at him to talk considering I was only five foot two and he was a good six foot. Even with six inch heels on, he towered over me.

I caught a glimpse of the time on his watch and said, "Well, I guess I should be heading home." I hoped he would ask me to stay. I shouldn't have, I know what Kat said, but I had to figure out what it was about this man that drew me in like a moth to a flame.

"Oh, really? Why don't we go back to my place? I mean, wait, that came out wrong. Ummmm." He tried to back track, but that only seemed to make things worse. He blushed a touch in his cheeks, and I laughed out loud.

"Well, how can I resist an invitation like that one?" I said, throwing my own playful smile his way.

"Yeah, um, well, I just meant that I could cook you something to eat. There's nothing open that has anything decent this time of night so," He finished, jamming his hands deep into his pockets and rocking on his heels.

"It's okay. Sure. Let's go back to your place."

"Okay." He turned me around and walked back in the direction of his house, which in fact, was not that far from Katarina's and mine.

His walkway was lit with solar lanterns and a hint of lavender filled the air as subtle as the breeze that wisped past me. I climbed the front steps with Nick's hand on my lower back guiding me as my hand glided along the railing to steady myself from going weak at the knees. He released me long enough to unlock the dark oak door and then repositioned his hand back on my back.

Gesturing me in, he said, "After you."

I walked in slowly looking around trying to get a feel for the type of person he was. Was he messy? A cleaning machine? A sports fanatic? What? You could tell it definitely was a man's house, but it also had hints and undertones of sophistication and femininity to it, as well, which was a huge surprise. The ceilings had exposed wooden beams, white round wooden columns and the hardwood floors were stained dark. All the wood was distressed and very masculine looking but hints of softness were throughout. The crystal vase full of fresh flowers on the table in the foyer was almost delicate. Beautiful crystal decanters full of, what could only be, his favorite expensive liquors were strategically placed on the bar and sweet berry scented candles in their beveled glass holders were strategically placed all about the house, as well.

"It's beautiful." That was not how I pictured his house or any single male's house, for that matter.

"Thanks," He said with a forced smile. I couldn't get a read on him at all. I know I should have run, something deep down told me to run, but something else, perhaps my own curiosity, willed me to stay. I should have listened to my gut, but I didn't.

Making simple conversation with him deemed almost impossible. It didn't go well at all. "I mean, my house is beautiful, but yours is cover of a magazine beautiful. Wait, no, that came out wrong." I tilted my head with brows furrowed. Did I really just say that? What was wrong with me? My face reddened from sheer embarrassment. Covering my eyes with my hands, I shook my head.

"Well, it's nice to know it's not just me that makes those kinds of faux pas," he said. I laughed a little as I hung my head in shame. The laugh he returned was more genuine than the forced smile from earlier. At that, I relaxed. "Yeah. So, are you hungry?" I was, but not for what he was talking about

"I'm really not. Sorry," was all I could manage after the gaff I just pulled.

"Well, that's okay. So … do you want to watch some TV?" he asked, switching the conversation.

"Sure." Relieved he wasn't pushing the issue; I took his lead and sank into his overly stuffed, cream colored sofa. His couch was soft, plush and the kind you could lose yourself in. We sat in uncomfortable silence while the minutes ticked by. I felt as if I had seen his place before. It all looked so familiar, but I knew I'd never been there. Something wasn't right, but I let it go. Another mistake.

The weight of his eyes on me, watching me, sizing me up caused me to shift my weight uneasily. With the tension mounting, I turn to see a .45 staring me in the face.

"Are you kidding me?" I asked. It was more of a statement than a question.

"No, I'm not kidding you." His irritated, angry voice stunned me. I had no idea where that came from. None at all. "My brother is gone because of you. What did you do to him? Where is he?"

"I didn't do anything. I didn't even know you had a brother, much less do anything to him. I just met you." I shoved the gun out of my face. Put a gun in my face? What was wrong with him? I didn't even know him before tonight. He definitely was not getting a second date after this little stunt.

"Whatever you did, you need to fix it. Because of you he's gone. I want to know what happened. I deserve to know. I need to know. Do you understand? Now tell me." Aiming the gun back at my head, he shouted, "Where is my brother?"

"I don't know what you're talking about. I don't even know your brother," I growled back at him.

"Yes you do." Snatching up a silver framed photo off the end table next to him, he shoved it violently into my face. Jerking my head back, I glared at him from around the frame. "You know him. I know you do. He talked about you several times. You did something to him. His name is Antonio. He is the only family I have left. Now, where is he?" He was hysterical by this point.

I grabbed the frame out of his hand and looked at the man in the photo. It all came flooding back to me. The night at the warehouse where I saved him. The day where I knocked him out. All of it, every little detail, came rushing back to me. So did Katarina's words. 'Everything you do will come back to you in one form or another', she said. Man, I hated it when she was right.

Pushing the gun away from my face again, I said, "Fine. I know him, but I didn't do anything to him. I saved him. Many times. The last time we met, well, I didn't kill him. So ... I don't know what you're talking about. I didn't do anything to him. You want to shoot me? Do you?"

His agitation grew at that point. "Yeah, I want to shoot you. I want my brother."

I shouldn't have added fuel to the already burning fire, but I couldn't stop myself. "Then shoot me!" I screamed, holding the barrel up to my temple. "Shoot me then, but it's not going to help you find your brother. Maybe you should be looking at the garbage I found him hanging out with." My voice was callus and cold, but I didn't care. He was lucky I didn't rip him up right then and tear out his throat.

Then a loud pop followed by a sharp heat tore through my flesh sending a burning pain shooting down my spine.

Chapter 7

Luckily or unfortunately, depending on how you looked at it, I wasn't dead. My warm blood splattered all over his couch, wall and his angered face. Turning my head slowly so he could see my eyes instead of the gaping wound he caused that poured blood and smelled of burnt flesh, I growled low and angry.

My eyes narrowed and lips snarled as I said, "That hurt." Jumping back, his eyes grew wide with fear as his heart sped to an unnatural pace. Caught between me and the arm of the couch, he did nothing but look on in disbelief. "Are we done now, Nick? Now, I do have to eat, and you're starting to look pretty good," I managed to get out between clenched teeth. Trying to control myself took all the energy I had within me.

"What are you?" He stammered and stuttered.

"What am I? Well, right now I am one very pissed off woman." My brows rose as I pursed my lips.

"I mean, how are you still alive? Who are you? What are you? Oh my … Antonio was right about you, wasn't he?" His voice now a mere whisper. Climbing backwards and inching his knees over the arm of the couch, he made sure to keep his eyes on me.

"I don't know. It depends on what he told you about me. I will tell you this, though, I'm not someone you want to mess with. I truly am sorry about your brother, but I didn't do anything to him. Maybe he just doesn't want to be around you anymore. Wow. Stupid me. I actually thought you liked me. My mistake. You shot me. Unbelievable." I stared at him in complete and utter disbelief.

A loud thud against his door caught us both off guard. In unison, our heads turn to face where the noise came from. Nick jumped up so quickly I couldn't tell if it was to get away from me, or if he truly was curious about the noise. Cautiously turning the gold handle revealed his brother Antonio's lifeless body sprawled out on the front steps. A wail laced with pain and anguish sent my head spinning toward him as he fell to his knees draped over Antonio's body cradling him like a baby. I used what little strength I had left to push myself off the couch and stagger his way. Collapsing next to him, I was extremely weak from the loss of blood that still seeped endlessly from the hole where my temple used to be. Antonio's blood smelled sweet and enticing. Fighting a war within myself, the smell was becoming too much for me to sustain from. I silently begged for Katarina's help. I knew there was no way for her to know or hear, but I desperately needed strength. I needed help. The beat of my own heart was slowing, and I was in serious trouble.

Katarina flooded the doorway in a matter of seconds. My eyes closing and head bobbing, she knew the situation wasn't good as she caught my slumping body. Against her own fears, and seeing time wasn't on her side, she made a decision to help me right then and there. I could hear her thoughts as though they were my own. She was not going to lose another sister. Not this way. Not when she had the power and resources to save me. Even with her fears running rampant, she stayed fixated on the task before her.

She was gone and back in the blink of an eye, or perhaps I was fading in and out of consciousness. Either way, when Katarina returned I was in a fog of haze. I felt her soft slender arms scoop me up and carry me over to the couch. She placed me gently down and through the fog that now covered all my senses, I saw her look around in anguish. Our secret was no longer a secret, and I lay dying. The prick from the I.V. stung for a second, but not enough to keep me from slipping into unconsciousness. After the sting it all went black.

My eyes fluttered as I forced them open. Everything was a blur and a little fuzzy around the edges. Uncertain of how long I had been out, I vaguely heard Katarina and Nick talking. About what, I was unsure of, but Katarina's voice was jittery. I'd never heard her like that before. Forcing my eyes to focus, I glanced around at the disaster of a room. Objects became clearer and so did the three empty I.V. bags of blood on the floor in addition to the one still flowing in me. By the looks of things, I must have been out for a while.

I stood up only to fall right back down. Still a little woozy from the loss of blood, I shook it off and tried again. Using my hands to push up off the couch, I stood back up, thankful the second time was more successful. Stumbling my way toward the kitchen, I ran my hand along the wall for support. Both Katarina and Nick stopped talking and stared at me as I entered clumsily. Katarina smiled, eyes filled with worry. The fear in Nick's told of both his terror and confusion.

Looking back at Nick I said, "I'm really sorry about the mess in your living room." He kept his stare locked on me unable to reply. Staggering, I closed the gap between Katarina and I and whispered, "What did I miss?"

"Not much," she replied. "simply explaining the situation to our friend Nicholas here." Her narrowed eyes and sarcastic smile was evident.

My eyes grew wide. "What? No. No one can know. You told me that."

"Yes, I did. However, given the circumstances, I saw no other choice. You left me no other choice, Alyssa. Now it's up to you on what we do next." She glanced Nick's way, who was staring at his brother's body lying cold on the bare wood floor.

His eyes were bloodshot and puffy from a long night of crying, and I paused thinking of my parents all those times I saw them hunched over crying. I understood what she was hinting at, but couldn't shake the feeling that this was my fault. I felt guilty for some reason and wanted, no needed, to help him. I needed to help him figure out what happened to his brother and why. I, in truth, had to find out if he died because of my actions, to ease my own conscience. Glancing over Antonio's body, I knew he wasn't much older than me. He had a family who loved and needed him, and somehow this was all my fault.

In a whisper of a voice I said, "I want to help you. I want to help you find out who did this to your brother." Katarina's eyes turned on me with a rage I had never encountered before. Chills ran down my spine as the fear crept through my body taking over and affecting every cell of my being. It had to be done for my own personal reasons. He needed help. I needed help. Perhaps this would help us both. "I think you're right. I think somehow this may all be my fault." I avoided eye contact with him at all cost. I would've rather risked the wrath of Kat's eyes then feel the pain of Nick's.

Kat's delicate hand stroked my back trying to comfort me, but it did little to ease the blame I knew was rightfully mine to accept.

"It's not your fault, Alyssa." Her words were kind but unconvincing. All I could do was shake my head. A second ago she glared at me with daggers for eyes, and now she was trying to ease and comfort me. I couldn't help but to not believe it. Kat definitely was showing she could have a different side to her. A mean, nasty side I never imagined. A side I hoped wasn't a constant.

"You should lie down." I wrapped my arm around Nick's waist to help him up was shoved off instead. I could do nothing but watch helplessly as he stood dazed moving slowly toward the staircase. I shot a worried look at Katarina before following behind him. He was sitting on the foot of his bed staring at the wall when I entered. "Are you okay? Is there anything I can do for you?"

I had no idea what to say to him. I wasn't allowed to speak to my family after my absence to try to ease their pain, and this pain, like that one, was my fault. There was no taking it back. In a situation like that, saying I'm sorry wasn't going to cut it. He lost his brother, his family, and I could've been to blame. I was to blame somehow. I knew it.

"Am I okay?" he repeated, anger flashing through his dark eyes as he spoke. "Am I okay? Is there anything you can do for me?" he shrieked. I carefully eased my way to where he was and sat down beside him. His pain was evident and rendered me more helpless than I already felt. "Can you bring back my brother? Can you do that?" he shouted at me.

He grabbed me, and, for a second, I feared he was going to fling me across the room. Instead he pulled me into his massive arms, clenching onto my back weeping silently into my shoulder. I wrapped my slender arms around him and pulled him into me even more. He needed comfort. He needed contact with someone. He just lost his only family. I knew how that felt. It had happened to me.

Not all that long ago I lost my own family. I knew the emptiness and the loneliness that loss brings to a person. The only difference was my family was still very much alive, and I was forced to continue on every day knowing I could never speak to them again or end the pain I put them through. It wasn't their fault. It wasn't my fault, but it didn't matter. It was for their own safety. I knew that, but it didn't make it any easier. I often wondered how my family reacted when they heard the news of my death. It's hard to imagine my dad crying or even my mom. That was a hurt I never wanted to inflict on them. That kind of pain they didn't deserve.

My parents are wonderful people, and they loved me very much. They still do. If they knew what I was now, I'm not so sure. We're the damned ones. That's what Kat repeatedly hammered into my head. Although, I still held hope in my heart she was wrong about that.

Of all the memories I have of them, I keep one in my mind always. My mother with her soft brown hair pulled back in a loose pony tail and her apron on making dinner. My dad, a handsome, kindhearted man with cool green eyes, would slip in the house undetected from work, sneak up behind her and kiss her tenderly on the side of her neck. It was a ritual I'd seen every night since I was a child. It always made me smile, and, when I got older, I knew that was what I wanted for myself. I wanted that type of love, the type that lasted forever. The kind of love my parents have for each other. They've been married for twenty-one years and still looked at each other every day as if it were the first.

I thought I'd found that with David. I loved him. I thought he loved me. I loved how my feet dangled in the air when he picked me up in his lean arms for a hug, swinging me around, laughing that soft, infectious laugh of his. David was always very tender, endearing and thoughtful toward me. Well, except for the last night we spent together. I still don't understand why he did what he did that night or said what he said. I personally saw how my death had affected him. It doesn't matter anymore. I would never get the answers to my questions.

Even still, I had everything I needed, an amazing family I could count on for anything. It's hard knowing you had everything you ever wanted at your fingertips, in the palm of your hand, and, in the blink of an eye, it all gets ripped away from you. Why? Why does that have to happen?

While sharing that intimate moment with Nick I suddenly knew what I had to do. There wasn't a doubt in my mind anymore. I had to help him figure out what happened to his brother and why. I owed him that much at least. It was my fault. Whatever happened to his brother, I had the sneaking suspicion it was because of my actions. If I hadn't had the smug attitude I did, I wouldn't have ever met Antonio. For that matter, if I had listened to Katarina, I wouldn't have gone after humans in the first place. Either way I looked at it, it was my fault. If I had listened to Katarina things would be a whole lot different, but I didn't. My actions and the results of my actions were solely my responsibility. No one else's. I had to take responsibility for them. Therefore, it was my responsibility to help Nick find out who did this to his brother and why.

His crying slowed, eventually stopping. As he remorsefully released his grip on me, I looked upon him with knowing eyes. "I'm sorry." His voice shaky. Using the back of his hand, to wipe his eyes, he inhaled deep slowing his breathing back to normal.

"It's fine. I understand. I lost my family, too. If anyone can understand what you're going through right now it would be me." Except my family was still very much alive, I thought to myself, and I am forced to live with the fact of being forbidden from ever seeing or speaking to them again.

"You lost your family too? How?" His damp eyes curiously grazed over me. He looked lost, so very lost that my heart ached to see the look of longing for answers burning in his eyes.

I couldn't lie to him. He deserved better than that, so I told the truth. "I died. I became what I am now, and no one can know. Not even them." I lowered my head. It was still hard for me to talk about. Even now, it's hard to think about them without regret filling my head of not saying I love you enough to them all.

"But I know." His intense stare studied my face waiting for an answer he feared, yet already knew.

"I know, but you're not supposed to. Technically, I'm not supposed to let you live." Those words coming out of my mouth frightened even me.

Tension filled his body as every muscle grew stiff. As much as he tried, he was unable to control his breath or his heart from pounding wildly out of control. He knew I was right, and, if I wanted, he could and would be dead at any point in time.

"I'm not going to though." Those words came out in a whisper.

"Why not?" He was right to question me. I would have questioned me. I did question myself as to why, but deep down I knew.

"I wasn't joking when I said I want to help you find out what happened and why. If I hadn't met him, if I hadn't been so egotistical and decided to kill those kinds of people, this might have never have happened. As I said earlier, this is my fault, and I owe you. Believe it or not, not all vampires are bad." It felt strange having that word come out of my mouth. Vampire. Katarina always said our kind. We never used the word vampire after the first night I woke. To hear it spoken aloud again brought back the same gut-wrenching fears of that night.

"There are more than just you two? Vampires, I mean." I laughed at the question even though it was a legitimate one.

"Yes, there are more. I don't know how many. I've only met Kat, but according to her, yes, there are many more besides ourselves."

Nodding he continued, "I didn't even believe in vampires until tonight. I still wouldn't believe in them if I hadn't seen what I saw with my own two eyes. Honestly, who would? I didn't believe Antonio when he said the crazy things he did. Although now, they don't seem so crazy. And what do you mean those kinds of people? What kinds of people? What are you trying to say about my brother? About me? My family?" His tone changed from soft to accusatory.

"Well, in my head, they were the low life scum that was killing this city. I chose the ones I felt no one had a need for or would miss. I was angry about my situation and about what happened to me, so I took it out on the world. Literally. I didn't choose your brother. Each encounter I had with him I allowed him to live," I answered as honest and truthful as I could. It came out harsher and uncaring than I meant for it to, but that's how the truth is sometimes. Harsh and uncaring.

To be completely honest, I wasn't sorry for the ones I killed. They brought chaos and harm to all they met. They weren't sorry, and they would have kept doing it if someone hadn't stop them. That someone just so happened to be me.

"So, it's true? You're the one who's been killing off our people? Antonio was right all along. It wasn't my brother at all?" A look of hatred overtook his gorgeous face. His eyes probed me for answers as they glared unrelenting into my own.

"Yes, I guess so. I'm sorry I got your brother into this. I know I can't make it right or fix it, but I want to help. I've seen a little of what my loved ones went through after they lost me. I never wanted to put anyone through that ever again. For that, I truly am sorry." I hung my head in defeat.

"I'm not going to lie," he started off, "I don't know you; I don't like you, and I don't trust you. In my heart I know my brother's blood is on your hands somehow. But I also know it takes a lot for a person to admit when they're wrong so for that, I thank you. In my family you don't get that very often, even when they know they're wrong. However, if we work together on this, it is going to be a tumultuous relationship at best. There is no trust between us," his words stern, cold, and hard.

"That's true. You don't trust me, and I don't know you. But by you knowing my secret, it puts me in a bad position. By me helping you, puts me in an even worse position. I appreciate your honesty. I do. I want you to trust me. That's why I've tried to be as honest with you as possible," I tried to sound upbeat but failed miserably at it.

"How does it put you in a bad position?" His skepticism was apparent. He thought I was lying. Why? To gain his trust? There was no reason for that. There was nothing I could gain from deceiving him. Trust is a funny thing. It takes seconds to lose yet a lifetime to regain.

"If anyone finds out my secret a few things could happen. Either one, the government could take me and do experiments on me." I laughed trying to lighten the mood. When silence was all that filled the air I decided to move on. On a more serious note I said, "Or two, it could get me killed by my own kind," I was firm while saying that.

"So, your world is a lot like mine then?" I could tell he wanted answers, but I wasn't sure how many I would be able to give him.

"Yes. I guess so. A sort of secret society I believe you would say." I gave him a half smile that wasn't returned. "Now you have leverage on me. Does that make it a little easier for you to trust me?"

"I guess so. I'm sorry, but I'm really tired." He said through a half yawn. "So, can we start tomorrow?" He yawned again, this time much bigger.

"Yeah, that's fine. Get some rest. It's been a long, exhausting day. I'll stay here, if that's okay, and tomorrow we will get started." I stood up and slowly walk out of his room, taking one last long look at him before quietly shutting the door.

There was something about him. Something magnetic. He kept me wanting to know more. I felt like a moth. You know the flame isn't good for you but you just can't seem to stay away from it. I was the moth and he was most definitely the flame. I had the distinct feeling I was going to get burned somehow. In some way I was going to go down. But was the fall going to be worth it?

Chapter 8

I headed downstairs to find Katarina still in the kitchen waiting for me. I sat down at the table across from her and, with tired eyes, picked at the white cloth mat that lay in front of me. I didn't want to hear the lecture I knew was coming, but there was no avoiding it. Better to get it over with now than constantly running from it.

"This is going to get us killed, you know. I told you not to get too close. Why would you let him shoot you? Why would you put yourself in that position? Why would you put me in that position? Why?" Her voice fell harsh and demanding on my ears. I'd never seen Katarina angry before, but I had a feeling I was going to tonight.

"I'm sorry," was all I managed to get out in my weakened state. The exhaustion setting in on my body from earlier was weighing heavy.

"You're sorry? You're sorry? Tell me how sorry you are when Dante kills us both, okay?" Pushing herself back, scraping the chair against the hardwood floor, she darted to the door.

Before she could shut it I hollered out, "I have to help him. Why don't you understand that?" I meant it to be a plea of understanding and sympathy, instead it was a screeching mess. I knew the mistake I made once the words were out of my mouth.

In the blink of an eye she was in my face forcing me back down into my seat. "Maybe it's because I don't want to die. I have done everything I could to help you. I have done everything I could to try to keep you safe, and all I seem to get in return is put in harm's way by you. So excuse me for not understanding why he is not dead, and we are not leaving this city right now." Kat's eyes were stone, her expression hard, and I sat down. I had never been in the unfortunate position to see this side of her before, and I prayed I never would be again. Not directed at me anyway.

"I'm sorry." The apology came out more shaken than I originally planned.

"You're sorry. Got it. You are always sorry, aren't you, Alyssa. Sometimes I'm sorry simply isn't good enough. When will you figure that out? This is why I do not deal with humans. This right here! "Katarina was gone in an instant, leaving an open door swinging behind her. She had never been that harsh or unkind to me. To be on the other end of her wrath was not a good position to be in.

I raced home in hopes to find her, but an empty house was all that awaited me. I hastily threw a change of clothes and a few personal items in my hot pink backpack and raced back to Nick's house. There was no way I was going to be able to go back to sleep, so instead, I slid into more comfortable clothes. My sky blue tank top and navy blue and black plaid boxer shorts would be easier to work in than the dress I had on previously.

After surveying the mess of blood in the living room, I quickly went on the hunt for his cleaning supplies. I needed something to keep my mind off my argument with Kat.

His house was bigger than Kat's and not everything was where I thought they should be. After locating the cleaning closet, I shuffled through all of the supplies. To my surprise, I found everything I needed. In that moment I was thankful I paid attention to my mother all those times she cleaned and scrubbed the house. She was always so meticulous to the point of being compulsive about every little detail. Every water spot and dirt speck had to be picked up and cleaned. Back then I laughed at her, but now I was just grateful. In my head all I kept saying was, *thank you, Mom because of you I know what to do.* Sighing and taking another good look around, I dug my heels in and attempted to clean the substantial amount of splatters and pools of blood that covered, what seemed to be, the entire room.

As first light of the new morning sneaked in through the windows, I finally finished and went to clean myself up. I let the hot water from the shower beat down on my back. Running my fingers through my hair, I watched as the red dripped down off of my chin and swirled down the drain. My wound was gone, my flesh had healed, but the heartbreak from Kat's disappointment lingered on. I wasn't trying to betray her, but I had to do this for me. If I had to live this way for all of eternity, I had to find my own way. Create my own path. Not follow others blindly and never question why.

I turned off the water and stepped out onto the cold marble floor. The shock of temperature change sent goose bumps racing up my legs and all the way through my body. The little hairs on my arms rose as I grabbed for the white chenille robe dangling from the polished nickel knob attached to the door. I slipped on the satin-lined warmth, and traced the silver initials that were hand sewn on.

Wiping the steam from the mirror, I glared at the reflection looking back at me. The porcelain complexion that was so perfect. Everything about me looked perfect. My mocha colored hair, my crystal blue eyes, even my sparkling white teeth looked perfect. What have I become? What have I done? These were the thoughts that kept running through my already hectic mind. I looked flawless, but everything about me was a mess. This was all I could do for him right now; all I could do to help ease his burden? Clean? Leaning over the sink, I shook my head at the thought.

"Ridiculous," I said aloud.

I quickly donned my favorite pair of already broken-in, holey jeans. They fit and curved to my body perfectly. Whenever I needed confidence I wore those jeans. I threw on a simple black t-shirt to go with them, brushed and swirled my hair around my fingers pulling it all back into a messy bun.

Antonio was lying in the dining room on a few blankets so I decided to carefully move him to a spare bedroom upstairs. Perhaps he would be more comfortable there. Silly thought, he was dead and couldn't feel anything anymore, but I would have wanted the same respect and regard for someone I loved.

Nick would be hungry when he woke, and, like my mother always said, breakfast is the most important meal of the day. Her advice had yet to fail me, so I rummaged around the pantry and easily found all the ingredients I needed. What the pantry didn't hold, the refrigerator did. I started cooking a typical, yet filling breakfast for Nick. He would need his strength. It wasn't fancy by any means; eggs, bacon, pancakes and some juice. I needed him to see I wanted to help not hurt him. Well, not hurt him even more than I already had. I needed his trust, I craved his approval, and I wanted his attention. Why I hungered for it so was a mystery even to me, but the desperation was always there.

The squeaking sound of his bedroom door sent me into a frenzy. The stairs creaked as he made his descent, and I frantically began making his plates. Eggs and bacon on one, pancakes on another. When he came in I had it all set up, ready and waiting for him.

Staggering sleepily into the kitchen he startled by my presence there. "Morning," he said groggily.

His sleepy eyes and bed head hair was not what I expected. He was real. More so than me. He wasn't perfect, and that's what I liked. Any girl my age would love to have my problem, I suppose. Perfect hair, perfect complexion, perfect teeth, but looking perfect wasn't all it was cracked up to be. Not when I was a complete and utter mess on the inside.

"Morning. I made you breakfast. I already ate mine." I gave a half-hearted attempt at a smile, but he didn't notice.

"Yeah. I was really hoping it was all just one big, bad, horrible dream. That it was Antonio down here cooking like he normally does, but I was wrong. It's a nightmare that will never end." Sadness radiated off his face.

"That was a bad joke. I'm sorry." Returning my attention to the sink, I went back to washing the dishes.

"This smells good. Thank you." He grabbed his fork and picked at the scrambled eggs. Half way through, he pushed his plate away and wiped his mouth. "Breakfast was good. Thanks, but I'm full." Pushing his chair back, he stood and turned to go back upstairs. Stopping dead in his tracks, he turned back around and scanned the room. "Where's my brother?"

Lowering my eyes from his stabbing gaze, I quietly stated, "I laid him upstairs in a spare bedroom. It seemed more dignified. He deserves that. You know, you should probably make the arrangements for him today."

"Yeah, I know I do. I'll make the calls after I take a quick shower." His voice nothing more than a hoarse of a whisper.

I nodded my head indiscernibly. He managed a slight smile before trudging upstairs. Once I knew he was gone, I returned my attention to the dishes. I couldn't get the argument Katarina and I had gotten into the night before out of my head. I needed to make amends. She was all I had left. I couldn't lose her, too. With a shaky hand, I picked up the phone and dialed our number but hung up before punching in the last digit. I repeated that vicious cycle five or so more times before I swallowed hard and listened to it ring.

"Yes, Alyssa?" Kat's voice was cold and flat.

"I wanted to tell you again that I really am sorry." Tears welled up in my eyes and streamed down my cheek faster than I could wipe.

"Just do what you feel you must do," her voice matter-of-fact and disconnected.

That hurt even more. Katarina was my only family now. I wasn't allowed to be with my human family. She was all I had left, and I was hurting her. This was not how things were supposed to go. I was trying to do the right thing, but I couldn't seem to make her see that. At that point I didn't want to try to anymore. I wanted to make it better for her and to stop causing pain in her life. I was stuck between a rock and a hard place. I wanted to reassure her I would take responsibility for my own actions. I wouldn't let anything happen to her, but I had to do this.

"All I want is to do the right thing for once. Kat, I want to do the right thing." I tried to control the quiver in my voice, but it was too much to bear.

"You should've done the right thing from the start and not gotten involved. But you do what you feel you need to do, Alyssa. You always do. I understand. It's fine." She said and hung up.

She was not fine. It was not fine. We were not fine. After she hung up I knew deep down it wasn't going work out the way I intended it to. The knot building deep down in my stomach only reiterating that fact to me.

After hanging up the phone I turned my focus back to cleaning the mess I made earlier. I was so lost in my own thoughts of my conversation with Kat I was completely unaware Nick had come back down into the kitchen.

"What are you doing?" His eyes followed my hand as I scrubbed the stove clean.

I stopped, smiled at him in the hopes he couldn't see the sadness in my eyes. "I'm just cleaning up a little. One less thing for you to worry about." I continued my scrubbing moving my focus onto the counter.

"Thank you. You didn't have to, though. I could've done that." He placed his hand on mine to stop me from cleaning the same spot I had been scouring for the last few minutes.

"It's not a problem. I was bored and needed something to do." My upbeat voice was anything but how I felt.

"Well, if you keep being helpful I won't have a stove or counter left." He carefully examined his granite countertop. Bending, he scanned them both at eye level.

"Look, it's undeniable you don't trust me. I don't trust you either, but at some point, if we are going to figure this out, we need to work together. It's inherent we trust each other or we will never find out the truth of what happened. I am risking everything to help you. Everything. Do you realize that?" I could feel my face heating up. I was losing everything I cared about, and all I asked for is a little respect.

"How are you risking everything?" The arrogance in his voice only added fuel to the already burning out of control fire that raged within me. "I'm the one who lost everything. My brother. Remember?"

That sent me over the edge. "Yeah? Well, I am going to die for you knowing what you know about me. Did you know that? And no, that is not a question, that is a certainty. Katarina, the girl you were talking to last night, she's the only family I have now. I told you, I lost my family. She's all I have left, and I'm putting her life in danger to help you. She didn't want this. She didn't want any this. She didn't ask for this, but here I am sticking her right smack dab in the middle. The rules state that you are supposed to die, but I am trying to make up, in some sick sort of way, the wrong I did to you. I am putting a lot of faith into you, and all I am asking for is the same freaking courtesy from you. I don't think that's asking too much considering all I have at stake here."

My whole body trembled. I gripped the counter to control myself from flying off the edge. He had no idea what I was risking to help him. My life was the least of what I was worrying about losing. Katarina was the first. Her life I was not willing to lose.

"Fine. Just realize there aren't a lot of people I do actually trust. It isn't just you. It's people in general. I just have more reason not to trust you." He stared at me intently watching my every move.

Nick's posture changed the more visibly upset I became, and, I am guessing, he was trying to judge what my next move might be. Gauging if I might turn on him.

"Fine. Now that we have that out of the way," I stated, calming myself down. "Let's get started on the issue at hand."

I walked into the living room, dug through one of the end table drawers and grabbed out a yellow legal pad of paper and pen I saw during my cleaning spree. While walking back into the kitchen all I could do was pray everything would work out in the end. Just in case Kat was wrong and he was still listening. For everyone's sake, I needed this to work out.

I placed the pen and paper down on the counter and pushed it into Nick's tapping fingers. "Let's start by making a list of everybody who could possibly have any reason to want your brother dead."

We sat for hours going over all the enemies he and his brother had acquired during their years working for the Campiato Family. That was how I found out about Nick and his brother worked for a very powerful family who had their hands in a little bit of everything. That explained why I always saw Antonio at those seedy places and with the company he kept.

The Campiato's were well known, well respected and, with good reason, well feared. Lucas Campiato had taken a liking to Nick and moved him up through the ranks rather quickly. He started out washing cars, and now he was one of Lucas' most trusted men. Nick never intended or wanted Antonio working for them, but, by the time he found out, it was too late. He kept his brother close at bay so he could watch over and protect him.

"It wasn't something I planned to do. It wasn't a goal I set for myself. No one says 'hey I want to work for a crime family,' but I had to take care of my brother. My parents were dead, and when my grandmother passed away, I had no other choice."

His words rang true, but something was off about them. He was hiding something or not telling, either way, it left me wondering. I let it go. I had already caused too many issues in his life already. At least he didn't pretend his brother didn't have enemies. Everyone has enemies whether they like to admit it or not.

71

"That's a good start, I think," I said flipping the notepad closed. "When do we want to start questioning the suspects?" Maybe I took my love of crime TV a tad bit too far. The baffled look he gave told me I had.

"For some of the people we are going to have to get Lucas' permission with them being business associates of his and all. We'll have to travel for some because they don't all live here. Some live in other states. I don't see many of them being too cooperative either. "He knew them better than me. I didn't know any of them, but I knew without a doubt I could get them to divulge whatever information we needed. I just didn't want to push too hard right then.

"Well then, do you want me to head home? Or I could stay if you want me too. You know, to make sure nothing happens to you." I kept my eyes focused on my shoes scuffing against the floor in hopes he wouldn't see the desperation that was too clearly written all over my face. I needed to show Kat I was more than just a screw up who made horrible choices. Above all, I needed to prove it to myself.

"No, you can stay if you want. I should probably eat something. Would you like to join me?" It was a sweet invitation, and I agreed without hesitance.

"I'll walk with you. I'm not really all that hungry."

I tried not to laugh. When a little snort managed to escape I was mortified. But it lightened his mood a little, and that satisfied me. There wasn't a smile, but I could tell by the look in his eyes. Eyes are the windows to the soul they always say and, with him, the logic appeared to be true. They weren't as brooding as they usually were, and his face softened a bit. I covered my nose and mouth as the embarrassment set inland laughed out loud at myself one more time.

Outside the day had turned into night while we had been inside tearing through every detail of Antonio's life. The city was alive with the sounds of cars rumbling and honking as they rolled by and people talking, laughing and hustling to get to wherever it was they were trying to go. The cool air tickled across my skin raising goose bumps all over. Once again the stars were blocked from sight that cloudless night by the bright glowing lights of the signs all around leaving me disappointed. The smell of hot dogs pulled Nick's attention toward the line for a stand on the corner. He ordered three with mustard, and I ended up holding two of them.

After taking a huge bite he said, "This way, you look like the pig. Not me." He laughed so hard I thought he was going to choke.

"Be careful," I said wiping mustard off the corner of that crooked little smile of his. "I don't know CPR," I retorted while laughing.

"What?" He asked, feigning shock. It was adorable, over dramatic, and I loved it. With a raise of my brow, I smiled back. "A person in your situation and you don't know CPR? What does that say about you?" That was the first hint of him actually having a sense of humor and that devilish little smile he gave me caused flutters in my stomach.

"It says I stay away from situations where I would have to use it." I couldn't control the laughter rolling out of me at that point.

He grabbed at his chest, "Oh that hurts. That really hurts." He was on a roll now. His seductive laugh echoed through my ears and that hypnotic smile drew me in.

I peered into Nick's eyes noticing there were little flecks of gold in them that lightened when he was in a better mood. In this light he seemed almost kind. *What am I doing*, I questioned myself? This isn't right, yet I was unable to take my eyes off him.

The feel of his hand accidentally grazing mine sent butterflies swirling around uncontrollably in my stomach. Regardless of it being an accident, I couldn't control my pounding heart. I smiled sheepishly as erratic thoughts ran through my mind. Impossible, inconceivable thoughts that would never manifest into anything real. Images of Nick spinning me around, dipping down low, and kissing me with more passion then I had ever felt before invaded my mind. Him telling me I was the only one for him and there would never be another. Wishes of him wanting and falling in love with me were childish and unrealistic. It would never happen. After all the grief I caused him, all the pain and suffering, there is no forgiveness for that. You can't turn back the hands of time, if I could, a lot of things would've been different. I pushed those thoughts out of my mind. You can't change the past so there is no sense in dwelling on it.

"You ready to head back to the house?" I snapped myself out of the dream that would never happen.

The eyes are the windows to the soul, and that saying has proved to be true. I hoped this time, with me, it wasn't. I didn't want him to see the thoughts and feelings my heart was creating. I didn't want to hear, right then, what his response would have been if he knew.

"Sure. Are you embarrassed to be seen with me now?" There was that playful smile of his again.

"No." I turned on my heels and hastened my pace.

I couldn't look at him. Not with that smile and not with knowing because of what I did, what I am, I could never have those feelings reciprocated. Not even a little bit. Perhaps it was the guilt I was feeling, or perhaps it was the undeniable truth sinking in. Either way, I knew there would never be anything more between us than what there was now, and there never could be. All I could hope for was friendship and even that seemed an impossible wish. According to Katarina I was the unlovable. The damned. It would never work between us. How could it?

Nick's sneakers hitting the hard cement as he jogged to catch up with me was only audible by my ears. His pace slowed to a steady stride once he was on point with me. I peeked to see his hair had fallen just enough to cast an edginess to his face.

"What's the hurry? Do we have to get back? People are coming to get Antonio's body right now so it would be easier for me to be out here instead of in there. Plus, if I'm in there too long I get claustrophobic and it starts to feel like the walls are closing in on me. It's just too hard for me to be at home right now. Do you mind if we just walk around for a little bit longer? Please?"

I watched as he scuffed his shoe against a crack that stuck up out of the pavement. His lighthearted mood was a ruse. Like my father, he joked to hide his pain. Always having to be the strong one, never letting on to how much pain and anguish he actually held deep inside. I love that about my dad. Always so strong but deep down he was nothing more than a big old teddy bear. I never let on I knew, and now he never will.

Taking the cue, I said, "Sure. We can do that. I love walking around this city. It always puts me at ease. There's always something new and exciting to see."

I looked around at the lights that were all lit up around us. Inhaling deep, I glanced over at him, and we set off again. There was a crisp, cool breeze blowing lightly, the sky was clear, and, by all accounts, it was the perfect night for a walk. We walked for hours talking, laughing and learning a little bit more about each other than we knew before. He was charming, engaging and innocent.

Only when the sun rose from the east over the tall statuesque buildings did we head back toward his house.

"You should get some rest," I stated as he opened the door for me.

"All right, Mom," he quipped back, turning to shut and lock the door behind us.

"No. I was only trying to say ... "

"It's fine. I should." Holding his hand up to silence me, he sauntered into the kitchen to grab a soda out of the refrigerator. As he popped it open, dark, sticky carbonation sprayed out everywhere. Laughing hysterically, I tossed a towel at him. He caught it gracefully with one hand and wiped off his face and shirt.

"I need to sleep, too. I didn't get any last night." I hadn't really noticed how tired I really was until I sat down. I was exhausted. Dead on my feet at that point. When I looked up from a yawn, his eyes lingered on me. I rolled my eyes, and I shook my head. Sliding off the stool, he started to say something, but no words came out. Pressing his lips together in frustration, he turned to go upstairs.

I watched as he walked away, stop suddenly, faced me and said, "Thanks for tonight. I needed it." He lowered his head, turned and finished walking upstairs.

"It was my pleasure," I whispered as the door closed shut behind him.

Chapter 9

Antonio's body was taken so it could be prepared for his funeral while we were out. Another benefit of working for the Campiato's, I suppose. No police. No questions. It left me wondering exactly just how many people they had in their pockets and how deep their pockets ran.

The funeral was to be held within a few days, and Nick needed a friend. I also had the task of trying to figure out where to start the search for Antonio's killer. I laid on the couch staring up at the plain white ceiling the whole night going through the list we came up with. When you don't know someone or their life, it's hard to decipher exactly what went wrong and when it got to that point. And I was finding out just how hard it could be.

The next few days were filled with Nick making preparations and phone calls for the funeral. What little spare time we did have together we spent trying to come up with reasons why each person on the list could've possibly wanted Antonio dead. Nick's face became lined with guilt from every one of those conversations. Those were not the final memories he wanted to have of his brother. Worn down and worn out, I knew the worst was yet to come for him.

"Do you mind if I attend the funeral, as well? I mean, I'll stay in the back out of everyone's way, but this way I can judge how the others act. Their behavior. This also cuts down on the need to travel because they're all already here. It's a lot easier this way. I'll stay out of everyone's sight and be your eyes. I'll be the observer you won't have the time to be," I offered. In truth, I knew he wouldn't be in any condition to notice much of anything at all. He was already a mess. When the moment came for that final goodbye, he would completely fall apart.

"Yeah, that's fine. You're right, it would be better that way." I followed his stare to the window. Gray clouds blanketed the sky preventing any light from escaping their clutches. The bleak atmosphere reflected his dark, oppressive mood.

"Do you want to go for a walk?" I learned quickly walking calmed him when he was under pressure or needed to clear his mind.

The exhaust-fumed air and noise-filled streets apparently soothed his soul.

"Sure. Why not?" He was so quiet, almost whispering.

He donned his black leather coat due to the weather taking a sudden turn these last couple of days. It was quite noticeable that Fall was upon us now. The leaves were turning and the air had more of a bite to it than usual. We walked for hours without speaking. I wanted to know how to help him, but I was quite sure even he didn't know the answer to that question.

My mother would have told me only time can help heal his wounds. She was always the first to admit she didn't have all the answers, but, somehow, she always knew exactly what to do to make me feel better. It was times like those when I desperately wished I could've called on her for help. I knew that was impossible so all I could do is reach into my past and try to do as she would have done.

My mother was the woman I aspired to be like. I always said if I could be half the woman she was, I would be doing all right.

I pulled Nick off to the side by his jacket sleeve and said, "I know only time will help you, but I wish there was something else I could do."

His nod gave me comfort, but I wasn't sure if I made the situation better or worse. "It will eventually get better. It has to, right? It has to get better than this. I'll be fine."

The day of the funeral arrived and the somberness hung heavy in the air. I didn't see anything out of the ordinary. There were no telling looks on any one person's face. There was not an exultant or elated look to be found at the gathering after the funeral.

I tried to mix in with the other people there, all the while watching without becoming conspicuous, when a man I didn't recognize from the funeral waltzed through the front door. There was a smugness exuding from him. His supercilious attitude irritated me. I burnt the image of his face into my mind so I could ask Nick about him later. At that moment, he was busy off talking in the corner with his boss.

Nick's boss, Lucas, was a very good-looking man, yet I could see how he could be considered very intimidating. To humans that is. His nefarious eyes drew you in and, no matter how hard you fought, you couldn't look away. His jet black hair worn slicked back added to the dominant, in-control persona he projected. Power and prestige emanated from his being. Even from across the room I could feel it. I had to stay focused on my objective and not get drawn in by the infamous man known as Mr. Lucas Campiato. I forced my eyes back on the abstruse man I didn't recognize. He seemed to know everyone in the room, yet there was not a friendly face toward him.

It worked once before so I decided to give it a try again. I called for Katarina in my head. I didn't want to put her into more danger, but I desperately needed her help. We hadn't spoken since our fight so I didn't have high hopes she would answer, if she could hear me at all.

'Alyssa? Are you okay?'

'I need your help. First off, the fact that you can hear me is pretty cool. Second, can you see what I see right now?' This was an interesting new skill to be able to do, I thought.

'Yes. I can see what you see.' While in my head she was able to see and hear everything going on around me. This could be a very useful ability. *Why didn't more vampires use it,* I wondered?

'Because not all vampires can do this, Alyssa.'

'How did you know what I was thinking?' The fact she could read my thoughts scared the crap me.

'Because I'm in your head. I hear your thoughts. That's how we're communicating.' Okay, now I felt ridiculous. There was my blonde moment for the day.

'Do you see that man over there?'

'Yes. I see him. He doesn't appear to be a very nice man at all. Alyssa, be careful around him.' Katarina always worried about me. It was endearing. *'You shouldn't be able to do this. The fact that you can is astounding.'* She sounded ecstatic. *'Try one little trick for me,'* she requested.

'For you? Anything.' It was true. For her, I would do anything.

'Go into that man's head. See if you can see anything.'

'Okay. But how do I do that?' I wasn't exactly sure how to do what she was asking. Through all our training, she never taught me how to dig through someone else's mind.

'Very carefully. That is how. Focus and see if you can see anything in his mind.' I wanted to do what she asked but it's a very

difficult and confusing task to attempt if you have no idea what you're doing.

I saw glimpses here and there but nothing consistent. Jumbled and mixed thoughts were all I received. I did get a scene of Antonio in what seemed to be his last days, though. This man, who I now knew was named Alonzo, had something to do with Antonio's untimely death. I was certain of it. I decided it would be best by all accounts to wait on telling Nick what I had learned. It was a burden he didn't need to bear right then.

Alonzo brazenly strolled up to Nick and panic seeped into my chest. I rushed over, close enough to protect him, but not close enough to be noticed. Alonzo embraced him like a friend giving his condolences for Antonio's death. I didn't like this man one bit. I had to admit, though, he had balls. Balls he had.

As the day wore on, the visitors slowly dispersed. A few actual family members stayed on, and I decided to stay at the house with Katarina. I hadn't seen her in days, and I missed her terribly. And, to be quite truthful, I needed to eat. Plus a few of Nick's family members stayed over to console and reminisce, and I didn't want to intrude on them during such a personal time. I walked in the front door and was greeted by a prodigious hug from Katarina. I hugged back just as tight, clinging on for dear life. That was when it hit me. I realized how much I needed to be missed. A few minutes pasted before we reluctantly released each other. Pulling back a few steps, I looked into her endless eyes then squeezed her one more time for good measure.

"Ahh, I missed you." I reiterated by taking her hands into mine.

"I've missed you, too. Come, we have lots to catch up on, and by the looks of things, it seems you could use a good meal."

She covered her mouth as she giggled which, in turn, caused me to giggle right along with her. I couldn't help it. Her being at ease and laughing helped me relax and enjoy being home. Cause and effect you may say. Holding her hand, I followed her to the living room and sat down on the couch. We spent the entire night talking. I caught her up on what was going on with my human situation, and she set me up with a tall glass of the yummy red goodness.

Eating her way was not that big of a deal to me anymore. It was easy, reliable, and we always had a supply waiting. Katarina was exhilarated about my newfound skill. She was going on and on about how rare of an ability it was. She thought it was a fluke at first when I was able to call her in my head, but the second time she knew I had something special.

"Not many can do what you can," she echoed over and over again to me.

I was happy for once I was able to appease her instead of disappointing her. It was an enormous weight lifted off of my shoulders. That was the homecoming I needed. It was nice to be home. It felt strange to me to say that, but that's what it was – my home.

The next evening was beautiful. A coolness flooded the city. Shorts and tank tops were traded in for jeans and sweaters. I slipped on my hoodie and stepped outside just in time to see the majestic glow of the orange and yellow sunset. That has always been my favorite part of the day. It signified the ending of one day and the beginning of a new one. Everything that had gone wrong was over and tomorrow you could start again. That was the way that I looked at it. Every day was a new chance to start over. To begin again.

I sat on my front stoop watching until the last rays disappeared behind the statuesque building and all that remained were the soft hues of lilac, rose and smoky blue. I rose, wiping the dirt from my jeans, and embarked on my stroll over to Nick's. It really wasn't that far of a walk at all. Down two blocks, over one, and there was his house. It was only a short ten-minute leisurely walk from Katarina's house. I wanted to give him a little time away from me, away from the situation, to have some time to reflect and spend with family before I bombarded him with my presence once again. I didn't want to wear out my welcome. I could only imagine in times like those, family would be the best thing to have around you. That's what I would've wanted. I didn't want to interfere or take that time away from him.

When I rounded the corner some of the same familiar solemn faces from the funeral emerged from his house. I hung back until I saw them load into cabs and disappear around the corner.

After making sure all were gone, I scrambled up to Nick as he turned back toward his house. "Hey," I said trying to act nonchalant. I didn't want him to know how much I had missed seeing his face, his smell or hearing his voice. That was when I knew in my heart I was falling for him. There was that indescribable quality he had I just couldn't resist, but I had to somehow learn how.

"Hey?" he said, more a question than a welcome. I handed over the white paper bag I was toting. "What's this?" He held it out in front of him, examining it, looking confused.

"Dinner," I stated simply.

"Thanks," he uttered.

I followed him inside and plopped down on one of the black leather chairs in the living room. His furniture was so amazingly comfortable and plush.

"It's supposed to be the best burger in town. That's what they claim anyway." A shocked and confused look was replaced by appreciation. "Is something wrong?" Did I do something wrong again? Things never manage to come out right when I tried too hard. My dad learned that the hard way from all of the homemade Father's Day gifts from me.

"No. It's great, actually." He sat there, eyes intently focused on the burger.

"Are you sure? I can go and get you something else if you prefer."

"No, its fine. It's just ... Never mind," he spouted.

"No. I want to know." I intertwined my hair in my fingers nervously.

"It's just normally women don't bring me things. I bring them things. This is a nice change of pace, for once. You thought about me." He picked up the burger and took a bite.

"Oh. Well, I figured you probably wouldn't be thinking about eating, and you need to eat to keep up your strength. So, I brought you food. My mother always fed me when I was upset. I don't know if that helps you feel better, but it always helped me, so ... "I smiled and pushed the fries at him.

He glanced down at them and chuckled, "Do you have any ketchup?"

"Yep. Here." I tossed him a couple of packets.

"You seemed to have thought of everything." He tore open the packet with his teeth. While squirting it over the heaping mound of fries, he continued, "I tend to buy the girls little baubles, trinkets.

You know, to dangle in front of them to keep their hopes up. To keep them interested. That's what they expect from me. That's what I'm supposed to do. I'm the man but they don't seem to know the difference between a gift from the heart and something trivial. To be honest, I'm not sure they even care." He kept eating.

"Well, that's not me. David would buy me little things occasionally, but if I saw something I thought he might like or that reminded me of him I would get it for him. That's how we were." I shrugged my shoulders. I had always assumed that's how every couple was with each other.

"Who's David?" He seemed intrigued, shocked even, that I might have actually had a relationship with someone.

"I told you, I wasn't always like this. One night my whole life changed. Well, in one night my whole life ended, but before that, I had a good life. I had amazing parents, terrific friends and a wonderful boyfriend. That would be David." I smiled while saying his name. It was a habit. I couldn't help it. I chose not to mention our last night together. That was not the memories I chose to remember or tell. "He was amazing. Everything I ever wanted."

I told him the story of how David and I met, things we did and how he asked me out. I told him about my parents, what my friends and I used to do and about school. He appeared a little saddened on that aspect.

"I was supposed to go to college," he replied while stuffing a French fry in his mouth.

"Really? Why didn't you? You know, it's never too late. They have night classes and online classes, as well." It was as if I was turning into the poster child for adult college. My parents would be so proud.

"Life got in the way. My parents died in an accident, and it was my job to raise Antonio. What I wanted didn't matter anymore and was put on the back burner. I don't mind. It's fine." Picking at his fingernails was a dead giveaway he was uncomfortable so I didn't push him on the subject. This was the most he had opened up to me. I wasn't about to blow it by being overly obnoxious.

I sat in admiration as I watched him eat listening to the stories he told about all of his and Antonio's little escapades from when they were younger. They were hilarious. He told them with such color and animation I could see them all unfolding and happening right in front of me as if I was right there with them. I laughed at the faces he made about the situations they somehow managed to land themselves into over and over again. Leaning in closer to listen, my hand took on a mind of its own and gently rubbed on his forearm. He stopped talking and glanced down at my hand. I jerked it back, running it through my hair instead.

"I'm sorry." My eyes were wider than I meant with my heart beat wildly out of control.

"It's fine." His dark eyes settled on mine. There was a look of confusion, but he didn't flinch or draw away like I assumed he would. He kept his attention on my face.

I swallowed hard. "I didn't mean to overstep my bounds. I know my place. I'm sorry." I tried to fix the issue, but all I could do was stick my foot even further into my mouth.

"What do you mean you know your place?" See. Foot in mouth yet again. I did not want to have to explain what Katarina had told me, but I left myself no other choice.

"Yes. I know my place. Look at me. Look at what I am, Nick." I felt my face getting hot, but I couldn't control it now.

"What? I mean, I know what you are but ... "There was no way he could possibly know or understand.

"You have your whole life in front of you, Nick. My life is gone. I'm not allowed to have feelings for anyone, and I certainly do not have the right to expect or ask anyone to have feelings for me. Let alone you. I don't have the liberty to fall for or care about anyone, you in particular. Especially considering what I am and what I have done to you and your family. It's not fair to you or me."

"You're falling for me?" He had a pleased with himself look on his face.

"You don't get it. Focus on what I'm saying." I stood, hovering over him trying to get him to concede my point. "I can't fall for you or anyone else, and why would you want me to? Look what I did to your brother. I'm a monster, Nick, a monster. I do nothing but bring hurt and destruction with me where ever I go!" I screamed, tears streaming down my face before collapsing onto the floor.

Kneeling, he wrapped his strong, capable arms around me and held me close. I could hear his heart beating and felt the warmth radiating from his body into my own. I tried to fight him off but he held me closer, tighter. Breathing in his soothing scent, I subdued myself and languished in his grip. I sat there hanging on to his arm, sobbing quietly.

Moments passed and I finally pulled myself together. As I wiped the tears away from my face, I peeked up at Nick's. He was focused on my eyes and softly caressed my face with the back of his warm, rough hand. Placing his finger under my chin, he gingerly bent down and kissed my tear soaked lips. I was not about to waste this one moment I had with him. I kissed his full lips back.

What started slow and easy quickly became hot and feverish. It was exhilarating to say the least. Finally pulling apart, we drank in the pure site of each other.

"What was that?" I asked breathlessly.

"I don't know. I liked it, though. I'm sorry?" It was more of a question than an apology. Either way I didn't want it.

"No. It's fine. I liked it, too. I really liked it, but I don't think we are supposed to be doing this. I'm going to get you killed, Nick. I don't want that." All the horrible things that could happen to him ran through my mind. What if I couldn't control myself around him? What if I hurt him? What if I turned him into what I was? What if Dante found out? What if ...

"Stop thinking so much," his soothing, rough voice interrupted my thoughts. "Stop and, for once, go with what you feel. What do you want? Do you want me to stop?" I shook my head no, and, before I knew it, he resumed kissing me, more vigorously this time. I never wanted it to end. I wanted him. There was no doubt in my mind. All I could think about was how could this possibly work, and then I stopped thinking. Right there in that moment I took his advice and went with what I felt.

That first kiss was everything I had imagined and wanted it to be. It was intense, breathtaking, dangerous and electrifying. I never wanted anything as much as I wanted it, that one magical kiss, to never end.

Pulling me onto his chest, we spent the rest of the night lying in front of the warm, lit fireplace on the floor in his living room surrounded by soft plush pillows. Talking for hours with our fingers interlocked in one another's, he softly brushed the hair out of my face. He needed me. I needed him. We needed each other.

Nick gradually fell asleep while I laid in his arms and, for once, my heart was at peace. But even though it was at peace, my heart could not stop my mind from all the horrid thoughts that kept racing through it. After lying there most of the night thinking of all the horrible and amazing things that could happen, I reluctantly slid out of his arms and scrambled back to Katarina's house. How was I supposed to explain this one to her? This was not going to go well.

Chapter 10

Upon entering our house, I quickly discovered things were moved, rearranged. "Hello?" Where was she? Normally Katarina always greeted me at the door. I turned around, and there she was. "Geez, you have to stop doing that. I almost jumped out of my skin."

She chortled and her eyes lit up welcoming me home. "Do you like the place? Since you haven't been here I found I have a lot of time on my hands." I wasn't quite sure how to take that. I wasn't sure if it was meant as compliment or an insult. I decided to take it as a compliment.

"I love it." I said, stretching out the words long enough to buy some time to find every little detail that was different. That way when she asked, which I knew she would, I would know what and where everything had been moved to. I wasn't sure if this was going to be a test of my new found ability or not. She was always finding new ways to test me.

I hugged her tight one more time. I was going to tell her, I had planned on telling her, but standing there looking at her face, I couldn't tell her. How was I supposed to disappoint her yet again?

"You know I care about you right?" I asked.

"Yes, and I care about you, as well. We're a family," she said, lovingly gazing into my eyes. I knew she wasn't lying. She truly did feel that way. That was the dagger to the heart with a little twist at the end.

"I just wanted to come and tell you that. No matter what idiotic mistakes I may make along the way, and I will make them, believe me on that one, I do care deeply for you. You are my family, my heart and I love you." Saying the words aloud made them ring even more real and true. "I'm going to get back now. I missed you and wanted to see your face. That's all," I said forcing back tears and putting on the most natural forced smile I could muster up.

Squeezing me until I was unable to breathe she finally let go. "I miss you too. Hurry up. Come home where you belong."

Letting a second pass, I smiled and said, "I will. I'll be home soon." Slowly walking out of the house, I prayed I hadn't just lied to her. I wanted to come home, but, considering all the rules I had already broken, I wasn't sure if that was a possibility anymore. And being honest with myself, I secretly longed to get back into Nick's arms.

I hoped he hadn't woken yet and noticed me missing. Sliding back into his arms was the most natural thing I'd done in a really long time. I closed my eyes, snuggled in and wondered if things had not happened as they did, would I have ever met him? If I was being honest with myself, the answer was no.

Wrapping my fingers in his, I gently rubbed his arm with my other hand. When he wakes I will tell him what I found out about Alonzo and his brother Antonio, I ordered myself. That should snap things back into reality. He would be done with me once he found out what happened. That's all this relationship was, a need to be close to someone until all the questions were answered. Right now he just needed to feel close to someone. Anyone. If I wasn't there, then it would've been someone else. Nothing else would come of this. But I wanted it to so badly it hurt. This, him, was clearly not my reality, and I needed to get back to my life. Do I really, I questioned myself. Yes, yes I do. Just not right now. Right now was not that time. For a second longer I wanted to pretend, pretend I was normal. That my life was normal. So I snuggled in a little closer, took in a deep breath and forced all the negative thoughts out of my head for this one moment in time.

He started to stir and nuzzled his face into the nape of my neck. This was it. The last few seconds I had in my make-believe, all is perfect right now, world. Soaking in all I could, as fast as I could, I found myself praying for a few more seconds of the life I wished I could have. I turned in his arms so I could look at his beautiful face. Memorize his perfect, full, mesmerizing lips, his glorious, well-defined jaw line and cheekbones and his dark, ominous eyes that always sucked me in.

When his eyes gradually opened, a warm smile made its way across his lips. "Morning." His raspy voice was masculine and inviting. It sent a buzz humming through my body and flutters racing in my stomach.

"Good morning," I whispered back. Reluctantly, I released my grip on him and wondered if he could tell. Would he even notice, or, for that matter, would he care? Why am I getting so wrapped up in him? Maybe because the only other guy you've ever been with was Andy, Alyssa?

Immediately whisking me out of my fantasy, he sat up, and I knew what I had to do. I would give him all the facts I knew and let him decide. Whatever his decision may be, I would respect and honor it even if it hurt.

Stretching his arms over his head, Nick made a grunting sound I'd never heard before that day in my life. Smiling, he bent down pressing his warm lips against mine then proceeded up the stairs to his room. When the shower kicked on I collapsed back down into the comforts of the rumpled blankets and pillows. Maybe last night did mean something to him. Maybe things could work out. Or maybe, just maybe, I was living in a fantasy world.

An hour passed before he finally ambled back in the room plopping down in the chair across from me with a thoughtful smile on his face.

I stopped picking up the floor long enough to say, "I really enjoyed last night. It was nice." My face reddened from the sheer embarrassment of the sound of my own voice cracking.

"Me too." His voice was like silk gliding across my ears.

"Nick, we need to talk. There are things I need to tell you, and I'm not sure how you're going to react to them."

"Okay, well, let's hear it," he said, clasping his hands together and sitting back in the chair.

"There was a man at the gathering following your brother's funeral. His name is Alonzo. Do you know him?" I inquired.

"Yeah." He let out a sigh. It was as if he knew where this was going, and I didn't blame him for the assumption considering how the others reacted to that man's presence. "My brother and I've known him for a long time. Since before my parent's accident. He helped me get into the family after it. He knew I didn't want Antonio in but he ... well, let's just say Antonio got in anyway. Things have been a little strained between us since Antonio and I moved up but ... Why are asking me about Alonzo? How do you know him? Did you meet him at the gathering?"

My mistake. He didn't have a clue of where I was going with this. "No. I didn't meet him, but I saw him there. I saw things in his head that... "

"Wait. Wait. Wait." He said, stopping me mid-sentence waving his hands around. "You saw things in his head? What does that even mean? You saw things in his head? You see things in people's heads now, too?" He sat straight up in the chair, brows pinched together, narrowed eyes focused on me.

"Yes, I can. I mean, I see inside people's heads. Read their thoughts. See things no one else is supposed to be able to see. Apparently, according to Katarina, it's a rare thing. I shouldn't be able to do it, but I can. What I saw was disturbing, to say the least, Nick."

"All right. What was it then? What did you see? In his head, I mean?" He didn't believe me. It was undeniable. He thought I was crazy, but I didn't care. He needed to know what this person he thought was a friend really was.

"He isn't your friend, Nick. I only got glimpses, images, flashes you can say. I haven't exactly learned how to use this ability perfectly yet. I didn't even know I had it until that night with you. I didn't even know it was an ability. I thought all of us could do it. Apparently, I was wrong. Because it is so rare, we're not even sure how to perfect it except with practice on my part." I hoped I made some kind of sense to him with my rambling, but the blank stare I received told me to keep dreaming.

"So you could be wrong? I know things have been strained, but he would never hurt Antonio or me. He loves us like family. Like brothers. You're wrong. So completely wrong. You have to be. Like you said, you haven't even learned how to really do it yet. Maybe you can't really do it. You could be making it all up for all I know. First you're a vampire, and now you want me to believe you're a mind reader, too? Come on." My jaw dropped. He was calling me a liar or a nut. Either way, I didn't appreciate it at all.

"There was another man there, as well. Alonzo was watching while this other man beat Antonio basically to death. This is your world. I don't pretend to know why this happen to your brother, all I know is what I saw. He was a white man, mid-to-late forties, a little heavier and about five foot nine. Anybody come to mind that you may know who fits that description?"

Shaking his head, I could tell he was going over things in his mind trying to think. "No. No one comes to mind. It doesn't matter anyway; I know Alonzo would not do this. I know him. You're wrong, Alyssa. You are dead wrong."

"Nick, if I could only take one piece of advice from Katarina it would be this; in the end you can only count on yourself. The only one you know you can really trust is you."

Looking defiantly, he said, "Well then, what makes me think I can trust you? Like you said, you can only trust yourself, and it is your fault he was in the situation to begin with. You're the reason he had to run in the first place. So ... "He stomped toward the bay window, plopped down refusing to look at me.

"I'm going to go. If or when you want my help, call me." Sliding over the yellow legal pad, I scribbled down my number and walked out. He didn't even try to stop me. I glanced back one last time only to see him still looking away angrily.

Outside, the sun shone down on my face. The air was chilly with only a few birds flying above. The blue sky was clear without single cloud to ruin it. Normally, I would be rejoicing over such a spectacular day, but right now I felt like my whole world was crumbling beneath me, and there wasn't a damn thing I could do about it. I had given myself to him completely, unabashedly and he rejected me. How else was I supposed to feel?

I walked lethargically back to the house, but my mind was racing. How could he think I would purposely lie or try to hurt him? We hadn't known each other very long, but I thought I had proven myself by now. I knew somehow I got his brother tangled up in God knows what, but it wasn't like I maliciously planned and executed it. It was never supposed to get Antonio hurt, much less killed. I could tell he wasn't a scumbag. Hell, I saved his life. Repeatedly. Why would he think that way?

The streets were filled with the hustle and bustle as always and, for once, I didn't find myself wondering where they were going or who they were. All I could focus on was the hurt and anguish I felt over Nick's reaction. His rejection of me. Walking up to the house I noticed Katarina had been gardening. Beautiful peacock orchids now lined the walk way as gorgeous multi-colored pansies hung from the windows in cute little white baskets. It made the place look more cheerful and feel a bit more like home. The beautiful smells of the orchids filled the air as I walked toward the door. Instead of heading in right away, I decided to take a minute and sat down on our front stoop. I needed to pull myself together before greeting Katarina, and I didn't want to have to explain to her what happened between Nick and me. To be honest, I didn't want to prove her right.

I sat there watching the people walk, drive, and ride by. Hours passed and only when it turned dusk and I had watched my favorite part of the day did I stand to go inside. Right then and there I made a choice. Instead of feeling sorry for myself, I was going to focus all my energy on figuring out this so-called ability of mine. Neither Katarina nor I had any idea how to do use it adequately, much less be able to perfect it. That was exactly what I needed to take my mind off Nick and the cruel accusations he made.

A sweet aroma surrounded me as soon as I opened the door. Katarina had decorated for fall and the smell of pumpkin spice reminded me of home. I looked around at the warm colors of yellows, oranges, browns, and reds. The whole house oozed serenity. The fireplace was going strong, and all I wanted to do was curl up in front of it, feeling its heat surround my body and bawl my eyes out.

Instead, I trudged upstairs to my room and put on the most comfortable pair of pajamas I could find. Looking into the mirror, I brushed my hair back into a ponytail realizing this was as good as it was going to get for the moment. I looked around my room noticing how bare it was. Well, at least now I have time to decorate, I thought to myself. I plodded my way downstairs sliding my hand along the dark sleek cherry wood banister when I noticed the intricately designed rod iron that was holding it up, daisies and leaves woven all throughout in a delicate design.

I sat on the stairs tracing the flowers with my finger, my mind wondering why I had never truly looked at the intricateness of it all. That's it. That was it. Sometimes you can't see what is staring you right in the face until you stop looking for it. If Nick would stop looking for why his brother was killed maybe, just maybe, it would smack him right in the face when he least expected it. Then he would see I wasn't wrong. He would see I wasn't trying to hurt him at all but help him.

Or maybe this was all just stupid, wishful thinking, and I needed to stop hoping for something that would never happen. Nick would never be mine. I wasn't allowed to have that kind of love anymore. Maybe Kat was right. We are damned. I hated being so damn logical sometimes. Sometimes I wanted to be able to live in my fantasy world without Kat's voice ringing in my head knocking me out of it.

"What are you in such deep thought about?" I about jumped out of my skin when her voice shattered the silence.

"What?" I stopped focusing on the daisies to find her practically nose to nose with me.

"I said, what are you in such deep thought about?" Confusion marred her perfect doll-like face. She sat down next to me still scrutinizing.

"Nothing. Just about how to perfect this ability of mine and the things I might be able to do with it. I mean, if I can get into people's heads maybe I could use it to keep us safe. You know, from the likes of Dante and others like him." It wasn't a total lie. I had thought about it.

"No. You do not want to try to get into his head. But we do need to work on it. Are you home for good or just for the night?" Her doe eyes anchored onto me.

"No. I'm home for good." I smiled, trying not to let my heartache seep through.

"Ahh. That's great news. Well, first let's get you fed and catch up. Then we can figure out what to do about that special skill of yours."

Sitting there talking with Kat, uncertainty crept over me. I felt something was coming. I wasn't quite sure what was it was, but I knew it was going to change all of us and what we thought we knew, forever.

Chapter 11

Weeks went by and my ability was even more of a mystery to us then it was in the beginning. At points, I could focus and see people's thoughts as clear as day, and at other times it was all a big jumbled mess of flashes and images I couldn't decipher. I focused and did every exercise Katarina told me to do, except it wasn't working. Nothing seemed to work. I wasn't strong enough to bypass all the flashes to find the information I was searching for. Most of the time it was their birthday or some other stupid, inconsequential bit of information, never anything too serious or private.

"You have to want it, Alyssa. You have to know what you want and focus on it. Only then will you see the information you're looking for." Katarina was beyond annoying me at that point.

"I am focusing, and I do want it. I am doing all I can, Kat. Why don't you do it since you seem to know so much? Oh wait, because you can't. That's right. So lay off of mean cut me some slack. Please." I hadn't meant to be so belligerent. I really did want it just as badly as she did, but, no matter how hard I tried, I couldn't will my mind to learn how. My frustrations got the better of me, and I, unfortunately, took it out on Kat. "I'm sorry. It's just that I am doing my best, and it doesn't seem to be good enough. It's so irritating." I parked myself on the couch.

"I know you're trying, Alyssa, I can see that. I truly do, but obviously we need to try a new approach. I don't know how this works, either. It is extremely rare. I told you that. So bear with me on the trial and error of what I'm asking you to do. Maybe you're right. We should take a break and perhaps go for a walk to clear our heads. Get a fresh take on things. What do you think?" A walk was exactly what I needed. I had been cooped up in the house for weeks. Fresh air would do me good.

"Yes. A walk would be great." I smiled at the thought of walking aimlessly. Not having to think to for a while. My brain hurt from all of her training exercises.

"Shall we?" I said, gesturing toward the door.

With a smirk, she said, "Yes. We shall." I started out the door when Katarina called out, "Alyssa?"

"Yes?" I replied back.

"Sweetie, do you think perhaps you should put on some clothes? I mean other than your pajamas?" How embarrassing.

"Yep."

I ran up the stairs taking them two at a time and quickly threw on a pair of jeans and a long sleeve t-shirt. I slid my favorite boots on and sauntered back down the stairs pretending as if the incident never happened. Kat, on the other hand, didn't get the gist and kept snickering. With my head held high, I walked passed her and opened the door pretending I didn't see or hear her laughing.

Outside the cold air blew through my hair and leaves rustled around my feet. The smell of winter in the air was undeniable. Being outside, walking around, awoke my senses, and I felt like a new person. Katarina and I started the stroll at a leisurely pace.

Watching the people rush by, Kat picked an especially hurried woman out of the crowd. "I wonder where she's going?" Katarina questioned.

I knew exactly where she was going with it. She wasn't very casual about it at all. "She's off to pick up her schnauzer from the groomers," I replied.

"And you know this how?" She once again questioned me.

"Because I saw it in her head." I looked at her, tipping my head knowingly.

"Very good, Alyssa." The excitement in her voice was enough for me to keep going without making too much of a fuss. We must have repeated that exercise for a good hour or so.

Finally, I said, "Enough Katarina. Let me enjoy my walk. Pretty please with a cherry on top?" I begged with my hands folded, pleading.

"Fine. I'm sorry. I saw an opportunity to challenge you, so I did. I'll stop now. I promise." She was smiling that innocent smile at me, but I wasn't buying it. Soon enough she would find another test for me. I felt it in my bones. It would come. It was only a matter of time.

We walked all around the city finding ourselves in central park. We sat there feeding the pigeons with the overly-priced pretzel Kat purchased from one of the stands and watched as the mass of people passed by in such a hurry. Flashes and images invaded my head. Nothing relevant to family, friends or fun, it was all about work, work and more work. It made me want to grab one of them out from the crowd and shake them. Tell them how important life is. They should enjoy it and spend it with the ones they loved and who loved them. In the end you only get one life so live it to the fullest. I couldn't though. We couldn't draw attention to ourselves.

The sun was starting to set as we began our walk back to the house, but before we could reach it, I saw Nick. It was the first time in weeks. He was smiling and laughing that intoxicating laugh I loved so much. Except … it wasn't with me. His arm was draped around a beautiful redhead with legs that went on for miles. I never wanted to rip someone's throat out as much as I did right then.

Control yourself, Alyssa, I said to myself. Katarina's stern hand grabbed onto my arm. Apparently, she sensed the tension in me, as well.

"Come, Alyssa. Let's go back to the house. Then you can tell me everything." Katarina was always able to sense when something was wrong with me. I wasn't sure if that was a good thing or bad thing, but I believe it was the mothering side of her she retained from raising her sister.

Nick and the woman walked right passed us and didn't say a word. He didn't even notice me. All I could do was stare in disbelief as they walked out of sight.

"Yeah. Let's go back to the house. I've had about all the fresh air I can handle." I snarled.

We weren't even all the way through the door when she started in on me. "What is going on, Alyssa?" She quickly shut and locked the door behind us.

"Nothing is going on, Katarina. Nothing, except for the fact that when you try to help someone out they do nothing but spit in your face. Now I know how you felt when I was an ungrateful little brat. That's what he is, you know, an ungrateful little brat."

"Uh huh?" She already knew where this was heading.

"Yeah. He doesn't even care that we're in danger or that I put my life on the line to help him. And why? Why did I do that? Because I felt guilty. That's what happens when you let your conscience take over. It will not happen again. Trust me on that." I couldn't stop myself from ranting.

"You care about him?" It was more of a statement than a question.

"No. No, I don't. I don't care one little bit about what happens to him. Not one bit. He could get hit by a bus tomorrow, and I wouldn't care." I honestly was trying not care. I really was, but she could see right through me.

"You're pacing around like a caged animal. You're ranting, and you're ... you're heartbroken aren't you?" I hated the way she could see right through me.

"No. Don't be ridiculous, Kat. That would be ignorant of me. I know what you told me. I know I can't fall in love. I'm not allowed. I know that. How stupid would it be if I did?" I stopped pacing and collapsed onto the couch.

"You are on dangerous grounds, young lady. Dangerous, dangerous grounds. Watch yourself or you'll end up walking right off the edge." She stared at me with such conviction I wondered how she knew with such a certainty what I was heading for. That is unless she had been there herself.

"Can I ask you a question, Kat?" I was almost whispering. I was petrified of what doors the question I was about to ask would open.

"Didn't you just ask me a question by asking if you could ask a question?" She chuckled.

"I'm serious, Kat."

"I know. Yes, you may ask your question." She already knew what I was going to ask. Why else would she try to deflect me from asking?

"Did it happen to you before? Being in love with someone you weren't supposed to, I mean. It's just, you seem so sure of the outcome, I have to wonder." I tended not to pry too much into her past, but this had been gnawing at me for a while.

"Do you want to know the truth? Well then, the truth is yes, I have been in that situation before. A few times actually. It hurts, and it's awful. You need to end it now. If Dante finds out, your lover is dead. And as long as we are being truthful, so are we. We should move. Find somewhere else to go. I hear Chicago is nice, a lot like New York. Busy all the time. We can be there in a few days if we start packing now. "There was something she wasn't telling me but what, I was unsure of.

"I don't want to move again, Kat. Why do we need to move? I'll stop seeing him. Hey, I already have. So there we go." It wasn't by choice, but it was true. I had stopped seeing him.

"Things are not that simple in this world, Alyssa. Just because you will it so, does not mean it will be so. Your friend Nick knows too much now, and we cannot help him. We can only try to save ourselves."

I contemplated exactly what she was trying to say. I didn't like how it sounded at all. She couldn't possibly be saying what I think she's saying, could she, I questioned myself. "Are you saying Nick is going to die?" The thought was too incomprehensible to conceive. Nick couldn't die. Not over me. Not over my mistakes. After all I had put him through, he didn't deserve that ending.

"What I am saying is that right now we need to be thinking of ourselves. We cannot worry about what happens to anyone else. Right now it's about self-preservation." It scared me to see Kat so worried. She was never like that unless she knew danger was coming.

"Why are you being like this, Kat?"

"Fine. I'll tell you. Then you'll see I'm right, and we need to go." She sat next to me and peered out the window. "It was a very long time ago. I met a man who was wonderful and intriguing. He had beautiful sandy hair and eyes as blue and wild as the ocean." A look of happiness settled in on her face. Both love and anguish poured out of her eyes as the story went on. "He was everything that I had ever asked for. He was well-spoken, kind, intelligent, and from a very affluent family. I fell in love. Eventually, I told him everything. Yes, that included me being a vampire. He wasn't afraid." She laughed at that. "He said it didn't matter to him what I was, and he wanted to be with me forever. He even asked me to change him. To make him like me so we could be together forever. On our wedding night," she started.

Shock was uncontrollably written all over my face and my jaw dropped.

"Yes, we got married. On our wedding night, Dante showed up. He told me I knew what I had done. He told me I had broken the sacred rules, and I must be punished. James, that was my husband's name, tried so hard to defend me." Tears filled her eyes. She tried to distract herself by staring at the sparrow perched on the branch just outside the window, but it was to no avail. The tears fell anyway. "He tried, Alyssa. He really did try."

"I'm sure he did, Kat." I shook my head in agreement and held her hands, but there was nothing I could do to ease her pain. She'd already lived through it.

"He didn't stand a chance against Dante. He did all he could, but in the end, ..." She couldn't bear to finish her sentence.

"He killed him?" It was an idiotic question, but I couldn't stop myself from asking. She shook her head.

"I barely escaped. Ever since then, I refuse to get close to any human like that ever again. That is why I told you what I did about falling in love. So, do you see why we must move now? It doesn't matter what you do or say, Dante will kill him. There is no stopping that, and he will kill us too unless we leave right now. You do not know him, Alyssa. Not like I do. He won't give up. Please, Alyssa. Can we go now?" Katarina was practically begging at this point. Fear and desperation were never a good combination.

"Okay. We can go. You go ahead. I have to warn Nick, and then I will meet you in Chicago. I'll be there in a few days. I'll be okay, I promise." I couldn't up and leave without informing Nick of the danger he was in.

"It's not smart to separate right now, Alyssa."

"I will be fine. Go. I'll follow in a couple of days." I tried to reassure her. It was painfully obvious it wasn't going to work. "Pack up your things, I'll have the rest shipped to you. This way you can find us a place to live and think of new ways for me to practice my skill, too. Think of the positive."

Shaking her head, she reluctantly agreed and quickly disappeared to pack up some of her possessions. Within a matter of hours, she was ready to leave. We said our goodbyes and she kissed my cheek one last time before turning to go.

"Remember, you can get in touch with me at any point in time with your newly found gift. Don't be afraid to say you need me. He is not one to be messed with, Alyssa. Stay away from him. I'll see you in a few days, yes?"

"Yes. I just have to warn Nick, and then I'll pack and be on my way. I promise." She squeezed my hand and handed her bags to the taxi driver waiting outside. I watched as the tail lights disappeared into the darkness.

The next morning, I raced over as fast as I could to Nick's house, not caring who saw me and rang his doorbell. There was no answer. I beat on the door, still no answer. Panic flooded me and my heart beat erratically. Had Dante gotten to him already? No, he couldn't have. Why wasn't he answering then? He should be home. I turned to go around back when the door suddenly swung open. I spun back around, and to my surprise, I saw the gorgeous redhead's face staring at me.

"Yes?" Her voice sweet. Too sweet for my taste, almost sugary sweet. I didn't like this woman one bit.

"I need to speak to Nick. Please." I tried to sound pleasant, but I'm sure it didn't come across that way to her. Honestly, I didn't care.

"He's a little busy at the moment. Anything I can do for you?" The sidedness rolling off her tongue was evident.

No, she couldn't help me, it was none of her business what I needed to speak to Nick about. What was her problem? I wanted to grab her and rip her heart out, but I had to control myself. I wasn't allowed to want him. He needed to be able to live a normal life. Well, as normal as a man in his line of work could live, anyways.

"No. You cannot help me. I need to speak with Nick. Now."

She irritated me to the core, and my patience was waning. I wanted her to go fetch Nick like the good little doggie she was so I could talk to him, warn him. Then I would be gone out of his life, and Kat would be safe. I hoped.

"Well, I'm sorry, but as I already said, he is busy." Before she could finish the sentence, I heard Nick walking down the stairs.

"Nick," I shouted.

He came to the door and said, "Alyssa? What do you want?"

"Can we speak in private, please?" I said gesturing toward her.

"Sure. Monica, go wait for me in the living room." She narrowed her eyes and stuck her bottom lip out, but it didn't seem to affect him too much.

"Come on in," he said, waving his hand toward the inside of his house.

He was annoyed by my presence there like I was a nuisance that he didn't want to deal with.

I walked in and ascended the stairs two at a time toward his bedroom. I made the decision to sit on the chair instead of the bed. It was made and tidied, but I still had my reservations.

It seemed like a lifetime ago I was last in his room. The last time was when Antonio's lifeless body had been left at the door. Nick hated me then, and I was pretty sure he hated me at that point in time, as well. It was the first time he had truly opened up to me, and it was the first time I felt his warm embrace against my body. The club didn't count. That wasn't sincere. In this room the embrace was true.

I didn't look around the first time I was in here. It was dark, and it wasn't the time for that. His room felt warm and inviting. The bed was big, king size, and dark mahogany. His dresser and armoire matched in color. The room itself was huge. He had a sitting area, intriguing artwork hung on the walls, and it was painted a beautiful calming blue with chocolate accents. It was all very relaxing, to say the least. I was noticing the shelves lined with leather-bound books when Nick finally sauntered in. I suppose he was consoling his new girlfriend. I don't know. It felt as if it took him forever to get in there, though. He slowly closed the door behind him and walked toward me.

"What do you want, Alyssa?" This was not my Nick. This was the Nick I first met, the cold, hard and distant Nick. He sat on the dark leather couch adjacent to me with his arms folded against his chest.

"I need to talk to you." It hurt and disappointed me all at the same time. I couldn't understand how he could go from the kind and loving person he was when I was in his embrace to this.

"Talk about what? What do you need to talk to me about, Alyssa?" He was frigid.

"First off, I don't understand why you're being so mean to me. I didn't do anything wrong. I told you what I saw. I told you what happened to your brother. I thought that was what you wanted to know." I tried to not raise my voice, but it hurt how malicious and icy he was acting.

"You don't understand why I am being so mean? All you did was tell me about what happened to my brother? What you did was accuse one of my oldest friends of murdering him. How about that? And according to you, you saw this information in his head. It's ludicrous, Alyssa. Maybe, just maybe, that's why I am being so mean as you put it."

"Got it. I just came here to tell you I'm leaving. Kat's worried about Dante. He's extremely dangerous, and she thinks he might know about you. He might know what you know about us. I told you what would happen to you if he found out. Do you remember what I said about him, Nick? I don't want anything to happen to you. Not because of me, not because of anyone, but definitely not because of me."

"I'm fine. I will be fine. I don't need your help for anything. I've taken care of myself this long without you, I'm good. You need to go." He opened the door and looked out ordering me to leave.

Standing, I nodded my head, took one final look around and walked to the door. Walking past him, I smiled sadly. I stopped when I reached the outside of the doorway. Turning to him, I said, "I care about you, Nick. I care more than I should."

I leaned in to softly kiss his lips when he turned his head before I could. I walked out of his house with my head held high until I heard the door slam shut. Letting out a deep sigh, I made the walk home with a lump in my throat but refusing to cry.

I returned to an empty house, and as soon as I closed the door, the tears fell like rain. I couldn't control them anymore than I could control the trembling of my body. In fact, I didn't want to. They were real. Real pain, real heartache, real emotions. I wanted to feel. I wanted to be real. I didn't want to be like Katarina and cut off from everything. After a few minutes of unbridled weeping, I stopped myself. I refused to allow myself to dwell on things I couldn't control any longer. I refused to allow myself to dwell on him.

Chapter 12

I packed for what seemed like hours. The house was dreary and empty, and I couldn't help but long to be with Kat again. I felt safe with her. She accepted me. She loved me. I looked around at the emptiness, it all felt so impersonal now. No pictures or paintings hung on the walls, sheets covered most of the furniture and cardboard boxes littered each room.

I lit a fire in the fireplace and sat on the hearth staring into the burning logs. My mind wandered off to different things. I thought about what my life would've been like had I not been so stupid that night and taken that deadly shortcut. Or what my life with Nick would've been like had I not opened my big, fat mouth about what I saw in that horrible man's mind.

That's when the most intriguing voice spoke to me in my head.

'Alyssa. Why are you so sad, Alyssa?' the stranger asked.

'Because I am not allowed to love or be loved,' I replied flatly. Great. Now I'm going crazy, I thought.

'You're not going crazy, and you can love, Alyssa. You just have to love the right kind. You should learn to love your own kind. Take me for instance.'

The voice was alluring, but that was all I had to go on. I couldn't see a face, eyes, nothing. My imagination was running wild. I imagined a tall, sexy, dangerous man who could fulfill my deepest desires. One who could have all the answers I needed. He wasn't saying I couldn't be loved as Kat had. She said not even our own kind was a good idea. He appeared to be taking the opposite approach. Kat never mentioned she had been with our kind before, just humans. Maybe she didn't know what it was really like to be with someone like us.

'Take you how?' I tried to sound uninterested, although deep down I longed to hear what he had to say.

He chuckled deep and seductive, and had I been standing, my knees would have buckled beneath me. The richness of his voice had my heart fluttering. *'Hmmm, I can help you. If you would like, that is.'*

103

'*Help me how? What makes you think I need help?*' Now it was plain old curiosity that had me.

'*Well, I can help you with your skill. Your ability that is. Also, if I were in your life, you would not be sitting around in pajamas watching a fire. I would have you out, showing you off. You would be my queen.*' I quickly fell under his spell. I wanted to see him, meet him, touch him right then and there.

'*Really?*' I could say nothing else. I was in awe. Someone wanted me. Someone wanted me when I was like this. A monster.

'*Hmmm, you shouldn't think of yourself as a monster, Alyssa. You are so beautiful. Exquisite, you might say.*'

'*Wait. How did you know what I was thinking?*'

'*I'm in your mind, Alyssa. I can see and hear everything you're thinking.*'

'*I knew that.*' I couldn't think properly with him in my head, but I didn't want him to know that, but I had the distinct feeling he already knew.

He laughed his deep, seductive, enthralling laugh. Something in my head was screaming don't trust him. DANGER! DANGER! DANGER! It felt like one of those annoying car alarms going off, but this one was in my head.

'*I should go.*' I had to say something. It was uncomfortable, and my stomach had a knot the size of a boulder in it.

'*How are you going to go when I am in your head? Hmmm, this could get fun, Alyssa. I'll leave you alone for now, but I will be back.*' With that, the mystery man disappeared from my head as suddenly as he had appeared.

The rest of my night was spent wondering who the mystery voice in my head was. Maybe he was someone who could help me figure out why I was able to do what I could do. Why I had this ability. Obviously, he was *my* kind so, therefore, I wasn't breaking any rules by telling him. Heck, he already knew. How did he know what I could do? How did he know me? Who was he? What did he look like? Had I met him before? There were so many questions and no real way to get the answers. He seemed to understand my abilities which was always a plus because I didn't at all.

The fire died down so I tossed a couple more logs on. After a minute or two, it came back as strong as ever. I started questioning if I thought about him hard enough in my head would he come back? Or, perhaps, if I thought about him long enough would I be able to get inside his head?

First, I concentrated on Nick. It was late, but at least, I would know if he was all right. He was fast asleep and dreaming. Dreaming of Antonio. I left it alone at that. It was personal and none of my business. I would hate to be invaded in that way, in something as personal as a dream. I switched my concentration to the mystery man. I focused on remembering the mysterious voice which had fascinated me so much. The deep, rich texture and the danger that lied within it.

'You're thinking of me.' And he was back. Yes!

'I have a lot of questions.' In truth, I needed to hear him again, but he didn't need to know that.

'I might have some answers for you. Perhaps we can make a game of it, Alyssa. What do you think? Do you like that idea?' More mystery.

'Yes. I like that idea a lot. You go first.'

'Good. Why would you waste your time on a mere human, one who would never fully understand or care about you the way he should, when you could have so much more?' The disgust his voice held when he said the word human was overwhelming.

'I don't know what you are talking about. I know my place. I'm not allowed. I know that.'

'Do you?'

'That's two questions. My turn.'

'No, no, no. Technically you didn't answer my question.' I hate technicalities.

'Fine. Because there's something about him I can't explain. He's different. Why do you ever care about someone? You just do. There is no rhyme, no reason. You can't force the heart to do something it doesn't want to do. The same goes for trying to force it not to do something it wants to do. Now, my turn. Do I know you?'

He chuckled again. *'In a way you know me but personally? No, you don't know me personally. Why did you want to hear my voice again so badly?'*

'I'm sure I don't know what you are talking about.' Laughter erupted again.

'Tsk Tsk Tsk. No lying. It is not becoming of you, Alyssa.' He was so aggravating, yet I didn't want the conversation to end, so I told the truth.

'Your voice is ... sexy, tantalizing, and also very sensual.' My face reddened with the revelation of that word. I'd never used it before, but nothing else fit so perfectly.

'That's the first time I have ever heard that. No one enjoys hearing my voice.'

'I do. I'm sure any woman you've talked to has.'

'No. They don't. I know this for a fact.'

'How could they not? That I don't understand. It's very alluring. Captivating.' I bit my lower lip while twirling my hair in my fingers. I couldn't tell him his voice excited me. It made me want to do things I know I shouldn't, for instance, find out where he was and run to him.

'Hmmm. I think that's enough questions for now, Alyssa.'

'Wait. It's my turn. You can't end it when it is my turn. There's still so many things I want to know like what's your name, what you look like, and where you are right now.'

'That's three questions. You're going to owe me, Alyssa. You may call me D. I look like most of our kind, perfect. Flawless skin, perfect teeth, and a decent body, I guess you might say. Right now? Right now I am looking right at you.' I looked out the French doors in the living room as the shadow quickly disappeared. I was excited and terrified all at the same time. What was I doing? What was I getting myself into?

'I owe you now, but it's just in the game, though, right?'

'Maybe. I haven't decided yet. I'll let you know when I do.'

I crawled over and opened the back door where the shadow had been standing. That was as close as I could get to him. I tried to get a whiff of his scent. That was another good thing about being a vampire, excellent sense of smell, and his smell was electrifying. I found myself wanting more, but inside I was screaming, what is wrong with you? He's trouble. Stay away. DANGER! DANGER! DANGER!

That was what I wanted though, a little bit of danger to keep me going. It wouldn't hurt me to have that, would it? I knew, in the back of my mind, that everything I did affected Kat, and I didn't want my little bit of danger to harm her, but, at least, he was our kind. I couldn't be with Nick. He didn't want me anyway, and Kat never said I couldn't be with someone of our own kind. Just it wasn't a good idea. Maybe this mystery man could be a great distraction for me.

Chapter 13

The next day dragged on sluggishly. Tick tock. Tick tock. The gold hands of the antique oak grandfather clock seemed to taunt me with its never-ending chatter that filled the house. Its sound was the only comfort I could find inside that empty space called a home, and it was turning into no comfort at all. It was as if the clock was moving in slow motion, and I was the only one who realized it. It was almost impossible for me to get even the simplest of tasks completed. I kept hearing that enticing voice inside my head. So seductive. So entrancing. I wanted to find him. I wanted to see what the person who had captivated me looked like. I wanted to feel his hard body wrapped around mine, his smell dancing around my nose, and me taking in every bit of it.

Seeing the cardboard boxes scattered about the house reminded me of how much work still lie ahead and how it desperately needed to get finished. Kat was counting on me to get all of this done and her personal possessions to her. *'Focus, Alyssa. Focus.'* I thought.

I forced myself to begin the tedious task of bubble wrapping all the fragile figurines and trinkets she'd collected over the years. It wasn't as if what she asked was too much for me to do. She'd done so much for me already. Letting out a forceful sigh, I started packing yet again. The gourmet kitchen wasn't as difficult as you would have thought. There was absolutely nothing in there. The dining room only needed the movers besides a few knick-knacks and pictures on the walls. I already finished Kat's room and bathroom. The furniture throughout the house was covered in pathetically sad, plain white sheet's and the artwork and pictures were down so I could cover and protect them, as well. Katarina left strict instructions for what was to be done to the house so it was prepared for the long absence that was coming. Most of it was complete.

The rapping on the door caught my attention, and I happily dropped what I was doing to run and open it. Unfortunately for me, I already packed up the rugs and slipped on the bare, newly polished hardwood floors. My hand, so fast it blurred, caught the banister just in time before I could fall hard and fast onto my butt.

Answering the door while still composing myself, I managed to mutter, "Yes?" Since it had all but lost its exciting façade due to my clumsiness.

"Hey, Alyssa." With the utterance of those two words, my heart stopped and my breath became shallow. I knew that voice. What was he doing here?

"Nick. Can I help you with something? Are you lost?" A girl doesn't forget when her heart's been broken, and he had broken mine. I believed in him, trusted him, and he betrayed me. I told him the truth about everything, and because he chose not to believe me, I was the bad guy. He should have been angry with Alonzo, but he wasn't. He believed I was the liar. I was the one who betrayed him. That I had, somehow, made it all up in my head. He didn't believe in my ability, and therefore, he didn't believe in me as the mysterious voice pointed out. If he doesn't believe in me when I tell him what I am capable of, how could he fully and completely understand me?

Even though my head knew all of that to be true, seeing him standing on my front step, hands in his pockets, I couldn't help but have to swallow hard.

"Ouch," he said, clutching onto his chest. Under other circumstances I probably would have found that cute, adorable even, but not today. I refused to let him wiggle off the hook that easily, if he got off the hook at all. "I deserved that one." Nodding his head in agreement, his eyes grew sad.

"You deserve that and a heck of a lot more. What do you want, Nick?"

His dark eyes focused in on me and sent tingles down my spine. The little hairs on my arms stood on ends, and I forced them down by rubbing hard with both hands. I would play it off by saying I was cold if he decided to ask. I'd already been hurt by him once, and I would not let it happen again. I was determined to focus on the pain my heart was feeling instead of his intoxicating scent. God, I loved that smell.

"I came to say I'm sorry, Alyssa. Things got out of hand before, and I overreacted. It's just … Can I come in?" His embarrassed glances around were followed by a nervous rocking from his toes to his heels. I gestured for him to come in with the same annoyed style he used on me. I wanted to make him feel as if he was a nuisance the same way I had last time I went to his house to talk and apologize.

He gawked at the bareness of it all. His face twisted in shock as he said, "You're really doing it? You're really moving? I didn't think you were serious. I've never been here before, but I'm assuming this isn't the normal look for you guys. Where's Katarina? That is her name, right? Katarina?"

The house did have a look of abandonment to it. It wasn't as luxurious at it was when I first laid eyes on it. "Yes. That is her name, and she isn't here. She's finding us a new place to live. Speaking of a place to live, how did you know where I lived at anyhow, Nick?" My narrowed eyes and flaring nostrils didn't seem to deter him in the slightest.

"It wasn't that difficult, surprisingly."

"That's good to know. Now that you have said your apologies, is there anything else?"

I wasn't sure how much longer I could stop myself from relinquishing all my hurt feelings I had toward him and forgive him instantly. Perhaps Kat was right. Maybe that's what I get for trusting a human. That's good, Alyssa. Keep reminding yourself of what he's done to you.

"Please, Alyssa, don't be like this. I truly am sorry. I miss hanging out with you. I miss being around you, and most of all, I miss looking into your beautiful blue eyes. I know we haven't known each other that long, but there's something about you I feel drawn to. I don't normally allow myself to feel that way about women, any woman really, but with you … I can't explain it. I can't stop it. There's just something about you."

I lowered my head. Those few little words were all it took. The fight inside of me was gone. I was tired of having to be in control of myself, of my feelings, and most of all, of my heart at all times. For once in this lifetime, I wanted to be able to give into what my heart wanted.

"I forgive you." The words escaped my lips in a hushed whisper. That night was to be my last night there, and all I could think about was how I wanted to spend what little time I had left with him. I wanted to spend it the way we did that magical night at his house. Together, close, almost inseparable. "Stay with me tonight. Please." I don't like to beg, but right then, at that moment, I was not about to let pride get the better of me. When that seductive smile slid across his lips, I knew my answer. I had to make it perfect. I ordered a pizza for him and made a nice warm fire in the stone fireplace. Running up to my room, thankful I hadn't packed it up yet, I brought the pillows and blankets downstairs making a picnic, so to speak, in front of the fire. "How's this?" I asked while glancing down proudly at the masterpiece I created.

"It looks great," Nick said while sliding down onto the floor and cozying up to a few of the pillows.

The doorbell rang, and I darted to get the food, putting the pizza more his way than my own. I don't eat human food. I could, but it wouldn't fill me up. Instead of tasting the warm gooey cheese and sweet marinara sauce it would be like chewing air, Katarina said. No taste. No point in pretending. I plopped down next to him and snuggled into a few of the pillows myself.

He pulled the pizza from his mouth with a long stretch of stringy mozzarella following. "Hot." He took a long swig of soda to cool his mouth.

His hair cast just enough edginess while his almost black eyes paved a dangerous road. They could be warm enough to lure you in, and in an instant, cold enough to freeze you to the core. His light blue button-up shirt only made them appear darker. He must have come from work because that was definitely a work shirt. When he wasn't at work, it was a t-shirt and jeans. After gulping down practically the whole can of Pepsi, he sat it down and looked over at me. It felt like it had been years since we last spoke cordially.

After a few minutes, it was as if we hadn't skipped a beat. Nick was soothing and steady. He was easy to talk to. I saw nothing wrong with what we were doing. I cared about him. He came to apologize to me, and I had forgiven him.

We talked and laughed most of the night away about nothing at all. I was always at ease with him, and that night I found myself praying daylight would never come. I didn't have to pretend with him. He knew my deep, dark secret, and he still liked me for who I was. He accepted what I was, for the most part. I could be myself no matter how silly or childish in some people's eyes that behavior may be. He accepted it, if not joined in. He laughed with me. The mysterious voice's theory was wrong. I was wrong for thinking he was right. Nick did accept me. He did understand me. He was only human, and humans make mistakes. Heck, I'm not human, and I still make mistakes. He was man enough to apologize for it so I would be woman enough to accept it and move on.

That was the moment I realized the truth. I knew I couldn't deny it any longer. There was no falling anymore. I was in love with him. I loved everything about him. I loved his eyes and how they twinkled when he smiled. I loved his smile and the devilish way it upturned just slightly when he was planning something mischievous and sneaky. I loved his walk, his smell, his laughter, and the way he seemed to pout when he didn't get his way about something. I loved the pompous attitude he sometimes got, even when at those times he got it, it made me want to smack him upside his head. How could something as pure as love be considered wrong?

It couldn't because it wasn't wrong.

I laid there staring at our hands pressed together for hours noticing how in this position, they looked like one. My hand fit perfectly into his when our fingers were intertwined. Looking over to tell him the little secret I just came to discover, I noticed the slight rise and fall of his chest. He was fast asleep. His face looked tranquil, angelic even. No worries hardening or twisting it, just calmness. I pressed my lips to his and lingered for a few seconds. Pulling away reluctantly, I couldn't help the smile on my face.

'Really, Alyssa? Really? I am gone for one day, and this is what you have reduced yourself to? A mere human?' His voice breaking through the silence startled me. I jumped which in turn woke Nick.

"What's wrong, babe? Are you okay?" He was still half-asleep but reaching for me.

"Yeah, sweetie, I'm fine. I'm sorry I woke you." Nick pulled me in closer to him and nuzzled into my neck even more.

'Ugh. How disgusting.' The mysterious voice was definitely not above letting me know of his displeasure tonight. *'Here I thought we had an understanding, you and I.'*

'What understanding? I don't know what you're talking about, right now. I don't even know you.' Which was the truth, I didn't know him. For all I knew he had been nothing more than a mere figment of my imagination or worse, a crazy lunatic hell bent on killing me.

'Ah, but you want to know me. Don't you, Alyssa? That's what you were saying last night.' His voice cool and hypnotic.

'I was lonely. Nick wasn't here then. Now he is.'

'You are choosing him over me? You want that over me?' I could hear the disdain pouring out of his voice. What was he talking about, me choosing Nick over him? Who was he? I've never even met him. I didn't know him. There was no choice.

'I don't understand what you're asking of me. I don't know you or anything about you. Nick knows and cares about me. There really is no choice.'

I could feel the anger rising within him. That scared me to no end. I had never felt anyone's emotions before.

'Please don't be angry with me.' For some unexplainable reason, I didn't want him to be upset with me. I liked the attention he gave me, but Nick had apologized. He admitted he was wrong, and I forgave him. What did the mysterious voice expect? Me to fall head over heels in love with him? A voice?

'Don't be angry. Don't be angry.' His voice growing more intense reverberated in my head, sending pain waves throughout.

I put my hands on my temples and started massaging trying to stop the spasm now rendering me helpless. It wasn't working. *'Please stop. Please. My head feels like it is going to explode. Please make the pain stop.'* I was begging, but I didn't care, I needed it to end. It felt like I was having an aneurysm.

As fast as the pain had onset it dissipated just as quickly. *'Thank you.'*

'You could feel that?'

'Yes, I could feel that. Was I not supposed to? Because it felt like I was being stabbed repeatedly in the center of my brain and then ran over by a Mack truck.'

'That is very good, Alyssa. That is very, very good. You are very special. Do you know that? You deserve so much more than that thing you're lying next to.' The contempt in his voice was easily recognizable and getting old.

'That thing is Nick, and he is a good person and my friend. I care about him very deeply.'

'You're so self-loathing right now, you would care about anything that gave you half a glance. You've been given a gift, and yet you squander and despise what it represents. Get rid of the snack you call Nick, or I will do it for you.'

The silence that followed was almost deafening.

What did he mean I squandered it? That I despised what it represented? Yes, I did despise what it represented. It represented death, destruction, despair and complete and utter alienation from all I knew and loved. I had been turned into a monster who could not love or be loved. So yes, I resented it.

I laid back down next to Nick and was comforted by his soft, warm breath on the nape of my neck. As soon as I settled back down and began to doze off, the pulsating pain made its way back into my brain once again.

'Last warning, Alyssa, get rid of that thing lying next to you, or I will.' His voice was seething with irritation.

"Get rid of what thing?" It was a groggy, slurred attempt at talking, but I was half-asleep when he decided to invade my head once again. The pain was so unbearable I could barely think, and it rendered me almost unable speak. Sitting up made it even worse.

"Are you all right, babe?" My rousing woke Nick again.

"Yeah, I'm fine. Go back to sleep."

"I sleep better with you in my arms." When those words poured out of his mouth and hit my ears, I was elated.

The angry growling in my head knocked me right out of my giddiness and the grumbling voice from the stranger sent piercing, throbbing, horrid agony ripping through my body. "What are you doing to me?" I grabbed my head, pulling my hair. I wanted to dig him out of my brain. Anything to make the pain stop. My voice cracked under the constraints of the torture my body was enduring.

"I'm not doing anything, babe. Are you okay? Come on, lay back down in my arms," Nick said, bewildered by the words I spoke aloud.

"I'm sorry. Go back to sleep. I'll be right back. I just have to get something really quick."

I was tired of being at the mercy of this intrusive stranger who had entered and disrupted my life so abruptly, and I decided to fight back. I gathered all the strength I had mentally to try to force him out of my head. He was strong. He was so very strong, but I needed the pain to stop. He was in control and definitely winning, but I refused to give in so quickly. The more I fought the less pain I felt, but he was still very much there in my head, laughing at me. Scoffing at me.

'Get ... out ... of ... my ... HEAD!' I screamed my thoughts at him through clenched jaws.

'Do you really think it will be that easy to get rid of me?' His arrogance was nauseating. *'What I want, I get. Do you understand what I am saying?'*

'You will NEVER have control over me. Do ... you ...get ... that?' I answered, seething with anger.

'I always get what or who I want, Alyssa. You will learn that fact soon enough.'

And with that, the pain was gone and only complete silence filled my head. It was a relief I welcomed, but an uneasy feeling filled my stomach. That was not the last time I would hear from him. I knew that for a fact. The stranger was becoming a pain, literally and figuratively. The sleep that came after was a gift.

Chapter 14

I woke in the morning to Nick lying next to me gazing into my eyes. Brushing the hair out of my face, he said, "You're in the sunlight."

"Yes?" I wasn't sure where he was going with it, but I decided to ride it out and see.

"Doesn't sunlight kill you? I mean, I've seen the movies. The sun's supposed to kill vampires, and you're lying in it." I tried to hide the giggle slipping out, but it was to no avail. A brief look of hurt flashed across his face.

I quickly wiped the smirk off of mine and said, "I'm sorry. No. That's not entirely true. Many things that are told about vampires today simply don't apply to us. Well, they don't apply to us anymore that is."

He already knew my secret; I saw no harm in helping him understand it a little more. Him asking questions was enough for me. He was trying to get to know me, and I wanted him to understand what I was and am.

"I mean, Kat said the Ancient Ones are like that. The Ancient Ones are a lot like what the movies portray us as, but today's vampires are just not like that. The farther down the line we go, the more evolved we become she said. When I was first turned, the sunlight did hurt me, sort of. I ended up getting horrible headaches and such, but as time passed and I grew stronger, the headaches seemed to dissipate. Now it doesn't affect me at all."

"That's good." It was obvious he was trying to understand, but when you've been taught one way for so long, it's hard to readjust your brain to a completely different truth. I understood what he was feeling. Not so long ago I felt the same way.

That day was to be my last day there, and the last day I would ever see Nick again. Kat was expecting me to be in Chicago by that evening. The knock at the door took us both by surprise. I'd forgotten about the movers coming. All three men were dressed alike in their navy blue jumpsuits. The pudgy, red-faced man, who was only about two inches taller than I, seemed to be the one in

116

charge. He introduced them all by name and asked what needed to be done. After a brief run through of the house, they all quickly dug in and began working.

After they were all situated with their supplies and boxes, I went back into the living room to see Nick. He had himself propped up against the frame of the French doors with that hint of danger I loved so much written all over him. A shadow from the large maple tree in the back fell across his eyes, making them look like two black onyxes. That smirk of his, that devilish little smirk, always lightened my mood. I couldn't help but smile and shake my head as I waltzed over, wrapped my arms around him, and nuzzled into his chest. His smell always intoxicated me, and it didn't seem to matter where or when.

"I have to go today." The dry, throat-catching whisper that crept out of my mouth was strange and foreign even to me.

"But … last night … I thought it meant? I mean, I thought we were … you know … together?" Confusion, hurt, and most of all, disappointment was all written on Nick's face. All I wanted to do was kiss away all of those feelings and reassure him I cared, that I didn't want to go.

"I don't want to go, Nick, I don't, but I have to."

"Then don't. Stay here. Stay with me." He gently pushed a lock of hair out of my eyes and tucked it behind my ear. Then, with his rough hands, he softly cupped my face upwards toward his. At first, it was a few short loving kisses that turned into a heart-stopping fire of raw emotion that left me not wanting it to end.

Then the sweetest most delectable taste seeped into my mouth. I wanted more. No, I needed more. I'd never had anything so delicious before, and I wanted it all. It was like pure ecstasy in my mouth.

"OW." Nick pulled away hard and fast, dabbed the inside of his lip with his fingers and stared at it. A puzzled expression, and if I'm not mistaken, a slight look of fear was aimed directly at me.

I felt a sharp pinch on my lower lip and noticed my canines were out in full show. I turned on my heels immediately. I had to calm myself down and control the animal inside of me. Mmmm … that was the most luscious, mouth-watering goodness I'd ever tasted. Maybe it was because I'd only hunted sleazy scumbags. Other than that, I'd only had animals or bags of blood. I'd never had a decent, willing participant before. That delicious goodness was so delectably satisfying. The best I'd ever had. My canines started descending again.

'Alyssa! Control yourself.' I yelled at myself in my head. I turned back around to apologize to Nick for what had just happened when the stranger popped back into my head.

'Why control yourself, Alyssa? This is what you were born to do. Why would you want to fight that?'

'Because Nick isn't food, that's why.'

'Yes, he is. They all are. Come on, come with me, Alyssa. I'll show you the way your life should be. Everything you deserve, everything you desire, you can have. I'll teach you how to get it all. I won't even hurt snack boy over there.'

'No. I'm not leaving Nick or Kat for that matter.'

'Fine! Always so stubborn, aren't you? I was trying to be nice, but apparently you don't respond to niceness. I'll just have to see what you will respond to then won't I?'

"Alyssa, yoo-hoo, Alyssa? Hello?" I snapped back to reality to Nick's hand waving in front of my face.

"Yeah. Sorry about that. I guess I spaced out."

"I'd say so. What happened? I mean, why'd you bite me? Did I do something wrong?" It crushed me knowing he could fathom the thought of me hurting him on purpose.

"No. You didn't do anything wrong. I have to learn how to control that part of myself better. I'm sorry, Nick. Maybe this, us, is a bad idea. I don't want to hurt you, and obviously, I can't control myself around you."

"Don't say that, Alyssa. Don't do this. Don't push me away. Not like this, not right now. I have never felt about anyone the way I feel about you. I can't explain it, and honestly, I don't want to." He held both of my hands in his, caressing them with his thumbs.

I had to ask, "What if I hurt you? I haven't fed in a measly couple of days, and I can't even contain my hunger long enough to not lose control with you. I could kill you, Nick. Or worse, I could turn you into this." I pointed my willowy finger at myself. "You don't want this. You don't want to be like this. Trust me."

"Trust me when I say I want you. All of you, exactly the way you are." He wrapped his warm, safe arms around me, and I allowed myself to sink into him completely.

Calling Kat was a terrifying, yet necessary thing to do. "I know it's not a good idea to separate right now, Kat."

"Alyssa, what happened? Why would you want to stay there? I told you what dangers are coming our way."

"I know, but I have to try to protect Nick."

"You cannot protect him, Alyssa. I'm not sure if you can even protect yourself. I have told you this many times before. This won't turn out the way you want it to. He *will* die, and then you will be left there to fight Dante by yourself. He won't hesitate to kill you. He will kill you, Alyssa. Do you understand what you're risking?"

"Yes, Kat, I understand, but I want you to stay safe, okay? I don't want to involve you in any of this. This is my fight, and I know that."

"If you need something, anything at all, you know what to do."

"Yes. I know what to do. Thank you. I miss you."

"I miss you, too. Be safe." At the click of her end hanging up, I knew that was one of the hardest conversations I would ever have to have. I couldn't leave Nick, not when he was that vulnerable to Dante. Or maybe it was simply the fact of I just couldn't leave him. Either way, I needed to know Kat would be safe, as well. As long as she was far away from me, she should be.

Exhaling loudly as I hung the phone up, I said, "All right, Kat knows I'm not coming to Chicago now." I tried to sound upbeat and positive, but my shaking body betrayed me. Katarina was my safe haven, my home, my family. Now I didn't have that anymore. I didn't have any of that. I'd just lost my support system; I lost my family … again. How many families can one person lose in a lifetime? I looked down to see Nick lovingly rubbing my arms. His rough, yet gentle, hands were warm and calming. I knew I couldn't lose him, but I didn't know how I would cope without Kat either.

"Are you okay?"

"Yeah. I'm fine. I'm here with you. Everything will be fine."

"Exactly. Now, about your house?" I followed his worried eyes around the empty room.

The movers were not amused when I asked them to unload everything they'd just finished loading. I sorted through all of the boxes and unpacked the things I decided to keep there. The rest of the things I boxed back up and had them reloaded into their truck. I gave them a hefty tip to ease the burden I'd put on them. I really hoped it would help ensure all of our household goods made it to Kat safe and sound and hopefully, all unbroken.

After hours upon hours of organizing, sorting, and hanging things, we finally had the house put back together. I realized I still hadn't eaten and the grumbling in Nick's stomach suggested he needed to, as well. "You sound hungry. Do you want to go get something to eat?"

"Yeah. What do you want?" It dawned on him after a few minutes. "Oh, I'm sorry, I forgot." Nick glanced around the room as his face reddened.

Smiling, I said, "It's all right."

"So, what do you eat? I guess I already know the answer to that one, don't I?" He sounded hesitant, unsure of whether he wanted to hear the answer come out of my mouth or not.

"Well, that part of the stories are true. We do drink blood. They did get one thing right." I tried to laugh but could see the uneasiness settling in on him. "At first, it was bags of blood. That's how Kat eats. I didn't find it exciting enough I suppose, so I tried animals. I didn't like that very much at all. They didn't taste right. Not like it was bad, just not right. You know? So I began to hunt humans." He tried not to show any reaction, but I caught his eyes widening a touch. There isn't a lot my eyes don't catch. "Now it's back to those lovely bags," I said while I gave a quick raise of the eyebrows.

"Yeah?" His acting skills needed a lot of serious improving, but I found it sweet and endearing.

"Yeah. Now that Kat's not here anymore, though, I'm not quite sure how I'm going to get them. She was the one with all the connections, not me."

"Let me move this last box, then we will figure something out," Nick grunted as he picked up the bulky, awkward box.

'Alyssa, you have food right there in front of you. Eat.' As those words entered my head, I felt an urge so strong I could almost

smell the blood pumping through Nick's body. I could actually see it coursing through his veins, and it was calling out to me. *'EAT HIM, ALYSSA!'*

Right then, a sweet sensuous aroma filled my nostrils, tantalizing my every sense. "Damn it!" Nick stuck his finger in his mouth, but not before I saw the glistening bead of bright red blood escape from his index finger. "Paper cut, box cut, whatever you want to call it." He shrugged as he sucked on it.

That was all it took. I couldn't stand it anymore. I had to get out of there. I had to get away from there and from him. I ran out the door not bothering to close it behind me. I ran as far as I could until I was far enough away where I knew I wouldn't hurt him. I finally stopped in a desolate part of town, and I walked toward the alley as something caught my eye.

I wouldn't hurt Nick, but the bum in the alleyway was a different story. I shoved him out of my way and dove for the orange and white tabby behind the dumpster. I devoured the poor creature and wanted more. No, I needed more. I stared at the bum who looked horrified at the sight of me licking the blood from around my lips.

I slinked up to him and whispered, "Boo." I would've never thought a man in his condition could run so fast. Boy was I was wrong. I looked around frantically. I needed to find something more to eat, and I needed to find it fast. I called on Kat. I had no other choice. I needed blood, and I needed it right then and there.

'I'm so very proud of you for calling, Alyssa. You have come a long way. I'll make a few calls. It should be there by the time you return home.' I could hear the smile on her face as she spoke. It felt good making her happy. I liked hearing her approval, and I wanted to do more for her. She had done so much for me. If me calling on her when I was in trouble made her happy, then that was the least I could do.

By the time I returned home someone had already delivered a cooler filled with bags upon bags of blood for me. Before I entered the house I checked to see where Nick was, thank goodness he wasn't there. I went against my own belief and peeked inside his head. He was at home eating a sandwich. I got out of his head as quickly as I could. I hated the fact I did that. I don't like going inside others head without reason, but I did have a pretty good reason. I needed to eat so I wouldn't hurt him. I grabbed the cooler from the front door and hauled it inside. Dumping the contents from one of the bags directly into a glass, I drank it straight up. Blood is so disgusting when it's cold, but it didn't matter. I needed to eat before I had a more serious accident with Nick. An accident we would both regret.

'Alyssa, why would you do this to yourself? You deserve so much more.'

'Go away!' I was battling a raging storm within myself right at that moment, and I didn't need him or his input to infuriate me even more.

'I can help you perfect your skill. Obviously, I have the same one. Therefore, I know how to teach you properly. I can give you everything you ever wanted, Alyssa. Anything your heart's ever desired. We could rule the darkness together. Forever.'

Picturesque images flowed through my imagination in such vividness they were impossible to ignore. I was with a man who I can only assume was my mysterious stranger. His face was a blur, but the happiness and love I felt surrounding me was anything but. There was a dangerous aura surrounding him, but somehow I knew he would never turn on me. I was dripping in diamonds and rubies. The strapless gown I wore was as white as the purest snow. Diamonds were strategically placed all over so no matter which way I turned it sparkled and shimmered. His kiss was the perfect combination of fire and ice. It was cold with a bite but scorched through my body with the intensity of an out of control blaze with no end in sight. We wanted for nothing. Everything we desired was ours. We were respected yet feared all at the same time. We were … untouchable.

'Do you see, Alyssa? You would be happy with me. We would own the darkness, together. Don't you want to be happy?'

I shook my head, trying to get out of the dreamlike state I seemed to be stuck inside. *'I am happy. I'm happy with Kat and Nick.'* His growl sent tremors through me, and I could hear his heart pounding, his breath quickening, and his anger mounting.

'You! I have given you ample opportunities to get rid of that human. I have shown you where you belong, and yet, you still refuse

me? I am done playing these mindless, childish games with you, Alyssa. I am the judge, jury, and executioner. You do what I say, or you will pay the price. You better be ready to pay when I come to collect, Alyssa.'

I fell to my knees covering my mouth with both hands. "Dante Ortello?" There was only silence.

Chapter 15

I burst through Nick's door with such force I almost took it right off the hinges. Slamming it behind me quickly, I immediately locked the deadbolt. Ugh. What was I doing? Like a locked door was going to stop Dante Ortello. *I swear sometimes, Alyssa, you can be so dense,* I scorned myself. I turned to see Nick eyeing me from across his long, shiny, black dining room table. The look was easy to decipher, he thought I'd lost my mind. Who could blame him, though? After running out on him like I had earlier that afternoon and then this? What else was he supposed to think? He had no idea what was going on or what was about to happen to us both. I'd tried so hard to keep him safe and now, because of my own selfishness, I'd placed him in even greater danger than even I was aware of.

"Nick, you have to go. You need to go. We have to go right now. You have to go."

The urgency in my voice obviously wasn't coming across correctly because he casually sat back and asked, "What are you talking about? I can't just go, Alyssa. I can't just leave. And, to be quite truthful, why would I want to?" He wasn't comprehending the severity of the situation at hand. There was no other choice. We had to go, and we needed to leave right then.

Hours of persuasion later and me teetering on the brink of just knocking him out, he reluctantly agreed to leave for a few weeks. "Finally. Now, can you go upstairs and pack as quickly as you can?"

"All right, all right. It's good to know you're that desperate to go away with me," he said while lollygagging his way up the stairs.

"Ugh. You are so frustrating sometimes," I screamed up the stairs at him.

How could he not understand the dire consequences we were going to face if Dante found us? I told him. I told him everything. I told him how, because I chose him, Nick, over Dante, bloodshed was wanted. Nick's blood, my blood, and maybe even Kat's. At this point, I wasn't even sure how Dante knew me or why he wanted me. It made absolutely no sense to me at all. He had power and prestige amongst our kind. Surely he could've found someone better, more worthy than me, to want. After all the horrible things Kat told me about him, how could he even fathom the idea I could ever want him? He was in my head. He must have seen what I was told. Oh no. Kat.

Nick sauntered his way back down his stairs with a small bag as though he hadn't a care in the world. "You're going to need more than that." I looked at the small overnight bag dangling from his hand in disbelief.

"Naw, I'll be fine. You ready to go? Since we're in a hurry and all," he said smugly with a pleased-with-himself look.

"Fine, let's go. I think I might have put Kat in danger as well. What have I done? What am I going to do, Nick?" The tears welled up in my eyes as I began to panic.

"Calm down. Calm down. I'm sure Kat will be fine, but if you're that concerned, give her a call."

How he could be so tranquil about the whole situation baffled to me. "You still don't get it, do you? This is serious, Nick. He will kill us. Do you not get that, or do you still not believe a word I say?" I became more frantic with every passing minute.

"It's not that I don't believe you or what you're saying, Alyssa. It's just I think maybe you could be blowing this out of proportion a little bit. Seriously, take a step back and think about it from my perspective. You, yourself, told me everything I have ever read, heard or seen in the movies about vampires is false. You have a pulse. You can go out into sunlight. You breathe and sleep. You're just like me except for your, how can I say this delicately, dietary necessities. Am I so bad for thinking maybe, just maybe, some of the things you have been told could be a little exaggerated as well? Think about it for a minute. I'm just saying."

"Nick." I had to take a minute because everything he pointed out was valid, but Kat wouldn't lie to me about something like that. She wouldn't lie to me about him, about Dante. All I could think about was how I needed Kat desperately, but if I involved her in this I was assuring her death. I couldn't do that. I wouldn't do that. "I understand where you are coming from, but right now we don't have time to argue. We have to go." This time he relented without an argument.

Nick opened the door to the sight of a nickel-plated nine millimeter berretta pointed directly at his head. I could smell who it was before catching a glimpse of him. That pungent odor was undeniable. It was Alonzo with a few hired goons in tow.

"Going somewhere, Nicholas?" The sound of Alonzo's voice made my skin crawl.

"Actually, yeah, I am going somewhere. What are you doing, man? What the hell is all of this?" I could smell the fear pouring off of Nick, and with Alonzo being the dog he was, I wondered if he could smell it, as well.

"Get back into the house, Nick. Get back." Alonzo shoved the gun hard into Nick's forehead.

Waving his hands in the air, Nick said, "Okay, okay." He turned with surprise and utter disbelief written all over his face.

Four of them entered the house bearishly ushering us into the dining room as one of the goons slammed the door shut behind him. Pulling out two chairs from the table, Alonzo pointed for us to sit with the barrel of his gun. I let it all play out because it was painfully obvious Nick needed to learn things the hard way. He didn't believe me when I tried to warn him before, and now he would see for himself. Looking back now, I should never have let any of it happen. It was a stupid, stupid move on my part.

"What are you doing, Alonzo? I thought we were friends. You're supposed to be my family, man. What is this?" Nick's hurt by this betrayal of his friend was evident. It broke my heart, but Alonzo wasn't affected. He didn't care. He was arrogant about it all. He enjoyed toying and tormenting Nick.

"Family? You're right, we were supposed to be family. That's why you left me in the trenches while you clawed your way to the top making friends with the boss man? Bringing your idiotic, incompetent brother with you instead of me? Who even got you in?"

"You did."

"That's right. I did. I helped you out when you were down, and that's how you repay me?"

"You know I never wanted Antonio in, Alonzo. Never. What do you want?"

The goons all stood behind Alonzo in a row. It looked like a scene from one of those really cheesy gangster movies, three big, burly men standing behind the man in charge. All three in gray suites that didn't quite fit right with their arms crossed against their chest. Two of them looked indistinguishable, but one was very recognizable. He was the one I saw in Alonzo's head. He was the one who'd beaten Antonio literally to death.

"I remember you," I spouted off, not controlling myself. The older one glared at me as I pointed my accusing finger at him. Nick, Alonzo, and the others all turned their heads toward me. "I saw what you did." My face was hardened now.

"Did ya now? And what might that be? That you saw me do, that is." The creepy smile he had on his pock-marked face made me want to knock some sense into him, and his rotting teeth made my stomach turn.

"I know what you did to Antonio. Both of you." My accusing eyes now focused in on Alonzo.

With a heavy smack, the back of Alonzo's hand flew crossed my face. I turned my head with the hit. I didn't want to let on that his puny smack didn't affect me in the slightest. That would've been too easy. I wanted him to admit what he did. Nick needed to hear it. The older man laughed at the smack as if he'd been the one who delivered it. Nick flew up out of his chair with cobra-like speed, knocking it over behind him. He was in Alonzo's face with his hand clenched tightly around his throat before any of them could react. Nick, with intense eyes focused solely on Alonzo's now purple face, was blindsided by the punch that knocked him off of his longtime friend now turned enemy.

"What did you do to my brother? What did you do to Antonio?"

Alonzo, with his twisted, little, sadistic smile, laughed. He laughed as though there was a joke told that no one else was privileged to hear. Nick struggled to get up, but one of the goons knocked him back down and held him in place. I wanted to know what was so funny, and as I entered his demented, little brain, I saw flashes of what he was laughing about. He was watching Antonio being beaten and demanding more pain to be thrust upon him. Antonio was screaming in agony, begging for Alonzo to make it stop and apologizing for whatever it was he did wrong, promising to never do it again. It was painfully obvious Antonio had no idea why this was happening to him. Tears streamed down my face. I'd had enough. I may be a monster, but he was the epitome of pure evil.

I flew up from the chair with such force that it slammed into the wall behind me, knocking some drywall out in the process. Everyone, Nick included, whipped their heads around to look at me. My face turned hard as stone as I stalked my way toward Alonzo. "You can stop your cackling at any time, Alonzo. Wipe that twisted, little smirk off your face while you're at it."

"Are you going to make me, doll? What are you, five-one? Five-two? Maybe a buck, buck ten, soaking wet? You think I'm afraid of you?" He chuckled as he looked around at his associates to validate his stance.

"Hmmm, all true points." I shook my head in agreement as I spoke. "But you see, there are a few minor details about me you are completely unaware of, Alonzo," I said showing my pretty sparkling white fangs to him. Slowly running my tongue across my teeth, I raised my eyebrows and smiled smugly at him.

"So you're a freak. Big deal. Am I supposed to be scared of that?"

This time I was the one laughing. "No. Don't be afraid. It's so much better when you're not." The other men, if you could even call them that, started toward me before Alonzo waved them off.

"Nick," I said.

"Yeah?" he replied, unsure how to take the situation.

"Do you want to know what he was laughing about?"

"Umm, actually yeah, I would like to know."

"Well, he was laughing at the thought of what he did to your brother. He was imagining Pat here," I glanced at the older man, "That is your name right? Pat?"

"Yeah. That's my name. How do you know that?" The older man was a bit baffled by all the knowledge I seemed to have but shrugged it off all the same.

"I'm that good, Pat. He was remembering what Pat here did to your brother. How he told Pat to inflict more and more pain while Antonio screamed in agony, begging for mercy, asking his friend here why. Asking what he did to deserve this from him."

My confident sneer focused right on Alonzo's ugly mug watching to see if there would be any change in his bearing, and there was. Slight, but it was there. Nick swelled with anger, and I saw a flash in his eyes that I'd only seen once before. That look of hatred was directed at me when he originally assumed I'd been the one who killed his brother. I knew what was coming next, and I knew what I needed to do.

I swooped over and attacked Pat. Not enough to kill him, I would leave that for Nick, but enough to incapacitate him. Pat's wound was fatal, but it would be days of agonizing suffering before he would succumb to it. As soon as I dove after Pat, Nick lunged at Alonzo. The other two were more fun. They were so horrified by my actions all they were able to focus on was me. They tried to run. Silly boys. I never heard grown men scream so shrilly before. I finished them in a matter of seconds as I didn't want to alarm the neighbors.

Nick had free reign to do as he pleased with Alonzo while I occupied the others. After knocking Alonzo to the floor, Nick threw a punch and the fight between the two ensued. "How could you do that? Why would you hurt Antonio?"

Another punch was thrown. Alonzo, getting his bearings, flipped Nick off of him and hit him square in the jaw. He quickly got up and kicked Nick one more time in the stomach to keep him down. Then, like a coward, Alonzo ran out the door. When I was done, I looked around for Nick, but he and Alonzo had disappeared.

I watched through Nick's eyes what happened next. I wasn't prying. I was simply protecting him in case anything should happen, I could get there in time.

I watched as he chased after Alonzo like a rabid dog catching up with him in an alley a few blocks away. Nick ran up behind him and slammed Alonzo into the cement and rock-embedded ground. Flipping him over to his back, Nick landed a few more punches to his face.

Alonzo scrambled away from Nick's grip. "You did that to your brother. I know what you are, Nicholas. You did that to your brother." With a shard of glass from a nearby broken bottle, Alonzo slashed the left side of Nicks face. "This is where you belong, in the alley with all the other rats. Rat." With Nick too stunned from the pain to chase after him, Alonzo ran.

I pulled out of his head after seeing Alonzo's cowardly move.

Nick staggered slowly back to the house where I'd already disposed of the two inconsequential bodies. I had Pat ready and waiting for him. The door slung open to a sight of blood gushing from the open gash on his now pale face as his body slumped over in the door way. He needed help, and I didn't have a lot of time. I raced over and gently wrapped my arm around his waist guiding him to a chair in the dining room.

"Are you okay? What happened?" It was a ridiculous question to ask, I knew he wasn't okay, but I needed to hear him speak. I needed to gauge how severe his wound was.

"Alonzo got away. How could I let him get away like that, Alyssa? I'm so sorry I didn't beli—" He slouched over in the chair fading in and out of consciousness.

"Nick? Nick?" He'd lost a lot of blood and coupled with the earlier beating, it didn't help matters. I had to do something and do it fast. Nick wasn't waking up, and the blood was still flowing.

I ran to my house and grabbed a few bags of the blood that matched his type. The little drop of blood I tasted from Nick's lip was turning into a blessing in disguise. Because of that one little drop, I now knew he was type A positive.

I brought the supplies back to his house and cleaned the wound as best I could. It was long and deep, deeper than I had anticipated, and needed stitches. I'm not a doctor so the butterfly stitches he had stored in his medicine cabinet would have to do. I may be small, but another advantage of my situation was my strength. That made it easy to scoop him up and carefully placed him on his sofa. I hate needles. I hate them with a passion. The sight alone was enough to frazzle me, but I had no other choice. Nick was in trouble and counting on me. I closed my eyes and tried to picture exactly how Kat had shown me to insert it. Taking a few deep breaths, I found a good vein on him and carefully pushed in the needle for the I.V.

Thank goodness I fed earlier because, even full, the smell of his blood teased and tempted me. With Nick still unconscious, I gagged and bound Pat hoping it would help Nick at least a little bit. Pat wasn't the one calling the shots, but he was the one who actually killed Antonio. Something deep down told me it wouldn't make a bit of difference, Antonio was still dead. Nothing could bring him back, and Alonzo, the mastermind, had escaped. Nick already beat himself up over that fact earlier, and I knew it was only the beginning.

Hours crept by and still no sign of Nick waking. I closed my eyes for what was only supposed to be a second but instead awoke to the sun shining in on my face. I looked over to see Nick removing the I.V. from in his arm. I was so elated, I pulled him to me hugging him tightly.

A painful groan snapped me out of it forcing me to let go. "Oh, I'm sorry. I'm so sorry. I wasn't thinking."

"It's okay," he managed out in a raspy, pain-ridden voice.

"Nick, you're really hurt. I need to get you to a hospital. There's not a lot I can do." I checked over his wounds a little more this time. There wasn't an inch on his chest not covered in bruises. His lip was busted open but not too deep, and his eye was black and swollen.

"No. I'm fine. I thought we were supposed to be on the run from a rogue, psycho vampire. Shouldn't we be going?" Every slight movement caused him to wince and groan in pain.

"Right now I think the only place we should be running to is a hospital."

"I said I'm fine. Come on, let's get moving." Nick stood but lost his balance falling back down onto the couch.

"You can't even stand, Nick. How are you going to go on the run? You could have internal bleeding. Please, just let me take you to the hospital."

"I'm fine. Really, I am, Alyssa. Can we please just go?" He was being more persistent than usual. He wanted out of New York and wanted out in a hurry.

"Damn it, Nick. I'm a vampire not a doctor. You need help."

A soft chuckle emanated from him as an appreciative smile. At least my Star Trek humor wasn't wasted on him, and it got a smile to boot.

"What about Pat?"

"What about him?"

"I have him waiting for you in the kitchen." I glanced toward that way.

Nick cautiously stood and stumbled over to the door where his bag was still at. Slowly sliding down the frame, he picked up the gray carry-on and slid back up the door. Slinging the bag onto his shoulder, he motioned for us to get going. "I'll make a call to Lucas. He'll deal with him." Nick glanced back toward Pat's direction and shut the door behind us.

I made one more stop at my house to quickly throw a few things into a bag and pack a cooler full of blood. I definitely needed those if I didn't want to lose control and hurt Nick even more. He still smelled of that delicious blood of his, and I wasn't going to take any more chances than necessary. I hopped back into the car, and we headed toward the New York state line.

"Spill it. What's going on?" I asked, still keeping my eyes on the road.

New York's streets were always crazy. Crowded wasn't even the word for it. I couldn't focus on what his expressions were, I had to go by his voice, and something wasn't right.

"You know what's going on, you were there, and I told you what happened with Alonzo."

"No. Something else is going on, Nick, something you're not telling me. I want to know what it is. You wanted to get out of New York awfully fast all-of-a-sudden. Something isn't right. What's wrong."

"Nothing is wrong, Alyssa. Don't worry about it. So where are we heading to?"

"I don't know just yet. Somewhere. You're not going to tell me, are you?"

"Let it go, Alyssa. Okay? Just let it go. Please?"

"Fine, I'll leave it alone. For now."

Chapter 16

We hit the Holland Tunnel and headed for New Jersey. Nick needed to make a phone call so we pulled over at a rest stop shortly after crossing the state line. After he eased out of the car and walked over to the pay phone, I tried with all my strength to locate Alonzo. It was to no avail. I couldn't see him or get into his head at all. I hoped that meant he was dead. Maybe, just maybe, Nick had gotten the better of him without even realizing it. I kept trying just to be sure, though. I glanced over to see Nick still talking to someone on the phone when the familiar voice, now known as Dante, rang through my head.

'Wherever you go, Alyssa, I will find you.' At least this time he kept it short and to the point.

Nick eased back into the car and buckled up. "All right. So, do you know where we're going yet?"

"Sort of. Are you up for a little road trip?" I scanned over him carefully. His face was bruised, but I could only imagine how bad his torso looked considering how he winced and groaned with every move. Even though he was severely banged up, I was more worried about internal damage, but, considering he refused to go to any hospital, I was left with no other choice but to watch him.

"I'm up for anything right now."

I already knew the answer, but I asked, "How are you feeling? I still think we should get you to a doctor."

"I'm okay. Seriously, stop worrying. Can we just go now?"

"Yep. Let's roll. First stop, Hershey."

Laughing, he replied, "Hershey here we come. Wait. What's in Hershey?"

Was he serious? Rolling my eyes, I said, "The candy factory, what else? I've always wanted to see it."

Still chuckling, Nick said, "Of course you have. What vampire hasn't?"

I playfully hit his arm and instantly regretted it. Hissing air as he sucked in, I pleaded for his forgiveness. "I am so sorry, Nick. I'm so sorry."

"It's fine," he said through clenched teeth. We rode the rest of the way in silence.

Upon entering the amazing city of Hershey, Pennsylvania the smell of chocolate filled the clear, breezy air. I'd wanted to visit the Hershey Factory ever since I was a child. I believe every child envisions it at least once in their life. My family always tended to stay closer to home when we went on family vacations. We took our trips to the lake since it was only a few hours away from our house and cheap. *This is going to be great,* I thought to myself.

Once we were in the factory different prices and packages were posted. I noticed we could sign up for special things to do, so I took it upon myself to sign Nick and I up for everything. I chose the chocolate enthusiast experience. It was the best deal and had the most bang for our buck you could say.

We prepared ourselves by putting on the hairnets and aprons provided for us. Our chocolate journey began by creating our own Hershey bars. I filled mine with almonds and other yummy little things I'd always loved. The best part for me was being able to make my own box. I was able to put any design and name I wanted on it. Nick looked ridiculous in the get up, but he was smiling and seemed to be in good spirit with it all. Children were all around us giggling and laughing joyously. It was everything I could have ever imagined until it came time for the taste-testing. That's when it all went downhill, for me anyway.

I looked over to see Nick stuffing his face with the free samples, and I laughed out loud at the sight of it. He reminded me of a chipmunk stuffing his cheeks, storing food for the winter. I wished I'd had a camera just for those kinds of moments. I took a sample for myself and couldn't wait to taste the sweet, smooth goodness. Except it was nothing like I remembered. There wasn't anything sweet about it. There was nothing. I hadn't had human food since I was turned, and I knew it had to be me. Kat warned me, but I'd hoped she was wrong. I looked around at everyone else who were smiling and enjoying all the sugary comfort. It was a devastating blow to me. One more thing I no longer was able to enjoy from my past.

Nick caught on to the disappointment on my face. "Are you okay, Alyssa?"

"I can't taste it, Nick." I shook my head.

"What do you mean you can't taste it? It's really good." He shrugged his shoulders.

"It means; I can't taste it." I let out a loud sigh.

"Okay. Do you want to go then?"

I knew he was trying to let me off the hook, but I didn't want to take this away from him. "No, it's fine. You're having fun."

"No, it's okay. I've had my fill of chocolate, anyway. We can go if you want." I instantly took him up on his offer. It was selfish, but I couldn't take it any longer.

Back in the car I laid my head down on the steering wheel. Yet another heartbreaking revelation in my new found world. I knew what Kat said about human food, but I never dared to try it so I didn't know for sure. I had hoped she was wrong, but now I knew she was right.

Nick's large hand caressed my back, and I slowly turned my head to look at his face. "Hey. Are you okay?" I shook my head as a tear slid down my cheek. He gently wiped it away with his rough fingers then leaned in and softly kissed my lips. He followed by gingerly kissing both my eyes trying to kiss away all the hurt and pain. "What's going on with you? You cannot be this upset over chocolate." He tilted his head meeting my gaze.

"I've wanted to come here since I was a child. It was everything I'd always dreamed it would be, except, now I can't even enjoy the best part of it." I sat up wiping the new tears now falling.

"I don't know what you're going through, Alyssa, but we'll get through it. We'll get through it together." The distant look in his eyes made me put my head down in shame. Here I was complaining about not being able to taste some stupid candy, and he just lost his brother. He just lost his only family a short time ago, and here I was acting like a child.

I exhaled long and deep, sat up, and said, "I'm being ridiculous. I'm sorry." Using the back of my hands to dry my face, I started the car.

"No, you're not. Everyone has childhood dreams they want to live up to their expectations. I understand wanting to hold on to something you've lost. Believe me, I get it." Nick, shaking his head in agreement, stared out the windshield with a distant look on his face again. I closed my eyes for a second and then slowly pulled out of the parking lot.

"Arizona here we come."

I drove right through Ohio and stopped in Indianapolis for the night. It wasn't a small city by any means. We pulled up to the hotel, handed the keys to the valet, and grabbed our bags out of the trunk. We walked through the sliding doors making a right toward the front desk. The lobby was beautiful and tastefully decorated. Nothing I would normally ever be able to afford. Nick set up the reservation and then led me to the elevators.

"Here's your key," he said, handing me one of the cards from his hand.

"Thanks," I said grinning at him.

"I mean, we're staying in the same room, I hope you don't mind? But I got us each our own key." That crooked little half smile came across his face, and I tried to hide my own.

"I don't mind."

"All right."

We stepped off the elevator, and I followed behind him to our room. Allowing me to do the honors of opening the door, I stepped in and was instantly taken aback. It was breathtaking. Making my way through the living room into the bedroom, I dropped my bags down. I walked over peering out the window to the busy street down below. The view was incredible. The glow of the lights and the hustle and bustle of the cars and people gave me a rush of excitement.

"Not bad, not bad." I turned to see Nick standing beside me.

I smiled. "Not bad? Admit it. This is a pretty great view."

"Okay, I'll give you that much. It's good."

"You're probably hungry, so, you go get something to eat, and I'll stay here and eat. Then we can meet up afterwards. Take in the town, maybe?" I was starving, and I didn't think it wise to take any more chances with Nick. He unfortunately took it the wrong way.

"All right," he said, shaking his head. "Do you always do that?" Nick stared at me, obviously irritated.

"Do what?" What the heck? I had no idea what he was talking about. I thought we were getting along and having a good time together.

"Do you always have to take charge of every little aspect that happens to be going on around you?"

"What?"

"Do you always have to be in control? Ever since we met, you've had to take charge of every situation that comes your way." I was completely blindsided. I didn't understand where any of this was coming from. That wasn't me.

"No, I don't."

"Okay then, well, I'm going to go get something to eat because, obviously, I'm hungry. Then I'll meet up with you afterwards to take in the town."

"No. That is not what I was trying to say. It's just …"

Cutting me off before I had a chance to finish, he said, "No. It's fine. I'm just going to go. I'll catch up with you in a little bit." He turned around walking toward the door.

Finally regaining enough of my senses, I said, "That is not what I meant." Waving his hand to cut me off yet again, he walked out with the door slamming shut behind him.

That wasn't what I was trying to do at all. I wasn't trying to manipulate the situation; I simply didn't want him around to see how I ate. What I ate. I know he knows but knowing and seeing are two completely different things. I didn't want him to physically see or know what I had been reduced to. I didn't want him to know I would never be normal. I would never be like any of the girls he usually dates. Right now we can still pretend. I was hoping to keep it that way forever.

Does it really matter, Alyssa? Soon Dante will come and kill you. There's no coming back from the death he will bring. You just have to figure out a way to save Nicki thought to myself.

I grabbed a bag from the bright red cooler. An appropriate color, if I did say so myself. Dumping it into a glass from the bar, I threw it into the microwave for a few seconds. The warm, red goodness danced playfully across my taste buds as I waited for the overly-sized bathtub to fill. Once it was full, I rinsed the glass and placed it in the sink. I slipped out of my clothes and sank into the hot bubble filled escape that I made for myself.

My head found the perfect spot to rest against the back of the tub as I closed my eyes drifting off into my own imagination. The tension was finally melting away when Dante's sultry voice echoed throughout my head.

'I don't want to hurt you, Alyssa. Just imagine it.'

With those words, my head began swimming with images instantly. Dante and I partners in every sense of the word. Walking side by side without fear, demanding respect from all others with passionate, loving embraces at night. All the thoughts and pictures swirling around in my mind were so mesmerizing it made it almost impossible to think clearly. It was all so very confusing to me. What was he trying to say? What exactly was it that he wanted from me? At the same time, it all seemed so real. It was as if I could feel his protective arms surrounding me. Embracing me. Comforting me. His kisses sending me into a frenzy of passion and desperation of needing more. Wanting more. More of him. All of him. I couldn't get enough.

'No. This isn't right. What about Nick? If ... if I go with you, what will happen to him? Will you leave him alone?'

'No. You know I can't do that, Alyssa. He knows too much now. He doesn't matter. He is not important. This is about you and I.'

That couldn't agree to. If I could save Nick it would be different. But to save myself and know what was going to happen to him… that was unthinkable. *'He is important. He's important to me. He's my friend, and I care for him deeply. I'm not going to let you hurt him. Not now. Not ever. Especially not to save myself.'*

I could feel tension creeping up inside him. The anger mounting. *'You can't stop me. This is what I do. If humans find out about our kind, they will hunt us down like rabid dogs. They won't stop until they kill us all. I'm sure Katarina has told you all about how I feel on this subject.'* I could feel the hatred dripping off of him as he thought about humans and them knowing of our existence. I wanted to calm him. I wanted to ease his hurt. I'm not entirely sure as to why, but it was something I felt I had to do. I was drawn to him. There was something that drew me to him from the very beginning. What it was I have no idea, but it wasn't something I was able to ignore even though I wanted to.

'Yes, she did. Kat said you weren't that nice about it, either.'

'Kat. That's a perfect nickname for her. It suits her. She knew the rules just like you do. You don't know what could happen if it gets out about our kind.'

'So tell me then. How do you know what will happen? What makes you so absolutely sure what they will do? Nick won't say anything to anyone. I promise.'

'That's a promise you can't keep. How much do you really know about this Nick? Not a lot from what I'm guessing because he is not at all what he says he is. I'm betting there's a lot you don't know. Me on the other hand, I'm an open book. Maybe another time I'll tell you how I am just so absolutely sure on what will happen. And it will happen. That I guarantee. Think about all I have said and shown you, Alyssa.' And again he was gone.

I flung my eyes open wide and sat straight up. Water sloshed out and the bubbles were all but gone. What was he talking about? I knew Nick. He told me things he didn't have to tell me. Huffing aloud I said, "Way to ruin my night, Dante."

Climbing out of the tub, I slid the white terry cloth robe over my milky white body and plopped down on the couch. Looking up at the ceiling, I couldn't help but shake my head in frustration at the predicament in which I have found us. How was I supposed to keep Nick safe when Dante was always two steps ahead of me? He could get into my head at any time he wished. He could see everything I thought and planned. He knew everything. Catching a glimpse at the clock on the wall, I realized the time. It was already seven thirty. There was no time for me to think about any of this right now. I had to go meet Nick.

Finding Nick at the hotel bar, I walked up and gently tapped his shoulder.

"Hello, beautiful. Look at you. You look gorgeous." He spun me around, slowly taking in what felt like every inch of me with his eyes. It was both flattering yet frightening at the same time.

"Wow. Thanks. That's nice of you to say. What's gotten into you tonight?" I asked, my wide smile unable to be hidden. I wasn't complaining by any means. It was nice to hear, but this was a far cry from the Nick that walked out of the hotel room calling me a manipulative, control freak.

"Nothing. Like you said, we're running for our lives. I don't want to leave anything unsaid." I didn't like the sound of that. I couldn't let him become hopeless. Not now. I was shaking up enough for the both of us.

"You're going to get out of this, Nick. I *will* get you out of this, even if it's the last thing I do."

"*We* will get out of this, Alyssa. Together." I smiled at the thought of that. That one little sentence coming from his mouth was all it took to renew my faith. We could do it as long as we did it together.

Downtown was comforting. The cool, crisp air was refreshing and the lights from the buildings were warming. We walked around for hours talking, laughing, and holding hands. The knot in my stomach grew, and the seed of doubt Dante planted earlier was beginning to take root.

All night, despite my best efforts, I kept having the sneaking suspension Dante was right. Nick was holding something back from me. What it was I had no idea, but my thoughts kept traveling back to the night he came back from the altercation with Alonzo. It had to be something to do with that. It just had to be, but what? I tried to see into Alonzo's head, but again I saw nothing but blackness. He must be dead, but the uneasiness in my stomach was convincing me otherwise. *You could break your own rules and look into his head*, I thought. No. I told him wouldn't do that. I wouldn't invade his privacy like that. *What is wrong with you, Alyssa? You are starting to act like... act like ... ugh.* I growled at myself for even considering that.

"I have no secrets from you. You know that, right?" I looked into his eyes questionably.

"No, I didn't know that, but that's nice to know." The little smile he put on wasn't going to get him out of this one.

"You're keeping something from me, Nick. I need to know what it is so I'll be able to protect you."

"It's nothing. It really is nothing. It has absolutely nothing to do with what's going on with this. It's fine." He tried to hide his laughter with a phony cough as he continued, "You protecting me. Now that's new. I can honestly say I have never been in that situation before. Usually it's the other way around. Usually I'm the one who's protecting someone. You know, saving the damsel in distress."

"Well, now you're the damsel." I laughed out loud with that image in my head. Imagining Nick in a pink, silk gown and a sheer cream colored veil covering his face was hysterical.

"What?"

With my own sly smirk, I answered, "Nothing. I'm just imagining you being the damsel." I giggled at the image in my head.

"Oh are you?"

"Uh-huh." I shook my head at him.

Nick pulled me toward him and tickled my sides. While I was squirming we locked eyes, and I realized we were nose to nose.

I stopped wiggling. I could hear his heart pounding and his breath was a warm breeze on my face. Slowly leaning in, he pressed his velvety lips to mine. The kiss was paradisiacal. It was just like the fairy tales that were read to me as a child. It was what we girls were taught since birth that kisses were supposed to be like. Picture perfect. Nick indolently released me, and I looked up sheepishly. Smiling, I bit my bottom lip and interlocked his fingers into mine. It seemed things were finally starting to fall into place for me, finally starting to come to some normalcy. If I had only known how soon it would all come crashing down around me.

Chapter 17

The next few days, and States for that matter, flew by. Phoenix was a few short hours away, and I was anxious at the possibility of seeing my family again. I needed to see them, and, considering it could possibly be the last time, I wanted to make it count. There were so many things I wanted to say to them, I needed to say to them. I wasn't even allowed to let them know I was alive. Well, not buried six feet under, that is. It wouldn't matter if I did tell them because soon enough I quite possibly would be.

Phoenix never looked more beautiful to my eyes than it did at that moment. I pulled the car over to the shoulder of the road to watch the blazing red sun slowly descend behind the peaceful looking blue-gray mountain tops. Hues of purple, pink, and orange illuminated the sky. It was majestic. I wondered why I never realized the beauty of this place, of my home. Why did I never truly appreciate all of its splendor?

Nick softly kissed my cheek, and I about jumped out of my skin.

"Are you all right?" Nick asked, a little taken aback.

"Yeah, I'm fine. I'm sorry. You surprised me a little. That's all. I didn't hear you get out of the car." I glanced his way for a brief second before returning my full attention back on the picturesque sky before me.

"I surprised you? Humph. And here I thought that was impossible." A self-pleasing grin plastered itself on his face. "It's beautiful here." Nick glanced all around. Inhaling slowly, he tapped the hood of the car and said, "Where are we heading to now?"

I smiled, closed my eyes for a second and said, "We're here. This is my home, Nick."

"Umm … did I miss something because I could've sworn you said you could never come back?" His confusion was obvious.

"I'm not going to let them see me. I just need to see their faces one last time." Sitting in the driver's seat before he could blink, I graciously leaned over and opened the passenger side door for him smiling while he just looked annoyed.

The drive wasn't a long one, in fact, we were only fifteen minutes away from where I grew up. After entering the neighborhood, I quickly pulled my dark hair through the white baseball cap I acquired at the gas station a few miles back and slid on the extra-large pair of dark sunglasses I purchased with it.

Children were playing and laughing in the backyards to the left and right. I parked a few houses down from mine and waited. The little three bedrooms, red, stucco house had not changed one bit. Star Jasmine bushes still lined the walk and the light pink Oleander tree was still as beautiful as it was the day Dad and I planted it as a Mother's Day gift for her. An hour passed before my mother came out wearing her oversized gardening hat I always laughed at her for owning. She started her usual ritual of pruning roses and plucking weeds in the front just as she always did.

I tapped Nick's shoulder without taking my eyes off of her. "Look. There she is. There's my mom. Isn't she beautiful? My dad always told me I looked like her. He called me her mini clone. I don't see it, though." Nick turned his gaze in the same direction mine was focused. My eyes lit up knowing what was about to happen when I caught sight of my father. "Look, Nick, look. Do you see that man right there?" I asked, continually tapping on his shoulder as I was rushed with excitement.

"Yeah, I see him." Scooting away from my hits, he followed my stare again.

"That's my dad. Watch. I've seen this a million times, and I never get bored of it." Wide smile and eager eyed, I watched my dad walk over from the neighbor's yard, kneel down and tenderly kissed the side of my mother's neck. She jumped a little, as she always did, took off her gloves and stood up. My dad slid off her hat and lovingly kissed her lips. It was a scene I'd seen played out numerous times before, but this time it was different. It was moving. Maybe it was because they seemed to appreciate each other just a little bit more, or maybe it was because this time I knew it would be my last time to ever witness it again.

"Hey. Are you okay?" The concern in Nick's voice was sweet. I looked down at his hand folded on top of mine.

"You know, Nick, I witnessed that same routine happens every single day. That one gesture, that one looks, was what I based my whole life on. Did you know that?" With lips pressed together, he continued to listen in silence. "That was what I wanted. That was what my life was going to be like. I was only twenty-years-old when I died. It was two days before my twenty first birthday. Did you know that?"

"No, I didn't know that. What are you going to do, Alyssa?"

"I'm going to do the same thing I used to do before Kat said we had to move. I'm going to hang back in the shadows and watch."

I stayed behind while Nick took the car to go eat and find us accommodations. I lurked around my old house keeping to the darkness, never getting too close. I watched them do the same things they had done a million other times before in front of me: make and eat dinner, read, and their usual nightly routine. My mom still slathered on the same nightly moisturizer before lying down for the night.

Sinking into my dad's old, broken, rusted brown recliner in his office, I waited for them to fall asleep. Once they were, I sneaked in closer to them. Brushing the hair out of my mother's face, careful as not to wake her, I could smell the coconut and jasmine of her lotion. It took me back to when I used to crawl into bed with her when I was a child after having a bad dream. She looked as though she'd aged a good ten years since the last time I saw her. Her sweet face carried so much worry on it that even in rest it could be seen. All of that aside, she still looked like an angel. My father, who was as handsome as I remembered, still looked like the strong, nobleman I imagined he was when I was a child. I could see grief had aged him as well. His cool fresh aftershave brought on memories of me pretending to shave with him in the mornings as he was getting ready for work. I was five, and he called me his princess.

Before dawn's light could break through the darkness, I was gone.

"What are you going to do now? What's the game plan here?"

Shaking my head in frustration, I replied, "I don't know. I just don't know, Nick. All I do know is I need to find a way to save you because I *am* going to die."

"Stop saying that. You're not going to die. You can't. I need you." Nick caressed my face slipping a piece of hair behind my ear.

Looking into his soulful eyes, a twinge of pain erupted throughout my body. *Why,* I thought to myself, *why when I wanted it all to end, it didn't? Now I don't want it to end, it is? So soon, at that?* I had to smile at the irony of the situation that entangled us.

"I'm sorry I've caused you so much pain, Nick. I got you into this mess, and to be honest, I'm not sure if I can get you out of it." I buried my head into his warm chest.

"While I do have to admit I wished it had been under different circumstances, I don't regret a thing about you. I'm glad I met you, Alyssa." Feeling him run his fingers through my hair affectionately made me believe he was telling the truth.

"Do you want to get out of here?" I blurted out after a deep breath.

"Sure. Where do you want to go?"

"Come on. I know just the place."

The cemetery was dark, quiet, and cold. In the distance I could hear the sounds of coyotes prowling for food, and the smell of freshly cut grass was unable to elude my nostrils. The cool wind whipped past us as I walked toward our destination. It didn't take long for me to find my headstone amongst the many dark, indiscernible others.

"Hey," Nick said as he tripped over yet another gray bevel marker headstone.

"Are you okay?" I questioned as I caught him.

"Yeah. I'm fine. I was just wondering why we're here."

"Ah, here it is." I walked a few more feet, crouched down, and slowly traced the outline of my name meticulously over and over again. "This … this is where my family now comes to grieve. Right here. They bought it after Kat and I moved. They used to have a memorial in the front yard for me, but I guess it got too hard to look at every day. I saw a picture of my mom kneeling beside it when I was in my dad's office last night." Nick clutched onto my moving hand. I hadn't realized I was still tracing the outline. I looked up at him and the somber expression he gave told me it was time to lighten the mood. "You should have seen me when I first woke up. I was terrified and screaming at the top of my lungs. I panicked and couldn't breathe. Little did I know I didn't *have* to breathe." I laughed. "I wasn't laughing at the time, but it's funny now. In retrospect, I guess."

"Yeah?" A slight smile graced his handsome face, and with a doleful look he asked, "Why are you doing this to yourself, Alyssa?"

"Doing what?" I tried to sound upbeat and innocent. The look I received in return told me he wasn't buying any of it. "Fine. I don't know why, Nick. I don't know. Maybe because that's where I feel I belong, or, maybe, it's because soon enough that's where I'm going to be. Except this time, it will be for real. Or possibly, because now I don't want to be there anymore, and I'm not going to have a choice. So I don't know why I'm doing this to myself. I just don't know." I rubbed my forehead trying to calm my nerves.

"Okay. I'm sorry. I just figured our time would be better spent devising a plan instead of just sitting here." I knew he is trying to help, but sometimes I just wanted to be able to not have all the answers all the time. I wanted to not have to know what to do all of time.

At that point I wasn't even sure what Dante's intent was. If he wanted us dead, we would've been dead. But Kat had said before he liked to toy with his prey to show how superior he was to them. Is that what he was doing? Was I just his toy, and he was having fun yanking the strings?

That was it. Maybe I might actually have a fighting chance of saving Nick if I did it that way. *Eureka,* I thought to myself. That might actually work. "I think I have an idea, Nick. Come on. Let's go."

I was in the car with it started before Nick was half way up to it. What is taking him so long. Come on. Come on. Come on. I let out an impatient sigh before it dawned on me, he's human, hello, he isn't as fast as you are, Alyssa. Plus, he's injured. Let's not forget that key point. I normally tried so hard to be human, little issues like those never came up. But at that moment, I was trying to be anything but human.

The ten minutes it took him to make it to the car seemed as if an eternity had passed. My mind was working overtime. The tapping sound from my black leather boot against the floorboard was the only sound I could process, and that was only because it was going about as fast as the jumbled thoughts in my head. Finally making it up to where we'd parked, Nick glared at me.

He eased into the soft leather seat, turned to me and said, "That was almost a mile, Alyssa, and the twelve-foot iron gate I had to hop? I'm still a little banged up here so a little patience would've been nice. I'm not as fast as you are. Obviously." He glared down at my boot still tapping away a mile a minute. I stopped.

"Sorry. I think I might have an idea. I'm not sure if it's going to work, but it's better than nothing."

"That's true. What do you got?" Nick was still breathing hard, and I could his heart pounding wildly against his chest. A glimpse of the huge, throbbing vein on the side of his neck caused my fangs to grow uncontrollably. Simply thinking about the delicious nectar coursing through his body caused me to inch ever so close to his tilted neck. "Are you able to turn someone like you or does it just kill them? I mean it's apparent that it is possible, but can you do it?" The question caught me off guard, and then I realized what I was doing.

I sat back upright and replied, "I've never tried to change anyone. I'm not sure I know how to. I do know, however, need to eat."

The blood bank wasn't too difficult to get in to. Then again, why would they be? I mean, who would want to steal blood, right? I laughed at the thought. I gorged myself while gearing up for the fight of a lifetime. I wasn't about to take any chances. I needed to be prepared in every way imaginable. I knew I needed more training to be fully ready, but if I involved Kat, he would surely punish her as well for helping me. I would have to do this all on my own. She warned me. She didn't ask or want any of this. I couldn't involve her. Not now. Not ever.

I needed to find an ideal location for my one on one with Dante. That was my plan. If I could get him isolated away from everyone and everything, my odds of beating him would be greatly improved. Then there wouldn't be anything he could use against me. His strength against mine, that's it. Maybe Nick was right when he said things could have been blown out of proportion. It kept repeating over and over again in my head. *"It's not that I don't believe you or what you're saying, Alyssa. It's just I think maybe you could be blowing this out of proportion a little bit. Seriously, take a step back and think about it from my perspective. You, yourself, told me everything I have ever read, heard or seen in the movies about vampires is false. You have a pulse. You can go out into the sunlight. You breathe and sleep. You're just like me except for your, how can I say this delicately, dietary necessities. Am I so bad for thinking maybe, just maybe, some of the things you have been told could be a little exaggerated, as well? Think about it for a minute. I'm just saying."*

Maybe he was right. Maybe Kat unknowingly exaggerated Dante's abilities. I had yet to see him and according to what she said, I should have by now. Perhaps it's more along the lines of the telephone game. One person whispers something to someone who adds something when they tell the story. Then the next person who adds something else when they tell it and so on and so on. But if Nick or I am wrong, hopefully, the fight I planned would leave Dante just exhausted enough that once he was finished with me, he would forget all about Nick. I could only hope. Either way, Nick would have a head start, and I would have my last stand. Where at? We were in Arizona so the deserts were plentiful, but the lack of knowledge on his powers forced me to make my choice wisely.

I checked my reflection in the mirror of the women's bathroom. I didn't even recognize the girl in the mirror when I looked half the time anymore. I raised my lips to stare at my canines. I shook my head in disbelief as if that would shake them out of my mouth. It didn't, it never did. I did that same routine every morning of my new existence. You would've thought I would've learned. You would've thought I would've realized this was my life, this was real, and I could never go back. If I ever needed all of that to hit me, right then would've been the perfect time for it.

I let out a deep breath and was outside in no time.

"I feel better now." I plopped down into the seat of the warm, still running car.

"Yeah? That's good." Nick looked disappointed, but about what, I had no clue.

"Is something bothering you?"

"No. Nothing is bothering me. I was just ..." His voice stopped, and he stared at his hands.

148

"What is it, Nick?"

"I was just wondering what it would be like to be like you. What it would be like to be what you are." He looked away from me out the window. After all of my warnings, complaining, stories, I would've thought that would've been enough to discourage him, but, apparently again, I was wrong. I gripped the steering wheel a little tighter.

Staring straight ahead through the darkness of the windshield, I answered, "You don't want to be like me, Nick. You don't want to be this. You don't exist anymore. You're dead to the world and dead to all you know and love. You can't see or be with your family, your friends, or anyone. You don't want that. It's a lonely existence, if you can even call it that." My words fell bland and flat.

"I already don't have any family now. I'm basically all alone as it is, and it's pretty much the same existence I have now. What's it like? Do you see things differently? Do you feel things differently? I mean, what is it like?" Nick's eyes were directly on me, almost burning a hole right through me.

"I see like you do but in more scintillating detail. The colors are more vivid and sounds are more clear and audible. It's all just … more. I can't describe it except it's more. The way things feel is indescribable. Imagine living all of your life wearing a pair of white cotton gloves. You can still feel things just not completely. Now imagine one day you take off those gloves. Everything is very different yet still the same." I looked over to his body inquisitively turned toward mine. The enthralled look in his eyes told me I hadn't done a very good job of discouraging his inquiry into this. "Nick, there was no other way for me. I was dying. I wouldn't wish this on anyone. Especially not on you. Do you understand what I'm saying?" I hugged his hand in mine, squeezing ever so slightly.

"I'm not saying anything. I was just curious. That's all. So, what's this plan of yours?" I threw the car into drive and headed back toward the hotel.

"Well, here's what I was thinking, if I could somehow get Dante off of you and focused on me, it would give you time to get a head start. Maybe I could get him to a remote area, that way he can't use anything or anyone against me. It would just be he and I."

From the corner of my eye, I saw his whole body tense up with the revelation. He didn't like my plan, or he was afraid I would fail. Either way, it wasn't a good sign. I ran my fingers through his raven hair, intertwining his silky strains around them to calm him down. It wasn't working.

"That's a ludicrous idea, Alyssa. Ridiculous at best."

"What?" What he was implying hurt. I thought it was a pretty damn good plan. I didn't see anything wrong with it.

"You heard me. Do you have a death wish? Because it sounds like a suicide mission to me." His narrowed eyes sent a shiver running down my spine.

Chapter 18

Walking through the hotel lobby we argued in hushed anger. Once entering the room, it regained its force. "How dare you, Nick, how dare you!" I shouted once the door was shut.

"How dare I? I'm being honest with you," he snapped back.

"And I'm trying to save your life!" I retaliated.

"By what, ending yours?" His quick comeback only infuriated me more.

"There's no other choice. You can't fight him, you'll die. You're the one who said things may be blown out of proportion." He was the one who said it. I was only going along with his thinking.

"And if you fight him? What? Are you guaranteed not to die?" He already knew the answer to that, and I knew I couldn't lie about it.

"No." My voice quiet. "No, I'm not. Do I want to die? No. For once, since I've become this horrible monster, I don't want to, but I don't want you dying for my stupidity. I care about you, Nick. A lot more than I should." I lowered my gaze to the floor at my admission.

"Then let's run together, or let's fight together, but in the end, let's be together. Yes, I did say that, but what if I'm wrong, Alyssa. I don't want to take that chance." I couldn't argue with his logic, or I didn't want to. To this day, I'm still not sure which it was.

"Okay," I whispered, nodding in agreement. "Then we need to get you prepared."

"Okay. Let's do this," Nick said, rubbing his hands together. "What do I need to do?"

I tried to remember all the things Kat taught me until I realized it had absolutely no relevance to a human at all. I needed to teach him things a human could do to hurt us. There wasn't a lot that could be done, but there were a few things.

"Let's work on some moves." It was a bad idea. I knew it, he knew it, but there really wasn't any other choice. He would be going up against a highly trained and much older vampire than I, and he had to be prepared.

After finding himself on his back repeatedly, he needed a break. Taking a swig of water, he wiping the beads of sweat from his brow and asked, "This is going to be tough, isn't it?"

"Yeah. It is. I'm not going to lie; it's going to be a hell of a lot tougher than what I'm putting you through. I'm taking it easy. I don't want to hurt you. Dante does. He isn't going to care. Dante will put you through a brick wall and not think twice about it."

After a huge sigh, he said, "Okay. So obviously I'm not going to be able to overpower him so what else can I do?"

Even he knew he wouldn't win the conventional way. I closed my eyes trying to think of something, anything, he'd be able to do.

Only one thought came to mind. "You are not going to like this, but I'll distract him while you move in for the kill." I gauged his expression on the idea, and luckily for me, he wasn't too against it.

"Okay. What do you mean exactly?"

"I mean, once I get his undivided attention on me, you move in for the kill. His throat, his heart, any area really that will make him bleed profusely, you cut. Got it? Cut long and deep."

"But I shot you, and you didn't die?"

I understood how he could get confused. I still get confused about some things, and it didn't help that I suck at explaining things.

"Yes, but only because Kat got there in the nick of time. Had she not gotten there with the blood when she did, I would have died. It's not the injuries that kill us, it's the loss of blood. Given time, the injuries heal, but losing that much blood is a death sentence to us. Got it?"

"Got it."

"Don't get me wrong, if you cut off our head, we're dead, but you get the idea." That was always something I wondered about. I mean, hello, if you stab anyone in the heart with a wooden stake they're going to die. Seriously.

Chuckling, he replied, "Yeah, I get the idea."

"Good," I replied with a roll of the eyes and a smirk. "Now, are you ready to go again?"

"Let's do this." His enthusiasm for the whole situation frightened me, but, maybe, it was a good thing. Maybe, just maybe, his fearlessness would work to our advantage somehow.

We continued for hours upon hours of grueling combatives. I finally had to say enough. Nick wasn't going to give in, but his bruised and battered body was calling out for me to stop. Standing over top of him, I reached out, grabbed his hands, and pulled him up to his feet. I walked over to the refrigerator, took out a bottle of water and tossed it to him.

"I think we're done for tonight." I couldn't do it to him anymore. It didn't matter how strong he was or how much we trained. The fact of the matter was he would never be able to out maneuver or overpower Dante. If he was trained with a weapon or two, we might actually have a fighting chance.

"Are you giving up?" he asked, breathing heavily.

Chuckling, I replied, "Yep. I sure am. I'm giving up on kicking your butt and thinking tomorrow we're going to concentrate on a different strategy." He was flustered, if not a little bit offended by what I said, but I didn't care. He already had serious injuries from before, this couldn't be healthy for him. "I'm sorry, Nick. I know you're trying. I really do. It's just that you're a human. Unless we wound him with no way for him to get blood, I don't see us winning. Don't you want to relax for a little bit?"

"That does sound nice." His neck cracked and popped as he moved it from side to side.

"You sit right here," I said patting the couch, "and I will be right back."

"Yes, ma'am." That smart-aleck smirk slid across his lips.

"Ugh," I said in playful disgust as I curled my lip up at him. I ran a steaming hot bath adding some bubbles, compliments of the hotel, then sauntered my way back up to him. I grabbed both his hands to pull him up, but instead I was pulled down onto his lap. We both busted out laughing, and it felt great. Laughter was a natural stress reliever and it was much needed. "What's this about?" That devilish smile I love ever so much was present.

"I'm trying to relax," he said before casually kissing my lips.

"I have a hot bath waiting for you. It'll help with the sore muscles. Come on." I stood and looked down at him, eyebrow raised.

"Okay, okay." He sighed and pushed his way up off of the couch.

"I figured I would order you something to eat. That is if you want me to." I presented my own cocky little smile at him.

He turned around in the doorway of the bathroom and said, "Yeah. Thank you. That sounds good. I'm starving."

With my own devious little smile, I said, "Well you could tell me what you want, or I could … sneak a peek and see."

"I thought you didn't do that." His snappish response froze me in place. The nervous glance and jittery tapping on the door frame confused me even more.

"I don't like to so I normally don't. It was a joke, Nick."

"I knew that." I hated the forced smile he always put on when he was trying to play it cool. "A burger and some fries will be fine. Thanks again. I'm going to go jump into the tub, like you said, for a little bit."

"Yeah."

I was more than a little puzzled over his behavior. I hated the knot in my stomach that was creeping up on me again. I really didn't like the fact Dante could be right. Why would Nick hide something from me, though? What would he hide for that matter? After all I've told him, why would he feel it necessary to lie to me? All those questions were dancing around in my head, but there were too many questions and no time for answers right now.

I ordered his burger and fries and sat back waiting for him to emerge from the bathroom. After an hour passed, I was done waiting. I yelled for him to see what was taking so long. He finally materialized, and his drooping eyelids revealed he'd fallen asleep. Nick stumbled over to the couch running his water-logged fingers through his dampened, glistening jet black mane. "Sorry. Time must have gotten away from me," he said groggily.

"I bet. Here's your food." I slid the plate across the teak wood coffee table. He devoured his food then sluggishly removed himself from the couch and headed toward the bedroom.

"Come on." He nodded his head toward the bedroom door. Sighing heavily, I pushed off the couch and went with him.

Nick was asleep within seconds of his head hitting the down-stuffed pillow. I, on the other hand, wasn't. There were too many questions floating around my head to rest. *What was tomorrow going to bring? Did Dante already know what I was planning? How was I supposed to defeat him when he was always two steps ahead of me? Poor Nick. He won't stand a chance,* I thought as I gently brushed the hair from his eyes. I finally drifted off, but that night's sleep brought me no rest. Horrible dreams, not dreams but nightmares, filled my mind the whole night. Nick and I alone in a dark alley, me being overpowered by Dante, Nick killed by some unknown assailant.

I awoke with a start with Nick lying awake next to me. "You were flailing around. Are you okay? Bad dream?"

Rubbing my hand on my forehead, I replied in a hoarse voice, "I'm fine. Yeah. It was just a bad dream. That's all."

"Do you want to tell me about it?" He softly stroked my back up and down.

"No. I'm all right. Everything's all right."

How could I explain I had a horrible dream in which he was killed, and I was powerless to stop it? If he wasn't deflated before, he most certainly would be after hearing that. I made my way out of the bed and to the bathroom. Closing the door behind me, I braced myself up by the sink splashing a handful of cold water on my face. I stared in the mirror at the cold reflection looking back at me.

Instinctively I let out a deep breath and whispered to the mirror, "This is not going to end well, is it?"

'That depends on your definition of well,' the voice snapped in my head.

'You know what? If you're the judge, jury, and executioner why don't you just kill me then, Dante?' I was sick of his pompousness. It was getting really old, really quick.

'If you remember correctly, Alyssa, I said I didn't want to hurt you.' With the utterance of those words, Dante appeared in the bathroom right behind me. His large hands found a home atop of mine. He was so close his soft lips brushed the side of my face as he spoke.

In a tone audible by my ears only, he said, "Look in the mirror, Alyssa. We belong together. We are perfect for each other. I understand you. I understand your needs, your wants, your desires." Kissing my neck in a way that sent shivers down my back, he continued, "I know your darkest secrets, and you know some of mine. You'll get to know the rest in time. Come with me. Let's end this now. You know I'm telling you the truth. You know I am where you belong."

From the mirror I saw him for the first time, except it wasn't the first time. He was the guy from the club who disappeared. If he'd come up to me I never would've even considered leaving with Nick, but he didn't. His dark eyes caught mine and I followed them toward the open window. Turning my head in the same direction, the cool breeze hit my face and rushed through my hair.

His grip loosened on my hands as I slowly turned to face him. I was in awe of how magnificent this man actually looked. His eyes were so dark and piercing blue it was as though they could see right through me and his jaw and cheekbones were defined and chiseled. His hair, his onyx colored hair, hung a bit longer which flattered his face and made him appear even more mysterious as it hovered just slightly over those sapphire eyes of his.

Pulling myself and my thoughts together, I asked in an equally muted tone, "And if I go with you? What will happen to Nick then? I know what you said would happen, and I know what I can't allow to happen."

I caught his eyes with my own. There was something between us. Something I couldn't explain or make go away. Chemistry, a spark, whatever it may be called, was growing more intense becoming undeniable. Dante's stare kept mine as he reluctantly surrendered me from his hold.

"Okay. I won't hurt your precious human, but if he utters one word, Alyssa." Seeing my name on his lips, hearing it come from his mouth, caused flutters in my stomach.

"He won't," I spoke softly not breaking my stare.

"If he does you know what must be done." He was only inches from my lips, and I found him leaning in closer.

Heart pounding, I wrapped my arms around his neck and ran my fingers through the back of his hair. I didn't know what was happening, but it felt magnetic. It felt as if I was being pulled to him by some invisible force. Was this what happened when we met our own kind? I was scared yet entranced at the same time. Was he using some power against me, or we're we more connected to our own kind? Dante carefully placed his hands around my waist. Before I knew it, he had us spun around, and I was up against the door. Propped up with one arm against the wall and one still around my waist, he pulled me closer to him.

"This is right, Alyssa. This right here is what's right."

With the utterance of that one sentence, he leaned in gracefully kissing my lips. The fiery ice of a kiss which followed was better than I could've ever envisioned. I didn't want that feeling or moment to end. Leaning down, Dante bit my neck. It was like an electric charge flowing through my body heightening all my senses to everything we were at that moment. It was the most euphoric sensation I had ever felt. A moan escaped my lips which was anything but hushed.

The door shook from Nick banging on it. "Is everything all right in there?"

I placed my finger over Dante's full, tempting lips right as he was about to say something. "Yes. Everything is fine. I'll be out in one minute." I shook my head no at Dante.

"All right. If you say so. I am going to order up breakfast." I listened for his footsteps to fade away from the door.

"You will never be truly happy with him, Alyssa. Not like you could be with me." Dante seductively ran his finger down the side of my neck. "Come with me. Let's leave now. We could be together, rule the night, you and I." His voice, mesmerizing.

"I'll go with you if you promise not to hurt Nick or send anyone else to hurt him either."

"I won't, if he doesn't say a word. I told you that already." He leaned in ever so close while tracing my lips with his index finger.

"Okay. Give me a few hours. I have to tell Nick what's going on and explain everything to him. I'll meet you in the hotel bar downstairs." I didn't want to leave Nick, but I had no other choice. One last soft kiss and Dante was gone. If this was what it took to save Nick, then so be it.

I walked over to the mirror straightening myself up before attempting to explain what just happened to Nick. I needed to explain everything, but I wasn't exactly sure as to how I was going to do it. I had to think. I splashed water onto my face again and looked at my reflection. I noticed there wasn't a bite mark on me. I took a closer look and again, still no mark.

That's when I heard it, the most awful, ghastly shriek from the other side of the door. The sound was so garbled it was barely recognizable. Oh no. "Dante, you promised." I flung the door open in time to see Alonzo pushing Nick off of the steel blade plunged into his stomach. Screaming in horror, I ran falling to Nick's side. Holding his stomach, Nick looked up at me with shocked, pain-riddened eyes. I glared up where Alonzo was standing only to find nothing but an opened door. Nick's eyes closed, and I could hear only a faint beat to his heart. Alonzo would pay for this. I would make him sorry.

I ran after Alonzo. I didn't care who or what they saw. All I cared about was making him pay for what he'd done to Nick. I ran through the lobby out onto the street in a blur. I paused for a moment to pick up his odorous stench of a scent, and then I was on his trail again. He was a mere human; no way he could get that far from me. I had him swooped up and in the alley in seconds. I didn't even try to conceal what I was about to do to him from the mortals walking the streets. I had him only a few feet back in that dark, dirty, death hole before I had him slammed up against the cement wall. "Now you're going to pay," I sneered at him.

"Screw you, bitch," he spat back. He fought with what little strength his pathetic body held. It was to no avail. I grinned at his horror-stricken face.

"I told you, you would pay, didn't I?" I was at his throat shredding it into a mangled mess of carnage before he could speak. Blood poured out splattering onto the wall and alleyway. I refused to taste one drop of that monster's life as it drained from his body. I dropped him like the garbage he was and turned and walked out onto the street. Blood soaked and canines out, I didn't even try to clean up or hide. Let someone see me, I didn't care, I dared a human to try to stop me. The last of my humanity died with the final beat of Nick's heart.

Not even two feet from the alley I was seized back into it by something, a blur of a person. I sneered and growled until my eyes fixated on Dante.

"What do you think you are doing?"

"What I thought would make you proud," I hissed back.

"Make me proud? You're going to get caught. If not by the humans, then by the Ancient Ones. Do you want us all to die?" Dante shifted his head keeping my stare.

"You're the one who kept implying we're superior to them. They're ridiculous creatures here on Earth only to supply us with food. Why should I care? This is what you wanted, Dante. This is how you wanted me to be, right? Well, now I am. Happy?" The sarcasm seeped out of my mouth without the slightest inclination of me trying to hide it.

"No. I am not happy. He was food. Nothing to get upset about and certainly nothing to get yourself killed over. The Ancient Ones are above me. I cannot help you with them. I cannot save you from them, Alyssa."

"Who said I wanted you to save me, Dante? Hmmm? Who?" The blank stare should have been an indicator that I didn't care what so ever if I died or not. I'd had enough. That was my breaking point.

"You are impossible, Alyssa. You're coming with me."

Chapter 19

"Are you all right, Alyssa?" The sound of Dante's voice pulled me out of my thoughts to see him kneeling at the stone fireplace that was alive with the burning and crackling of logs. I watched as the fire danced wildly.

"I'm fine," I said, entangling myself in my oversized gray hooded sweatshirt.

Dante nodded his head returning his gaze back to the crackling fire. I returned mine back outside through the oversized windows running floor to ceiling. It was a quiet night. The pine trees swayed slowly, dancing with an invisible partner. The mountains in the distance had a touch of snow on their peaks as if strategically painted there by some unknown artist. If this had been different circumstances, I would've been able to enjoy it. Considering why I was there, I wasn't.

I turned and walked over to the bookshelf lined with all the classics. I ran my finger lovingly over each and every leather bound title and not one caught my interest. That, for me, was strange. I would get lost in books for hours upon hours with no end in sight. Whenever something went wrong, I would immerse myself in a book until I forgot what I wanted to escape. Instead, I settled into the brown leather couch facing the fireplace.

I looked up to a glass being held in front of my face. The thick redness filling it was unmistakable and Dante holding it as though it was peace offering was unexpected. Graciously accepting it, I peered up and smiled. "Thank you. I'm sorry about earlier. It's just … it was my fault. I should've known he wasn't dead. I should've been watching Alonzo better. But I didn't see anything when I tried to get into his head. I only saw darkness. I thought it meant he was dead. I was trying so hard to protect Nick from you I forgot about everyone else."

A slight smile encroached on his face before he wiped it away. He obviously wasn't one for emotions, I remember telling myself. "I accept your apology, Alyssa. It may sound cruel, but this should just reiterate why humans are not a part of our world." He was right.

It was a cruel and unnecessary thing for him to say. "I'm sure you did your best, but you are still so young in this life. You should be focusing on learning how to survive. I'll help you. If you would like, that is."

"Sure," I said. "Why not? I have nothing better to do, right?" I said, my voice betraying me. It quivered just a touch at the end. I hoped Dante hadn't caught it, but he seemed like the type that didn't miss too much going on around him. "Is there somewhere I can lay down at here?" I scanned the cabin with my eyes before returning them to him.

"Yes. I'll show you to your room." I followed behind him up the stairs and to the second door on the right. He opened it and whispered, "Good night, Alyssa. I'll see you in the morning."

With a fake smile, I whispered back, "Good night, Dante," and entered into the darkness. He closed the door behind him as he walked away.

Looking around, I switched on the table lamp next to the bed. The walls upstairs were smooth, normal, and drywalled unlike the downstairs wooden logs. The calming light sky-blue color balanced nicely with the walnut floors. The spindled log bed was beautifully crafted out of white cedar, and I slowly ran my fingers along the footboard on my way to the window where stared out at the quiet unknown.

The next morning came all too soon. I laid in bed tracing the intricately laced designs stitched into the quilt. The little white daisy outlines seem too symmetrical to be hand sewn, but I had a distinct feeling they were. The image of Nick staring wide-eyed at Alonzo haunted me throughout the night. I couldn't seem to get the image of Nick's face twisted in horror as he was being pushed off Alonzo's knife out of my head. I decided to check to see if I could have been wrong, if Nick was still alive and somehow managed to be saved. Darkness. All I could see was darkness. I knew he was dead, but my heart rejected what my head was telling it. I heard that last faint beat of his heart. I knew there was no way for someone to survive that kind of injury. No human anyway.

'Are you coming downstairs, Alyssa, or are you going to lie in bed all day?' Dante bellowed in my head.

'I'm getting up. You could have come upstairs and asked me that. I hate you going into my head.'

'That is what I do. Why does it bother you so much?'

'I don't know, it just does. Now get out!' I replied flinging the soft, hand-sewn quilt off of me. I lied. I did know why it bothered me. It was my head, my private thoughts, but trying to explain it to him seemed pointless.

I threw on my purple turtleneck sweater and a pair of faded jeans with annoyance and stomped down the stairs to see what Dante was doing.

"Ah, you are finally up, I see." His smile lit up his sapphire eyes, turning them more playful.

"Ah, you're finally talking to me like a normal person, I see," I retaliated back. I wasn't in any sort of mood to play.

"Nothing about us is normal, Alyssa. The sooner you are able to realize that, the better off you'll be. Stop fighting what you are. Stop fighting what you've become. You, more than most, were meant to be this." He shook his head scornfully at me for my lack of appreciation for what I had become. What was he talking about, me more than most was meant to be this?

"What do you mean by, I, more than most, was meant to be this?" I stared at him through narrow slit eyes waiting for his answer.

"There is a lot you don't know about our kind, Alyssa. Information Kat, as you refer to her as, was never privileged enough to know. I want to teach it all to you, the true and correct information. Take you for instance." Cocking his head to the side, he had a matter of fact look to his face.

"What about me?" Taken aback a bit, I was a little offended by this remark for some reason.

"You go against all I believe in. You go against all I have ever been taught, yet here you are in front of my very eyes."

"What does that mean? Why? How do I go against all you know?" My mind kept screaming, what's wrong with me? What is he saying is so wrong about me? But outside, I kept my composure.

"It means you're capable of doing things only a true vampire should be able to do."

I didn't understand what he was talking about. A true vampire? Was there a difference between us all? What things can only a true vampire do? What does that even mean, a true vampire? What makes a vampire a true vampire? "Such as what?" I asked, my defiant attitude slowly waning.

"Such as *'talking in your head'*. Only those who are of pure blood have powers such as those. We're all fast, even the mixed bloods, but only the purest are able to have the power such as that." Mixed bloods? What was that?

Confused and curious, I asked, "What is a mixed blood?"

Smiling, pleased I was paying attention and hungered for more knowledge, he replied, "Mixed bloods are those who were humans and turned by a vampire. They're not born into this life. They're made a vampire. Their blood is mixed; human and vampire. Hence mixed blood." For once, something actually made sense to me. "There is so much you need to learn, Alyssa. So much Katarina was unable to teach you because she, herself, is a mixed blood. She's not privy to most of what you need to know. You're different, Alyssa Saunders. You're like no one I have ever met."

Dante's eyes turned softer, gentler somehow when he looked at me. Forcing myself to look down at the floor, I knew if I lingered in his eyes any longer I would get lost in them. I inhaled softly and lifted my head to him standing so close I could feel his breath on my face. I licked and then bit my lower lip in habit. Nervousness set in, but a voice deep down was shouting this is right. This is what is supposed to be. I fought it the best I could. It felt as though I would betray Nick somehow if I gave in to this. Gave in to him.

Before it was to save Nick's life, or at least that's what I told myself. Now, I wondered if I had wanted this all along. Not Nick's death but Dante. I didn't fight it in Arizona when he kissed me, and, to be truthful, I didn't want it to end. It hadn't been that long since Nick was murdered, and here I was thinking of another man. *What kind of person did that make me,* I wondered to myself. I cared about Nick. I loved him, and now I feel as though I can't resist a man who, until the other day, was going to kill us?

'Were you this critical of yourself when you were human?' he muttered in my head.

Why must he do that when he knows it annoys me to no end? "Why are you in my head, Dante?"

"You looked lost in your own thoughts. I wanted to see what was keeping your attention so closely. Again, were you always so critical of yourself when you were human?"

Ignoring him, I walked to the living room and plopped down on the couch. I couldn't be that close to him and think straight. "Yes," I said.

"In this life being what you are is as much about instincts and feelings as it is about thinking. Your mind can trick you. That primal instinct you have to stay alive will never deceive you." I didn't doubt what he was saying, but I didn't whole heartedly believe it either. "Alyssa, I never let anyone get close to me, but there is something about you that keeps drawing me in. Something keeps drawing me back to you. I have no idea what or why, but I do know I shouldn't fight it. I feel I need to save you. I need to protect you, if only from yourself. I've heard others say it. I've heard them talk about that primal instinct to protect the one they love, but I'd never encountered or felt it myself. Not this strong. Not as powerful as what it is between us. I know you feel it. You just have to allow yourself to believe it's right."

Dante was right. I did feel something. I felt the urge to protect him, to save him, but how could I reason with myself it was okay when just a short while ago I thought I felt the same for Nick? And what's even more confusing was Dante was saying the same thing Nick said, he was drawn to me for some unexplainable reason. Why? Why were they all drawn to me, I questioned.

Dante followed me and sat down in the matching leather chair catty-cornered to the fireplace. Burying his intense eyes into mine, he said, "I know you don't want to, Alyssa, but let it go. Let go of all the things holding you back and causing you pain. You couldn't help what happened to you, and had you not been turned, you would be dead. I know what I'm asking is a lot, but you deserve to set yourself free. You deserve to allow yourself to be happy. Nick was nothing more than you trying to hold on to your humanity. That's it. Nothing more. I don't understand it, but you can't tell me in all honesty, that you felt for him as you are feeling right now with me."

I refused to admit I knew what he was saying was true. I did want to hang on to being human, but he was wrong on one fact because that was not all Nick was to me. I loved him. That was not just me trying to hang on to my humanity, but something inside me was ablaze. Burning with an intensity which was frightening yet exhilarating all at the same time.

"What do you want me to do, Dante?" The throaty whisper that escaped my lips caught even me by surprise. The recognizable yearning in the whisper was more power than I wanted to give away to him. Now he knew he was right. Dante knew he was winning, but once it was out I no longer cared about winning. All I wanted was for him to tell me what to do, tell me how to end the pain from losing Nick that was slowly killing me and for him to tell me how to control the ache crippling me from not having him, Dante, in my arms.

"Do you feel it, too?" he asked, kneeling in front of me, rubbing ever so tenderly on my thighs. "That's love, Alyssa. This is love. We are the same you and I. You don't have to pretend with me. I already know." His fingers slowly slid up to my hips and as he pulled me in closer, I succumbed to all the feelings I'd been trying to fight all along. The first moment he spoke to me I knew it. I knew I wanted him, but I refused to acknowledge that desire. I didn't have the strength to contest it any longer.

Sitting there with Dante's eyes fixed on mine, the fire raging behind him, I stopped fighting. I leaned in and the kiss which followed was beyond anything I had ever experienced in either of my lives. It was a fiery ice of a kiss that sent chills tingling down my spine but burned me inside me like no other. It was impassioned. He kissed me as though he desperately needed me, as though he couldn't live one more day, one more second, without me. I'd never had that before, and I didn't want to lose it either. Dante lingered on my lips for a few seconds longer before ever so cautiously pulling away still keeping his eyes anchored onto mine. In the intensity of it all, we laughed in unison. His laugh was intoxicating. I'd never heard it before, and it comforted me. Its deep richness reverberated through my body warming me. I would take all the comforting I could get at the moment.

"Fine." I had to smile at the revelation of it all. A short time with him and I was ready to accept the fate of what I had become, whereas all my time with Kat had never made me want to relinquish. "On one condition," I continued.

"What's that?" That sweet smile of his and those gentle hands almost made me forget what I was going to say. Almost.

"Tell me about you. Tell me everything. Unlike you, I don't go inside people's heads to get the information I want. I don't like to do that."

"First of all, there's a reason you have the ability you do. You should use it and use it more often than not."

"I don't like to. Thoughts are private and not to be known by anyone other than whom you choose to share them with. I don't like to invade people's privacy like that. Now, tell me about you, Mr. I-Don't-Have-Any-Secrets. I want to know it all. Tell me everything."

Dante stood back up and positioned himself at the other end of the couch. "Well, I was born this way."

He started when I interrupted, "Wait. What? What do you mean you were born this way? How is that even possible?" With confusion swirling around in my mind, I tried to grasp onto the possibility of what he was saying. He removed the knee-high boots from my feet strategically and purposefully pushing and kneading my arches and instep to relax me into submission.

My head fell back against the couch as I enjoyed the message and he continued, "As I said before, there's a lot you don't know about our kind, Alyssa."

"Okay. I see that now." I was still reeling from the fact of vampires having the ability to procreate. I always assumed it was impossible.

"My name is Dante Michael Ortello. I'm a lot older than you are, obviously, and I am as awful as you've been told. To those who break our rules and put us all in harm's way, that is. I do not let others get too close to me. I have my own reasons for that, but as I said before, there's something about you that makes me want to let you in, but I guess that's what love does to a person."

"Have you ever been in love?" I questioned.

"Not like this."

166

"So, why do you think you're in love with me then?"

Letting out a heavy sigh, he said, "Because I've been told love at first sight does exist, and when you meet the one who causes all the world to make sense, you don't lose them. You don't let them go. You know you're more like me than you think, Alyssa."

"How's that?" I was nothing like him. If anything, he was more like Kat; cut off and distant. Kat just wasn't as cold as he was.

"Well, you hunted the ones you felt deserved it. You became the judge, jury, and executioner, and you felt no remorse about it. Why? Because you knew what you were doing was for the greater good. I know what I'm doing may seem harsh, but in the end, it is for the greater good of us all. You, above all, understand what and why I do what I do. You understand me." He was right. I did feel entitled to make those decisions. I knew, in the end, it would help other women, other people. I never saw what he did that way, though. I only saw the horror stories that were told to me. I never stopped to consider maybe he had good intentions.

The weeks flew by, and I barely noticed. It was like I'd found my home. I finally found where I belonged in my new life. I was still mourning Nick, but I'd finally found peace in what I was. Dante helped me find peace in my existence. I stuck with Kat's way of eating and hoped to turn Dante onto it on a more permanent basis. He would appease me every once in a while, which was becoming more and more frequent. I hated when he left me to find other means of eating. Sometimes it was only a few hours, other times it was a few days. On those occasions he came back with food for me, as well. A horrible feeling crept over me before his last trip. I gave no credence to it. I should have. Dante told me to listen to my gut, to my instinct to stay alive, but I didn't. Looking back now, I definitely should have.

I loved the little seclusion of paradise Dante had. We were away from everything, everyone. It was quiet, clean, and pure. I never thought to think of enemies. I never gave thought to harm coming for me. Why would I? I was warned of Dante. He was the one to fear. He kept track of all the ones who broke the rules. Now that he was on my side the others would be, as well. He was my protector. Nothing could hurt me while he was around. The problem was, he wasn't always around. The last thing I remembered was the searing pain ripping through my body and me screaming in agony until blackness settled upon me.

Chapter 20

The memories of my past fade into the background, and I open my eyes only to realize I'm still in this dungeon. Sliding up the stone wall, I stagger over to the metal door. Whoever brought me here must have drained me almost completely dry because every fiber of my being aches as it screams out for blood. As I try to walk, my legs buckle, and my blurred vision isn't helping me at all. Unfortunately, though, it's not blurry enough to see I can't find a way out of this rank room.

I bang my palm against the door screaming, "Hello? Is anybody out there? Hello?"

It seems like forever since the man has come in to taunt me. My vision was so deteriorated at that point; I couldn't make out any features or tell anything distinguishing about him. Why am I here? I don't understand any of this. I want answers. I need answers. If I am going to die, I deserve to know why. I bang on the door again and again until I slither down into a crumpled, crying mess on the floor.

Waking in the darkened room, goosebumps cover my arms and panic takes over me. Someone's in here with me. I can feel their eyes watching me as I scan the room methodically. Looking, searching one wall at a time. In the shadowed corner across from me, steel gray eyes pierce through the darkness, aiming directly at me.

"Ah, you're awake now." The tall man glides toward me, and in response, I scoot to the wall as quick as my arms and legs will allow. "Don't cower, it's unbecoming, Alyssa," he sneers, still gliding toward me, his eyes never releasing mine.

"Who are you?" I manage to get out but not without a tremor.

Laughing, he replies, "I'm your only salvation. I am, for all intents and purposes, your best friend, your only friend, right now." The laugh echoes off the walls bouncing back into my ears causing them to ring, but I stare at him defiantly regardless. I refuse to let him win. I refuse to let him get to me.

"You are not my friend. Dante will come for me, and so will Kat. Then you'll be sorry."

This time, his laugh was louder, more smug than before. "Your precious Kat doesn't even know you're missing, and, as for Dante, well, he works for us. Did you honestly think he just found you? Did you think he simply happened to befriend you? No, no, no sweetheart. He's under our orders. I admit he has taken a shine to you and not fulfilled his duty to us as we had hoped, but that will be dealt with soon enough. Even though I must say I am glad he didn't carry out those orders, he still disobeyed. He will be appropriately punished, but don't worry your pretty little head about that. You, on the other hand, you are special, Alyssa. You're not like the rest of the mixed bloods. Your blood runs deeper than that."

What is he talking about? My blood runs deeper than that? My blood runs deeper than what? And I don't believe a word he says about Dante either. I can't, because if I do it means all Dante has said and done is a lie, and it can't be a lie. It just can't.

Crouching down in my face under the dim light of the candle, the man says, "How rude of me. I do apologize for not introducing myself properly earlier. My name is Roman." Tilting his head from side to side, he examines me as if I'm a specimen he's studying. Clumsily grasping at the wall, I pull myself up to my feet. He's a good foot taller than me with striking gray eyes like magnets I can't pull my gaze from. With his long, dark blond hair tucked behind his ears, I can see he's more wirythen not. Pushing up against the wall, Roman moves with me, mirroring me, copying me, still studying his little specimen. "You are smarter than the rest. Do you know that?" With him still in my face, what I really want to do is reach out and bite him. Right here, right now.

Laughter rings throughout the room again as he turns and walks away clapping his hands.

"How am I smarter?" I question.

"You have more dignity, as well. There is more fight in you. You know why you are here. You know what is about to happen to you, and yet you do not beg. You do not beg for mercy or another chance. It's in your blood not to."

Staring into those cold, metallic eyes, I show no fear. I know he can sense it, but I will die with dignity. I refuse to degrade myself to

170

any of those things the others do or have done. I'll accept responsibility for the things I've done and take what is due to me, but I will not stand idly by and be toyed with and openly mocked. "Are you going to kill me or not?" It sounded more threatening in my head than aloud. Aloud it was meek and timid. Not the strong, intimidating voice I aimed for.

"Do you want to die?" His hands steeple together, head tilted looking directly at me waiting for me to surrender to pleading.

"No," I say with an edge to my voice. "I don't want to die. No one wants to die. You may think you do until you lose the option to live."

A smile crosses his lips as he says, "You really are living up to my expectations, Alyssa. Bravo." Roman clapping his hands in approval is anything but favorable to me. "I am not going to kill you … just yet, that is." Spinning around on his heels, he's mere inches from my face before I can think of a witty response. "I think I may keep you around for a bit. You're rather entertaining to me."

"You think so?" My body in spasms from the lack of blood renders me helpless in making any real smart-aleck commentary back to him. All I am able to retort with is, "I'm glad I can amuse you, Roman, is it?" I narrow my eyes trying to decipher exactly what it is this man could possibly want from me. Better yet, what he feels my crime has been. To no avail of course, but what I really want to know is what he's planning on doing to me.

"Well, I see we are beginning to become foul in our mood. So I will leave for now, but I will be back."

As he turns to leave, I yell out, "Wait."

Smiling in triumph, he turns slowly on his heels again to face me. "Yes, Alyssa?" Roman says drumming his fingers together, impatiently waiting for me. I have the distinct feeling his smugness thinks he already knows what I'm going to say. But he's wrong. He has no idea.

"Are we fed in here, or am I to die a painfully, slow death of starvation?" Loud, sadistic chuckling emanates from him before the door quickly slams behind him.

There's nothing for me to do in this dungeon except sleep and pace. Pace and sleep. It must have been days since Roman was last in here mocking and tormenting me. Not that I would know for certain considering there are no windows in this room, cell, whatever it is. There are only candle sconces on the walls slowly burning out.

Taking what little strength I have left, I study the room compulsively to see if I overlooked something, anything, I could use to get out of this vile place. Nothing. There is absolutely nothing I have overlooked. Cooling my head against the stones of the wall, I pick at the mortar holding them all together with my nail. Maybe I'll get lucky and the wall will fall with all the stones crashing down on my head, crushing me to death.

Nice try, Alyssa, you're a vampire, not that easily killed.

If I only knew what Roman thought I did wrong, I could try to rectify it. I could offer a solution to the situation, but he isn't talking. Instead, he would rather slowly kill me by starving me to death.

Roman insinuating Dante only feigned interest in me because he works for them haunts my mind. Questions buzz through my head as I chip away at the wall knowing I won't even make a dent. First of all, who are the "them" he spoke of? The Ancient Ones? Second off, what did I do to have them send Dante after me? Dante, one of the most feared vampires of all. If that's even what happened to begin with. Was it my relationship I had with Nick? Or was Kat right and my past of hunting scumbags has finally caught up with me?

Dante was not just using me. He couldn't be. I saw into his soul when I looked into those dark blue eyes of his. The kind of emotion I saw radiating out from them couldn't have been faked. Did Dante set me up? No, that I refuse to believe. I refuse to give Roman exactly what he wants, which is for me to doubt Dante. It won't happen. Dante has been nothing if not honest and truthful with me. Even at times when I preferred anything but the truth, he still gave it to me straight.

"I brought you something," Roman's voice echoes outside the impenetrable shield otherwise known as the door. The grinding sound of metal against metal sends my head whipping toward the sound. A little girl about the age of eleven or twelve is shoved violently in, and the slamming sound that follows causes us both to flinch. "Enjoy, Alyssa."

His fiendish chuckle mixed with the clanking of his footsteps fades away. The dirty, disheveled girl crouches in the corner as far from me as she can possibly get. The smell of fear emanates off of her, and I wonder why I'd really never taken notice of that before this moment. I smelt it back when I hunted human prey, I just never focused enough to know what it was. Shame overtakes me knowing this poor girl, this child, was put into this position and fears me like she does. Even though I know she should, I wonder how she knows it.

Roman's intentions are clear, and I'm fighting every urge in my body not harm this innocent child. She's smart, I can tell by the way she observes everything around her. I wonder how she knows to stay away from me the way she does. I see no visible bite marks on her, but that means nothing. If they tortured her already, she knows what they, we, are. I'm no different than the rest of them. I'm a monster just like them, but maybe I'm the only one with a conscience.

"Hey, what's your name, sweetie?" I smile.

I don't want to move too fast and startle her, but I want so badly to ease and comfort her. Ease her fears the way my mother used to do for me when I was terrified of the boogieman. Her dark almond eyes widened with fear as she stares at me, but she's also battling with herself on whether or not to trust me.

"My name is Alyssa." A sharp pinch on my lip steals my attention from her, and I know my canines are now in full show. I press my lips tightly together, but it's too late. She scoots back and bangs against the wall repeatedly while little whimpers escape her tiny throat. "Okay. Okay. I'll leave you alone, but if you want to talk, I'll be right over here." I walk back to the opposite corner hoping this will help calm her.

Her sweet smell teases my nostrils as her heart beats rapidly through the silence. I pace back and forth along the wall like a caged animal waiting for Roman to return. He'll be sorry for this. I will make him pay dearly. A scuttling noise catches my attention and I pounce like a tiger onto the rat. It hisses and squirms trying to get away, but I sink my pointed teeth into it before it gets a chance. Two seconds is all it takes to drain it bone dry, and I let it flow to the ground. That rat didn't have enough blood in it to even be considered an appetizer.

I look over in time to see the girl making a disgusted face toward me. "Hey, beggars can't be choosers," I say. "It was the rat or you." As soon as it's out of my mouth, I know it's a huge mistake. I shouldn't have said it. Not then. Not ever. Her eyes grow wide with fear again and she returns to her fetal position of safety. "I'm sorry. I didn't mean it. Well, I did mean it, but I shouldn't have said it. I don't even know if you can speak English," I say with a sigh. Shaking my head, I return to my spot on the opposite side of the room.

Right as I drop my head on my knees I hear a little angelic voice say, "My name is Amaya." Her voice is shaky and timid, but her eyes are alert and keen.

"Well, it's very nice to meet you, Amaya. Your name's very beautiful. "I catch the twinkle in her eye but can't determine if it's a flicker from the candles or a glimmer of trust toward me. I'm hoping for trust, although I'm not quite sure I deserve it just yet.

Another rat scurries by, and I snatch it up and drain it before she can blink. I toss it into the shadowed corner so she doesn't have to look at its lifeless body any more than she needs to.

"Tell me about you, Amaya. How did you get here?" I was trying to lull her with the ease of my voice as Kat had done to me so many times.

"I don't know how I got here." Her tiny voice shakes as tears stream down her dirty face leaving a path of clean streaks after it.

"It's okay, sweetie. I don't know how I got here either."

"Really?" she asks, wiping her cheeks dry with the back of her hand.

"Yeah. No idea. I was sitting on my friend's back porch daydreaming when I felt a sharp pain in my neck. The next thing I know I'm waking up in here." I look around, but still no way to escape can be seen. "It's okay," I continue. I pull her into me and rub softly on her fragile arm.

I'm going to get her out of here if it's the last thing I do.

She doesn't deserve this. What could she have done? Nothing. That was my answer. There was nothing she could've done to deserve this. I have to be very cautious in my planning. If what

174

Dante said is true, then Roman can read my mind and know all of my thoughts before I have a chance to do anything. What am I thinking? Of course, Dante was telling the truth. I have no reason to doubt him. None whatsoever. Don't think. I'll have to do whatever comes to me at that moment so there's no premeditation, and hopefully, if I'm right, no way to guard against it.

Chapter 21

Her warmth pressed against my skin relaxes me before I plummet into a world of darkness and dread seeing no immediate way of stopping it. Hitting a nonexistent floor with a thud, I look around to see images of my family swirling around me like a carnival ride I can't stop. Finally, the swirling ceases, and I'm trapped in the middle. My family on one side of me; my mother, father and my dead grandfather. On the other side of me is my newly acquired family; Kat and Dante, and others I can't decipher. My head in a constant swivel side to side knowing I have to choose, just not knowing why. Feeling the sadness and despair filling my every fiber, and me unable to decide or take a stand.

Grinding and screeching of metal on metal causes me to jump to my feet, quicker than I thought I had the strength to do, and throwing my body in front of Amaya, protecting her from whatever it is he has planned. She shouldn't have to suffer for his amusement. My hair drenched and clinging to the side of my face, I stare into his cold gaze.

"I am very disappointed in you, Alyssa," Roman hisses as he stares at her slinking back into the corner. "I thought you would have rid us of this little atrocity by now." He continues his cold stare at her.

"Keep dreaming," I spat. Lunging forward, I sink my now aching teeth into the tender spot between his neck and shoulder. We fly back against the wall behind him as I give in to the need of my body. I haven't drank nearly enough before he rips me from his being and slams me into the wall just beside Amaya. Roman stumbling, finally collapses to the floor. I see my opportunity and snatch Amaya's hand and run. Picking her up a few feet from the door that once trapped us, I piggyback her the rest of the way until we're outside.

Sliding her off of me, I look in her big brown eyes. Eyes I now notice seem to be too old for her, as if they've seen way too much to belong to such a young child. "You have to listen to me. If something happens, no matter what is going on, I need you to run.

Run as fast as you can. Get away from here and don't worry about me. Okay?" I stare at her intently hoping she understands. "Whatever you do, though, do not, I repeat, do not mention vampires, biting, or drinking blood. Others either won't believe you and think you're crazy, or they will believe you and come after me and a lot of others to hurt us." She only stares at me. "We aren't all bad, and you telling our secret would hurt us all. That includes me, and I hope by now we're friends." I need her to understand how important this is, but I don't want to put her in danger either.

Keeping my back toward the house, I focus only on Amaya. Wood splinters right before two hand-carved French doors fly through the air right at her and I. I push her out of the way into a soft bed of red and yellow daylilies leaving me to be hit right across the back of the head by a large chunk of the wood. Grabbing grass by the handfuls, I try to drag myself out of his path as he strides toward us with his eyes of steel fixated on me.

"Run, Amaya, run," I yell, focusing only on the sound of her shoeless feet high-tailing it out of there. I peer up as he towers over me with a look of consternation on my face. "That's not possible. You can't go out into the sunlight." I say, only able to gawk with wide eyes.

"Says who?" he scoffs.

"But … you … you're an Ancient One, right?" I finally sputter out.

"Yes," he flouts.

"Then it isn't possible. This isn't possible. I heard the stories." I say, still trying to skirt away from his intended path.

An upturning of his lips shows his amusement. Roman squats down by my ear and whispers, "Again, from who?" His soft chuckle sets my stomach uneasy. Everything I know, everything I've been taught was a lie. I have nothing to go on, to believe in, or to use to my advantage. "You are all that I hoped you would be, Alyssa," Roman says as he stands, extending a hand toward me. My refusal to take it only causes him to laugh more. "Very, very good, Alyssa. Never trust an enemy, except … I'm not your enemy." The look of truth in his eyes frightened me even more. If he isn't my enemy, I would hate to see who is.

I stand but fall right back down hitting the ground hard. His memories flowing through my mind at such a speed it knocks me off my equilibrium. Hundreds of years, centuries upon centuries of memories dancing around in my head. Things I don't quite understand but know somehow I should. "Is it hitting you now?" Roman nothing but a dull background noise to what I'm seeing.

Roman sitting around a large pine table with other men and women discussing something I can't quite make out. It's a serious discussion but with bouts of laughter here and there. A fire roars and women serve glasses filled to the brim with red wine, which was more than likely blood, on silver platters.

Suddenly, someone, a boy dressed in plain pants held up by suspenders and white shirt rushes in with news of one of their own being killed by a human. Anger and panic set in as he's told his friend's dead. Attacked by humans after them somehow finding out what he really was. I see Roman rushing through the busy cobblestone streets in his carriage to his beloved's house.

"Abigail, we have to go. The people are working themselves into hysteria. It is not safe here anymore." Roman ever so lovingly grabbing for her hand to lead her away, but she stops him.

"There are monsters roaming our streets. That is not hysteria, that is a fact. They are going to send them all back to Hell where they belong. What could be more safe or sane than that, Roman?" Abigail asks, her eyes questioning.

"Surely you cannot believe all of this?" He asks, hoping she truly didn't feel this way. "Even if it is partially true, you do not believe they are all bad, do you? What if they are not? Who are we to judge?" His eyes pleading, but she's unwavering in her beliefs.

"They are monsters, Roman. Monsters. It is our job to protect what is ours. That is how it is supposed to be. They are the damned." Her eyes wild and set. He nods and walks out, never to see her again. His love turned against him, his friend dead, his whole world turned upside down.

"That's how it all started, Alyssa." Roman's voice pulling me back into this century.

"That's how all what started?" I ask, still a little dazed.

"The refusal to have anything to do with humans. Before that, we tried to coexist. We tried to blend in. We even fell in love and some chose to take them as their spouse. Humans started the war because Alexander chose the wrong one to love. Her name was Miriam. It was later discovered her father caught them in an intimate moment and saw his fangs. He told everyone Alexander was an animal and tried to kill his daughter. Her father told the other humans your grandfather tried to bite her and drink her blood. In retaliation, we killed him and left him on display for all to see. His name was Michael." Curling his lip, he asks, "Do you know what Michael means?"

Shaking my head, I reply, "No. What?"

"He who is like God." He sneers with a look of disgust on his face. "And so … the war began."

"What happened to Miriam?" I ask timidly.

"I don't know. After we found out it was her father who started all of this, we focused on him and the others who killed Alex. She slipped away, and now we know why. Don't we?" he says, looking me up and down.

"I don't understand any of this." Shaking my head, I was still sitting on the cool grass under the shade of the line of red maple trees.

"You will, Alyssa, you will."

"So, what does this all have to do with me?" I don't understand how I have anything to do with this at all.

"You are Alex's family. His blood courses through you. That is why you are so special. That is why you are able to do all that you can. You are from an Ancient One, Alyssa. The original untainted blood courses through your veins." Seeing Roman stare at me, trying to gauge my reaction, sets my stomach uneasy again. "You deserve to take your rightful place by our side. Make no mistake, you will have to earn it, Alyssa. It won't be handed over easily." What rightful place? What was talking about?

Unsure of the part Roman expects me to play, I try to call for Dante. He has to know what Roman's thinking and how exactly I fit into all of this. Again all I hear is silence. He hadn't answered me before, but I thought maybe now, being outside, he would.

"He can't hear you, Alyssa. I have forbidden it. Obstructed it, if you will."

Narrowing my eyes, I ask, "Why? Why would you do that?"

Romans eyes dance excitedly as he says, "I had to test you. I had to see if you would live up to everything I expected from Alex's descendant."

I purse my lips pushing myself up off the hard ground. Keeping my eyes locked onto his, I intend on showing him just exactly what I'm made of and how I have absolutely no fear of him.

My voice grows in strength as I say, "You're telling me this was all a test?" I can feel the anger rising in my body, and I clench my fist to calm myself as best I can. "And when did you decide to put me through this test of yours, Roman? How long have you known about me?" I scowl at him with a low growl coming from somewhere deep and foreign within me.

With a snake-like smile he says, "Once I bit you, I knew. I could see it in your blood. I can see things about you not even you yourself know. That was the only single reason I did not kill you right then and there. I was going to. Trust me, I wanted to, but once I saw that, I knew I couldn't. I knew you didn't know about it, so I decided to put you through a little series of tests. I needed to know what you were capable of doing. I wanted to see if you were as useless as the other mixed bloods or if you took after your great, great, great, well you get the idea, grandfather's side of the family." A faint hint of a smirk appears as he says, "Now I know. You are so much like him, Alyssa. More than you know. Much more than I would have ever thought." Crossing the distance faster than I can blink, he looks down at me staring into my eyes as if delving deep into my soul. I turn my head to break the uncomfortable gapeonly to have him lift my chin and force it to resume. "It is your duty. You must uphold your family's name." His cool breath stings my face as his intense, frighteningly glacial eyes hold onto mine.

"How am I supposed to uphold my family name?" My voice so soft and low it is barely audible.

With Roman's finger still holding my chin, I'm not sure if I can't or won't break the resolute hold his eyes have on mine. Finally, he releases my eyes as he walks away saying, "I'm not sure yet, but I don't believe in coincidences. You were brought to us for a reason. The fact it happens to be now leads me to believe there is more to it than you or I know at the moment."

Kat always said she wasn't sure what made her look at me that night. She never understood what caused her to go against her own convictions and help me, but she said it was as if she was pulled toward me. There was something different, something special about me, and it was undeniable. Was it this? Was it that I was meant to do this? To help a civilization in which I knew nothing about? Was my ancestor's blood so strong and powerful it could pull others to me just because it coursed through my veins? Does Kat know who I really am? If so, why didn't she tell me? I doubt it considering she wasn't even entitled to know most of the truths regarding the Ancient Ones.

"What was he like? My great, great, great grandfather? Why was he worth starting a war with the humans? I'm sure others had been killed by them, why was he so special?"

I hope if I figure out the answer to that, perhaps it can help me understand why I've always felt like somewhat of an outsider. Thinking back, I've always felt a little lost. Not quite like everyone else. I had a few close friends, but I was never what you would consider popular. David had my heart from the beginning, and I thought I had his. I longed to be around others, but still felt alone even when I wasn't. Was it because I was always different and never truly like anyone else? Is that why Nick and Dante felt so drawn to me?

Roman cuts me off mid-thought. "I will tell you all about him, but first we should go. The girl is gone, and there is no telling when the others will come here searching for us."

Chapter 22

Being back at Dante's house gives me a sense of safety. The crisp, clean, pine-scented air cleanses my lungs as I inhale long and deep, and the sight of the snowcapped mountains put my mind at ease. The rising sun sends strokes of colors whisping across the sky as if it were painted with watercolors by a delicate hand. The sound of forest creatures waking and scuttling around searching for food made the picture even more surreal. If I had to imagine Heaven, I'm not quite sure how it would compare to the sight my eyes behold at this moment.

"What did you do to her, Roman?" Dante demands to know, furious at my appearance. Rushing to the kitchen, he warms a few bags of blood and hurriedly pours them into a glass for me. "Here, Alyssa, drink." Holding the glass forcibly up to my lips for me to sip, I gently place my hand on his slipping it away from his grip. The concern his eyes hold for me is warming, and I can't help but smile at him lovingly. Narrowing his eyes at my appearance while looking me over, Dante hardens his glare as he turns it back onto Roman. "What were you thinking, Roman?" Dante's hands turn white under the pressure of him fisting them, and his jaw tightens as he speaks. Whether it be from fear or respect, I can't tell, but he doesn't make a move. The desire he has to lambast Roman is apparent, but instead he chooses to control himself.

It's obvious Roman senses it as well by the way a smug smile slides across his lips, and just as quickly he turns it into a scowl before saying, "I was thinking I needed to do what you were supposed to do, Dante. Or did you forget? We sent you after her. We gave you a job to do, and you failed miserably. Dare I ask why?" Roman's words dripping with accusations caught me off guard as if any reason would be dirty or tawdry.

Dante's jaw clenches even tighter as he sucks his teeth trying to push down the rage encapsulating him. I feel anger mounting inside him, just about to boil over when I decide to interject and try to diffuse the situation. "I'm right here, and I don't like to be spoken about as if I'm not." I look back and forth staring at both of them.

Dante nods but continues to hold his stare on Roman as he digs his nails into the palms of his hands. "What job were you sent to do, Dante?" With my eyes puzzled and my brow crinkling, I stare at him waiting for the answer.

"What?" He looks away from Roman in confusion at me.

"What job were you sent to do?" I restate my question again frustrated at having to repeat myself. Curling his lips, he shifts his eyes toward Roman and lets out a low growl. That smile just continues to tug on Roman's lips.

"Yes, Dante. What job were you sent to do?" Roman was having fun at the thought of him coming between us, his words causing me to doubt Dante and his intentions. That isn't the truth. That wasn't it at all. I know that, and I hope Dante does, as well. I only want to figure out what's going on. I'm sick of not knowing what I'm involved in or what pertains to me. This, I deserve to know.

"I was sent to kill you. Roman ordered it, but I couldn't. You were different. I told you that. There's something about you, and ..." His eyes shift back to Roman again not wanting to say it in front of him.

"And?" I prod with eyebrows raised. I want to hear it. I need to hear it. I want Roman to hear it. I'm not sure why, but it's as if the validation of it being said in front of Roman will make it real. If he truly does believe he loves me, then he'll say it.

"And ... I fell in love with you. I told you this already, Alyssa. I don't know why. Sometimes there is no reason why. It just happens." When the words flow from his lips to my ears, my body warms from the inside as my heart pounds wildly. His fingers stroke my sunken in cheek cautiously. Their warmth penetrates my skin as they graze so effortlessly from my cheek to my chin, then my lips. Their warmth. Normally he's the same temperature as I am, but now he feels warmer. How close to death had I actually been?

"How touching," Roman bellows, clapping his hands together for nothing more than sheer dramatic effect. "Did you fall in love with her before or after you bit her? Go ahead, be honest now."

I shoot a confusing glance at Roman then settle my gaze on Dante. "What does that matter?" I ask, still looking at both of them.

Roman glances at Dante. When Dante refuses to answer, Roman purses his lips and explains, "Well you see, my dear Alyssa, the moment he tasted your blood he saw exactly what I saw. He saw your lineage and knew the same things I now know since biting you. Your importance. Your strength." Focusing in on Dante, he continues, "He knows how valuable you are. So, if he supposedly fell in love with you, I am left to wonder why. Aren't you?" Tilting his head letting the blond locks fall over his cement colored eyes, he catches my eyes as they move toward Dante.

"Dante?" It can't be so. My eyes beg him to tell me it isn't. My heart sinks to think he could be so callous as to use love against me for his own gain. But it makes no sense if he's on their side as Roman has pointed out repeatedly. He works for them, so why use that? Why lie about it? And if it's all true and his love is nothing more than a ruse, then what would he have to gain from it?

"Power, Alyssa. What he has to gain is power. Dante knows how important your bloodline is. How much power it holds. He's greedy. When he bites you, he grows stronger," Roman answers my thoughts as if I spoke them aloud.

"Shut up, Roman. He's lying, Alyssa. It has nothing to do with that. It's about you and me. Nothing else." Dante tilts my chin up so our eyes meet. His pouty lips pressed together, eyes willing mine to believe him.

When I'm finally able to break the hold between us, I glance at Roman and say, "Tell me about my great, great, great, however many I need to add, grandfather."

"Not about that, Dante? Really? That has yet to be proven."

"Roman," Dante's voice is a hoarse, agitated growl.

"I would watch myself if I were you, Dante. Now, about your lineage, Alyssa. Let's drop the great, great, great and just call him your grandfather, shall we? Your grandfather, Alexander Wyatt Campshire, was a great vampire. He was a vampire of honor, integrity, loyalty, and most of all, compassion. Too much compassion for those who were unworthy of it if you ask me. He was a dear friend to me and helped make most of the rules in which we followed until his death. We followed his lead on being merciful to the humans. He foolishly believed we all could coexist; humans and vampires. Under his influence, we stopped feeding on humans

184

as much and switched to other means. We fed on animals and those who were already dying. It was a blessing, an easier death for some, and they welcomed it willingly. We mingled amongst them as if we were one of them and welcomed a chance to spend a long happy life with a human if we fell in love. If we did fall in love and marry, those were the few we divulged our greatest secrets to. We only turned those we chose to make a life with and only if they were accepting and wanting of it. Alex believed one day we would all be able to live together harmoniously and that humans would accept us. That thought led to his demise."

Roman turns sharply, the memory is too painful for him to remember. Gliding over to the oversized windows, he peers out into the never ending forest. Running his long, slender fingers through his mane, he drops it to his side before beginning again. "After his death, we changed it all. All the rules. We no longer trusted humans. No longer empathized with them. Why would we?"

I look over at Dante stretching my hand out for his. I let him lead me over toward the soft leather couch and burrow into him as we listen to details I doubt even he has heard.

"How could we trust them? They killed Alex. Alex, the most human-like of us all. He identified with them and tried to do right by them. He loved their humanity and tried to save them. He accepted all their faults and flaws and tried to bring peace. And, in the end, they took his life. And for what? For loving one of them?" Roman lets out scoffing noise of disgust. Turning toward us just as sharply as he turned it away, Roman narrowing his eyes at Dante, asks, "Do you see why there are rules? Do you see why the rules must be followed? Why the rules must be obeyed? It is the lack of obedience which has led us here to this precarious situation in which we find ourselves now, or have you forgotten the rules you were appointed to uphold?" Roman slams his fist into his hand, and Dante's jaw contracts and his back straightens as Roman snarls the question at him.

Feeling uncomfortable, I move from Dante's side making my way into the kitchen. I fix myself another glass of the red goodness and listen attentively as the two of them berate each other.

"No, I did not forget my duty, and I also did not turn her or any of the ones that have caused this. Need I remind you of that?" Dante's words bitter and barbed. He rises to meet Roman's eyes.

"No. You did not turn her, but you did turn Katarina. Did you not?" Roman hisses at Dante.

What did Kat have to do with any of this? She has never, as far as I know, hurt anyone. She doesn't have anything to do with the human or vampire world at all. She always stays to herself, and now I'm starting to see why.

"Katarina was turned by you, and she, in turn, turned her. Did she not? So obliviously she doesn't have a problem with going against the rules either. The chain of events is what I am speaking of, Dante. One thing leads to another which leads to another. Humans cannot handle the power in which we possess and can give to them. They are ruthless, selfish, and baleful." His disdain for humans being turned and for humans period is blatantly clear, even more so than Dante's. For someone who holds my family's name in such high regard, he doesn't seem to approve of me at all.

"Yes, I turned Katarina, and yes, she turned Alyssa. May I add, had Katarina not turned her, you would never have known of Alyssa's existence or of Alex's blood living on." Raising a brow, Dante's point is valid and truthful.

"One does not make the other acceptable. Rules are rules, and they are in place for a reason." It was clear Roman would not be swayed.

I clear my throat pointing out the fact I'm still here, but I doubt either one really cares right now. They both turn. "Again, I'm still here and can hear everything you're saying, if that matters to either of you at all." Dante shakes his head as Roman continues to stare blankly at me. "It's obvious, Roman, you hate humans and can't stand the fact I was turned. So how am I supposed to help when you don't want anything to do with me?" I stand there, hand on my hip, waiting to hear his reply. Roman doesn't even flinch at my question.

Turning back casually toward the window, he says, "I do not agree with the means which have led you to us, but I do appreciate your ancestry. I'm not sure how, but I know you're here for a reason. I'm just not sure what that reason is yet."

Roman's voice was sure and strong, and I found myself believing him. I'm not sure how I'm supposed to help but deep within my heart, I know I am. Was this why I was born? I never thought of myself as having a purpose to my life. I thought we all are born, live and then die. I never thought there was a higher purpose, until now that is. Perhaps there is a higher purpose for us all. We just need to find it, discover it.

Regardless of what Roman says, I know he still cares about humans. I learned many things through his blood. Such as, he chooses not to feed on them still and, in the wake of things, seems to still be trying to protect them. But I have to ask myself why? Why continue to follow rules that were established to protect the humans? If he detests humans so much why does he care what the mixed bloods do to them?

"Why indeed, Alyssa, why indeed. Unfortunately, you're correct in your assumptions. What Alex instilled in me all those years ago has still endured through all these trials and tribulations. It's not that I care what happens to the humans, it's simply I don't want our kind discovered. If bodies are left, evidence found, we will be exposed, and that helps no one."

"First off, please stop reading my thoughts. Second off, why do you hold my grandfather in such high reverence? What did he do that was so great?"

His hands tremble just a touch. So slight, in fact, that if I weren't looking for it, I would have missed it entirely. Placing them behind his back, his hard gaze regains my focus. "He saved my life once." Dante's eyes widen. Roman stiffens his stance and catches my hand in his. "Alyssa, we need you. I need you. We are being extinguished. Someone is hunting us, maybe you'll be the one to put an end to it and save our kind." I look down at his hand cocooning mine, his touch not quite as warm as Dante's. His fingers are slenderer and smooth, though.

The one thing I wasn't told before was why me. Neither he nor Roman explained to me why I'd been targeted. Why Dante was sent after me specifically. "Why, Dante? Why were you sent after me? What did I do to cause you to be sent to kill me?" I slip my hand from Roman's swallowing hard waiting to hear his response, unsure if I want to know the answer now.

"That is what I do. I kill those who choose not to follow the rules, and I was sent to kill you." Dante already told me this once before but it still hurt hearing the words trickle out of his mouth as if it were nothing. "Roman had been tracking you since you were turned." His voice mechanical and matter-of-fact.

"Why?"

"Because I turned Katarina. Like he said, we aren't supposed to turn humans, and I broke that rule. The only rule I have ever broken, I might add," he says, turning a glacial glare to Roman. It softens when returning to me. "You were acting erratic and out of control. You were killing off humans, at a rapid pace I might add, and it was becoming noticeable. Also, you were making friends and relationships which you shouldn't have been with humans. Nick in particular. Not only that, but you told him what you are. All those things are against the rules. You were breaking every single rule there is, Alyssa. I thought perhaps if I lured you away from him, from that behavior, from that life, you could be saved. I never fully informed Katarina of all the rules. I felt it unnecessary considering she stayed pretty much to herself, but when she turned you it caused a ruckus. Turning Katarina was a mistake, and I didn't want to take more away from her than I already had. Roman didn't give me a chance to tell him what I'd seen when I bit you before he snatched you while I was gone." Dante turns an ice cold stare toward Roman once again.

Smiling Roman says, "Had you told me what you found out instead of keeping her shacked up here with you, for however long it was, we would not have had that problem, now would we? You had plenty of time to tell me, and you chose not to. How long were you two held up here anyway, Dante?" Roman glances around the room before fixing his stare on me.

"Are you jealous, Roman?" Dante sneers.

"You flatter yourself, Dante. As if you could keep something away from me if I truly wanted it." The two men circle each other, eyes wild.

Turning the focus, I ask, "Why does it matter? Do you want me dead, or am I supposed to stand beside the Ancient Ones you keep talking about because I'm getting really confused here?"

"If I wanted you dead, Alyssa, you would be," Roman says, his voice cold and calculated.

"Then why does it matter how long we were here for? You want me to, as you put it, earn my rightful place amongst the Ancient Ones, correct?"

"Yes."

"Then can someone please explain to me what an Ancient One is, considering it might fall upon me, at some point in time, to save them?"

Dante clears his throat, grabbing my attention. "Your bloodline is a very special one, Alyssa. It dates back to the first of our kind. Your grandfather was turned by the original vampire himself. The one who fathers us all chose your grandfather to continue his legacy. Each person he chose has an ability within them. Those abilities are what keeps us safe and alive. They are what give us the power and the line of succession to the throne, one might say." Dante says.

"Throne? You have a king and queen?" I question.

"Sort of. The bloodline closest to the original vampire is the one who's in power."

"Okay? Who was in power after the original vampire? I mean, if he turned them all, then they were all the closest, correct?"

A smooth, alluring smile slides across Dante's lips, and my heart skips a beat.

"You're correct in that assumption if it had been the original that bit them all, but it was not he who turned them. He only turned your grandfather. Your grandfather is the one who turned the rest. Between the ones he turned, it goes to the one whom he bit first," he says with that seductive smile still planted on his face.

"Okay. I get it, but what does all of that this have to do with me?"

"His blood courses through you. You may have been born human, but you've always had vampire in you. You are his descendant, and therefore, in line to take over."

"What? Wait. No. I can't take over. Not me. Not right now. Maybe not ever." I shake my head trying to shake out the words Dante just uttered, but I can't. So fear takes over instead.

"You don't have to, Alyssa." Roman interjects, casting a displeasing glance at Dante.

189

"But Dante said …"

My sentence is cut short by Roman as he says, "Dante is not an Ancient One. He doesn't make the rules. He only enforces them. If you choose to not accede the throne, you would still be a very vital asset to us. No one would think any less of you."

The sickly, sweet smile planted on his boyish face makes me nauseous. His gray eyes are heavy-lidded, his sun-kissed blonde hair tousled, and his pointed nose gives a look of superiority to him. His thin lips and five o'clock shadow add to his good looks but give nothing to the lack of sincerity radiating off of him.

"If I choose not to accede the throne, as you put it, who does? Who is next in line to take over then?" Directing my glances between the two, I catch Dante lowering his head.

"Well, I suppose that would be me." Roman's false realization is the epitome of bad acting.

"Is that so?" I ask, acting as much surprised as he did.

"Yes, it is. Roman would continue his reign as he has since your grandfather's death." Dante informs me.

"Is that right? Since my grandfather's death?"

"Yes. He's the next in line after your family. He was the first your grandfather bit."

"And if I choose to take my rightful place since there seems to be issues within the ranks?" I ask, directing it more toward Dante.

"Then he will have to step down."

"I need time to think. I need to go somewhere. Everything is happening all at once, and I don't even have anyone to talk to about it because every one of you has an invested interest in my decision in some way, shape or form. The only one who doesn't is dead. I need him now more than ever, and it's my fault he's dead." I growl as I run my fingers roughly through my hair. "Give me a few days, okay? Alone."

"Okay." Dante's voice is nothing more than a rough whisper of hurt.

"I guess, if I have no choice." Roman is not above letting me know of his displeasure of my decision.

"No, you don't. I just want to go back to being the normal, dysfunctional girl I was before."

"There is no going back, Alyssa."

"I know that, Dante. I know. I'm going to go. Give me a few days."

Kat was in Chicago, but I need New York. Maybe I would call her once I made it there, although she had an invested interest in my choice, as well. God, I hate feeling like this. Now I truly am completely and utterly alone.

Chapter 23

The townhome sits just as empty now as it was the day I left New York with Nick. Walking through the house, hints of a woody, Mediterranean scent hit my nose, and I realize it's Nick's cologne. I can still smell him. Oh God, Nick, what did I do? The couch deflates underneath my weight as I collapse on it cocooning myself in the blanket from our last night here. Inhaling long and deep, his smell fills my senses, and the tears flow uncontrollably. It was my responsibility to keep him safe. He was my responsibility, and I couldn't protect him. I can't even protect myself, how am I supposed to protect a whole secret society of vampires? I can't, but everything inside me screams Roman shouldn't be either. I don't trust him. I can't trust him. To be honest, I'm not sure if there's anyone I can trust. Kat had to know about me. She saved me yet said nothing. Dante knew and grew stronger with each bite all the while saying nothing. Then there's Roman, who has everything to lose and, not to mention, tortured me relentlessly. Now he asks for my help? Nothing's adding up, and I'm left alone to figure it all out.

"What am I supposed to do?" I cry out as if an empty house could answer me back.

"Follow your heart," Kat's soft voice answers back.

"What are you doing here? I thought you were in Chicago?" I'm not sure whether to be shocked or elated.

"I was. Dante insisted you might need me." She answers, sitting down next to me.

"I don't even know what I need so how can he? I don't know who I can trust anymore, Kat." My eyes well up at the admission.

Hurt rushes over her porcelain face before she quickly gets it under control. "You can trust me."

"Can I? You had to have known who or what I am yet you said nothing to me, Kat. What am I supposed to think?" I shake my head. I want to believe her, but how can I? She told me absolutely nothing.

"What would you have liked me to say, Alyssa? I told you from the beginning you were special. I told you there were things you were able to do you should not have been able to. You were already so scared and afraid. I didn't want to add to that fear. I didn't know what you were exactly just that you were special. I apologize for not telling you, but I truly did have the best of intentions." I know she did. Kat would never purposely hurt anyone, and that's what makes it worse for me. Her sadness washes over me, and I am drained of any resistance I might've had to stay angry at her.

"I know you did, Kat. I'm sorry. I don't know what to do. I don't know who to trust. I don't even know what I'm supposed to do for the Ancient Ones. I have no idea what they want or expect from me. How am I supposed to know what to do if they don't even know what I'm supposed to do? I don't understand what any of this means." I say, my tears flowing freely now.

"I know you're confused right now, but it will all work out, Alyssa. Dante explained what the issues are. I believe he's hoping I may be able to reason with you." Her delicate hand rest upon mine squeezing ever so lightly.

"Well," I say, wiping my eyes and pushing off the couch, "I'm starving. How about you?" I ask, trying to regain control of my emotions and the conversation.

"Yes, I'm hungry. I'll make some calls." With pressed lips pretending to be a smile, she reaches for her cell phone as she walks toward the kitchen.

Resting my head against the cool glass of the French doors, I stare out praying to find the answers I seek amongst the vast array of midnight enveloping everything this dark, ominous night. The darkness gives way to different shapes and sounds encroaching on my senses. Grass gives way to paver stones, trees give way to old style brick and wooden buildings, and quietness gives way to the sounds of people buzzing by and horses clacking down the road. Turning from the view of outside, I, or whoever it is that I am in this vision, walk down a candle lit hall turning sharply into a darkened room. Flicking a flame and tossing it into a darkened pit, the fireplace roars to life as another person enters the room, closing the door quietly behind them. I turn and Dante is in my view.

"What did you wish to speak to me about, Roman?" Roman? This was Roman's memory?

"Alex is becoming out of control. He is too complaisant to the humans. Something must be done."

"What are you saying?" Dante's brows furrowing.

"If this behavior continues, we will all perish. He is making us weak. We must stop him." Roman slams his fist against his hand as his voice rises in anger.

Dante's eyes widen at the divulgement. Taking a step back, Dante finds his way to the corner and pulls over a wooden chair to sit down on. Did Dante and Roman kill my grandfather? No. Oh no. No. It can't be. He couldn't have, could he?

"No." Dante stood and was in front of Roman in an instant.

"What?" Shocked and appalled, Roman couldn't believe his ears.

"I said no. I will have no part in this. I am not your confidant. I am not your friend. I am a protector of the bloodline. He is the bloodline. Alex will kill you when he finds out about your betrayal," he said with eyes hard and cold. A look I've been privileged to never see toward me.

"You are correct. I do not know what I was thinking. It was a moment of weakness. I do apologize," Roman replied facing the crackling fire.

"I will not speak of this to Alex, but if you attempt any harm to him in any way, I will kill you myself." Dante's words were strong and Roman trembled with the utterance of them. Roman's afraid of Dante. That's an interesting new turn of events.

The setting changes again, and now I'm now outside in a darkened field conversing with a man of stocky stature and dark, unkempt hair and clothes. His light eyes lined with wrinkles from a hard life flares with anger. "What do you mean my daughter is being seduced by a vampire? Those creatures do not really exist. It is simply fairytales."

"Oh, they do very much exist, my good Sir. What I am saying is she is being beguiled by a vampire who is going to defile her. You should rescue her before he does the unthinkable. You must hurry while there is still a chance to save her."

Watching as the man rushes off, tripping and falling over his own crops, Roman lets out a loud, boisterous, howl of a laugh that fills the air. Within minutes the small house in the distance is ablaze, and a feeling of gratification overwhelms me.

With outrage overtaking me, I find myself staring into the face of Katarina instead of an image of the past. Did I just see what I think I saw? That son of a …

"Alyssa, are you okay?" Katarina's words stop me mid-thought.

"Yeah. Zoned out for a minute. Sorry," I say, pressing my lips into a forced smile.

"Zoned out is an understatement. I've been watching you move around this room for fifteen minutes now. The blood is here. Would you like some?"

"Yes, please. Thank you."

Katarina's eyes focus back on mine after shoving the red wine box now filled with our food supply back into the refrigerator. Easing onto the chair across from mine, she asks, "What did you see?"

"What are you talking about?" I try to pretend as though I don't know what she's talking about, but she knows me all too well.

"You know exactly what I am talking about. What did you see?" Her curious, narrowed eyes cause me to shift uncomfortably.

"It's hard to explain."

"Try, Alyssa. I may be able to help you, if you'll let me." Her tone sweet yet firm.

"It was before my time. There were images, sounds, smells swirling around in my mind. Things I've never encountered yet I knew them. A time before my own yet I was seeing it as though I was there. I was Roman. It was his thoughts and ideas filling my head. His beliefs fueling me to do things I know are wrong."

A soft gasp escapes her wide open mouth before she forces it shut. "Are you seeing Roman's memories? How is that even possible, Alyssa?"

"I bit him." I shrug, turning and meeting her eyes with my own.

"What do you mean you bit him? It is impossible for a low level to bite an Ancient One." She didn't believe me. It was written clear as day all over her face.

"Well, I did. I started seeing things soon after, but he laughed. It took a while for me to see it, according to him. I didn't know what

195

it was until Roman told me. Now I'm seeing more, and I'm going to rip his throat out."

"Memories are hard to decipher and sift through. You may not have seen what you thought you saw."

"I know what I saw, Kat."

"I'm not saying you didn't see it, Alyssa. I'm simply saying it's hard to decipher through memories sometimes. What did you see?" Her soft hand reaches for mine, but I recoil. Rage boils up inside me again as I think back on everything I saw, heard and seen.

"Roman tried to plot with Dante to kill my grandfather, and when that didn't work, he went to Miriam's father. He ratted out my grandfather. He told her father my grandfather was a vampire. He set him up to die and laughed when he did." I stalk toward the window only able to see my own reflection looking back at me.

Katarina's face appears next to mine, her hand resting gently on my shoulder. "If this is true and we can prove it, he will have to answer to the council. He'll have to pay for the treason he has committed. These are serious accusations; we'll definitely need proof."

"All the proof I have is what I see in my head."

"You look exhausted. Rest. We'll figure out the rest tomorrow. I want you to know you can and always will be able to trust me."

"I'll see you in the morning." I yawn before turning and trudging up the stairs to the seclusion of my safe haven. I didn't acknowledge what she said about trusting her, and I did it on purpose. I'm still not sure who I can and cannot trust.

This night it isn't dreams or nightmares that invade my sleep, it's memories. Memories of different era's, different places and different faces. Roman's memories.

A black and silver silk ball gown and diamond encrusted necklace accentuate the woman's perfect alabaster skin. Her auburn hair is pulled back with curly tendrils framing her long neck and soft features. With piercing green eyes, she scans the room searching, inspecting it, to see if there's danger amongst them. She doesn't see the danger lurking right in front of her.

By the look of the tuxedo's and dresses, I can only guess it's the early nineteen hundreds. A sideways glance in the mirror reveals Roman's sadistic smirk and soulless eyes. Excitement and fear fuel him. This was his first attempt at killing another vampire. He had gotten humans to do his dirty work on my grandfather, but now, now he was going to do it himself. Nerves were starting to get the better of him the more and more he thought of the council. If they found out, he would be dead. She, herself, was a council member.

Margaret was younger than he but almost his equal in every other way. She was intelligent, strong, beautiful, fierce and a stickler for the rules. Margaret, or Maggie as she was lovingly referred to by many including Roman, was Roman's biggest threat as far as power goes. If she wanted to she could give him a run for his money for the position of head council member, if not win it entirely. That was why he plotted this. He was afraid. Just like with my grandfather, Roman needed to be in complete control. He craved complete and utter power.

Pulling her around a darkened corner, she giggled in surprise. Her gentle caressing of his face told she had other plans in mind. It was obvious she cared for him, she trusted him. That was her mistake. Gentle, subtle kisses on her neck turned into one ferocious tear of her throat. His powerful fangs tore into her soft skin ripping out her trachea with one powerful bite. There was no chance for her to scream, no chance for her fight back. There was no warning. Tossing her into a deserted room, he cleaned up in the basin and returned to the party as if nothing had happened. Her sweet blood still coated his tongue as it coursed through his veins giving him a high of power. He wasn't remorseful or saddened. In fact, he was elated and wanted to do it to every vampire in that room. He wanted more.

Roman wasn't caught that time, but it had been close. A poor mixed blood, as they call them, was accused and killed for Margaret's murder. Roman interjected himself early on into the investigation and had a major influence on the outcome. He weaseled his way out of suspicion by casting it onto the poor mixed blood servant of Margaret's. That, in turn, filled Roman with a whole new high. He was now manipulating the most powerful of vampires and getting away with it.

Times raged on and so did Roman's thirst for his own kind. He didn't limit himself solely to women. He targeted the men, as well. Each time growing more gruesome than the last.

The most recent was only a few years before I was turned. A vampire known as Monte was now in Roman's sights. He'd risen to the top due to all of the deaths of the other Ancient Ones. There'd been eight deaths in all. He'd risen to the top because of Roman, and now Roman had him in his sight. His button down gray shirt accented his cerulean blue eyes. His chestnut hair hung low on his back and kept in place with a simple rubber band. Roman wanted this one to be gruesome. He wanted Monte to suffer and he was going to enjoy it. Roman wanted him to scream and wither in pain. He wanted it to be torturous.

I feel the anticipation mounting inside him. I'm him in all of these memories. I know what he wanted, what he planned and how he felt in each and every horrendous moment. My skin crawls but there is absolutely nothing I can do about it. They are Roman's memories. I'm powerless to change any of it now.

"Roman. How are you this evening?" Monte's smile warmed his face.

"I'm good, Monte. You're looking well." The sadistic undertone was transparent on Monte's ears.

"Thank you. You, as well." Monte had no idea what Roman had planned for him.

"After the meeting, you should stay. We should catch up on old times," Roman said, his mouth watering at the thought of Monte's blood coursing through him.

"That sounds fantastic."

And with that, the four of them took their seats. The numbers had dwindled, and there were no more to take the dead's place. The only person capable of creating new Ancient Ones was my grandfather, no other. They would only create mixed bloods because they, themselves, are mixed bloods. No others had been bitten by the original. My grandfather was the only one. He drank the blood of the original vampire, and in doing so, it changed my grandfather's blood forever. He became a true vampire, not a mixed blood. The others were more powerful than the mixed bloods of today. They were bitten by one with the original's blood coursing through him. That gave them stronger powers but not as strong as he and not as pure, either. They're still mixed.

The meeting carried on as planned, but instead of paying attention, Roman's mind wondered to thoughts of slowly bleeding Monte. The pleasure he would get from bleeding him for days, months even, bottling some of his blood for later. Then it turned to visions of him ripping through the flesh of Monte's throat and hearing that last ghastly, blood-curdling scream. I don't want to be here, but I have no choice. I can't get out. I can't escape it. I have to see it through.

Everyone else left, and Monte and Roman sat alone by the roaring fire of Roman's eerily quiet den. Watching as Monte's eyes focused on the glistening white, marble fireplace, Roman saw his chance. Quicker than lighting, Roman had Monte pinned against the adjacent wall before he could blink. Roman's cool hand wrapped around Monte's bulging neck cutting off his circulation instantly.

"What are you doing?" Monte garbled out through the crushing of his larynx.

"What I've wanted to do for years," Roman sneered.

"Why?" Monte's questioning only fueled Roman.

"I'm tired of all of you trying to contest my authority. I'm the one in charge. I'm the most powerful. Alex's death left me the Lord and Master, and I will reign supreme. All vampires will answer to me. No one will be above me. Ever."

Roman sunk his razor-sharp fangs into the tender flesh of Monte's neck. Monte retaliated by digging his nails into Roman's face with one gouging deep into his eye socket. It was Roman's blood-curdling scream that filled my head, not Monte's. Roman tried to block out the pain, but he wasn't used to being challenged. It had been centuries since someone last threatened him. Roman was out of practice and stunned. Monte seized the opportunity, flung Roman off of him, and ran.

Monte had gotten away. That's the reason Roman wants me. He wants me to go after Monte. The vampire had beaten Roman at his own game, and now he can't find him. He knows Monte now has the power to bring him down, and Roman honestly believes if I'm on his side, Alex's last descendant, the remaining Ancient Ones will be as well. Boy is he wrong. I will never be on his side.

Chapter 24

Jerking up, my eyes shift around frantically until I wake enough to realize I'm safe and sound in my own bed. Roman's thoughts, his memories, disgust me. His sick, twisted way of thinking is appalling. Why hadn't he killed me? Maybe it was his desire to torture his own kind, and he was fulfilling it through me. Maybe …

"You're finally awake." Katarina's voice breaks through my thoughts as the smell of the blood she's carrying rouses me from my bed.

Snatching the glass from her hands, I gulp the contents down glancing around for more.

"Slow down, Alyssa. Would you like more?" she asks in her concerned, motherly voice.

"I feel like I haven't eaten in days. I don't know what's wrong with me," I reply, looking at her apologetically.

My hunger's never been this bad with the exception of when I was first turned. Then again when Roman tried to starve me, but now there's no reason for this hunger. I just ate the night before, and I'm definitely not a new vampire. I haven't been for over three years now.

"You *haven't* eaten in days, Alyssa." Her furrowed brows show her concern.

"What? No. I ate last night before I came to bed." Now I'm the one with furrowed brows.

"Alyssa, you've been asleep for days. I came to check on you several times, but you were lost in your dreams. Tossing and turning with an occasional growl. I didn't know what to make of it, and to be quite honest, I still don't." Her voice is filled with worry.

"What do you mean I've been asleep for days, Katarina?" My voice came out sharper than I intended.

"Would you like some more?" Katarina asks while slipping the glass out of my hand.

"Yes, please," I reply, my voice gentler as I follow behind her.

"Oh, I forgot to mention," she says, stopping and turning toward me, "Dante and Roman are here."

"Excuse me?" My heart races at the utterance of Roman's name.

"They said you told them to come here. Alyssa?" Katarina's voice follows me as I dart past her down the stairs.

"Dante," I say, stopping short of running into him.

"Alyssa, have you thought more about what we discussed?" Dante's dark blue eyes bury themselves deep into my own making me lose focus on everything except him.

"Alyssa." Roman's voice pulls me out of the hypnotizing spell of Dante's eyes and back to reality and my hatred for him.

"You," I growl at him.

"Is there a problem, Alyssa?" The serpentine grin splashed across his smug face infuriates me.

"You're damn right there's a problem," I say, my eyes narrowed and lips curled.

"What is going on, Alyssa?" Dante moves directly in my eye line, blocking Roman from all sight before affectionately tucking my hair behind my ear.

Sidestepping him, I shove into Roman sending him smacking into the wall, plaster crumbling around him. Dante and Katarina look on in shock yet neither steps in to interfere. After picking his crumpled mess of a body up, Roman stalks toward me like a lion on the prowl. The lunge from him with his teeth bared frightens me to my core. Inches from my neck, Roman is caught midair hanging a few feet above me. The look of panic is written all over his face this time as I stand frozen in astonishment.

"How did you do that, Alyssa?" Dante's voice both frightened and amazed.

"I don't know. Who says I did?" I reply unable to take my eyes off the hanging vampire.

"Let me down," Roman growls.

"Alyssa, no one else could have done this. You're more powerful than we thought," Dante says still staring at the vampire frozen midair.

"What?" I ask, walking around the airborne snarling vampire.

"We knew you were powerful, but this is incredible," he says while standing slack-jawed at the sight of the still hovering Roman. "We have to go, Alyssa. We have to get out of here. You don't know what he's capable of, what they all are capable of." Clutching my arm, he drags me out of the house and toward the woods. Turning around to make sure I'm keeping up, he stops and asks, "Are you okay?"

"I'm fine. Why?"

"You're bleeding." His brows furrow as he points at my nose.

I wipe my nose smearing the blood in the process. "Why am I bleeding?" I ask, hysteria quickly taking over.

"It has to be the strain of using your powers too much too soon. It'll stop. I hope. We have to keep moving before…" The ground shakes sending us staggering and knocking us both off kilter. "We have to go." His strong hand grabs my arm once again pulling me up off the ground and dragging me away.

"No, Dante. I am not running anymore. This ends here." I stop, planting my feet firmly into the soft, wet ground.

"You don't know what they'll do to you if you go after him. What if he kills you? We need you, Alyssa. I need you."

I can't look at him and say what I need to say. So I avoid his eyes, opting to look toward the house instead. "Dante, if you honestly believe I'll make a good leader you have to trust me. I am going to kill him, and the Ancient Ones that are left won't do a thing about it after they find out what I know." And with that, I dash back toward the house.

Busting through the back door, wood cracks and splinters around me as the glass shatters sending shards flying through the air. Finding Katarina trapped in Roman's clutches stops my heart. Everything around me ceases to exist, and I can only focus on the terrifying screams pouring out of Kat's mouth. His teeth piercing her neck, letting the blood trickle down, was more than I could handle. Rushing toward him, he stops me dead in my tracks by holding Kat hostage in his arms.

"Tsk. Tsk. Tsk. I wouldn't do that if I were you," Roman says, blood still dripping from his fangs.

"And why is that?" Disdain dripping off my tongue.

"Because I will kill her, and you wouldn't want that now would you?" Her quivering broadens his smile.

"Roman, please." Kat's begging excites him even more.

"Shut up," he says violently shaking her.

"If you hurt her, I will kill you." His taunting laugh only infuriates me.

"Roman, what do you think you're doing?" Dante's voice is shaky. He's obviously apprehensive questioning Roman. It's not like before. Roman is now the head vampire, and as a protector of the bloodline, it is Dante's job to protect him. Before he meant nothing to Dante. Alex called the shots. Alex is no longer around.

"Nothing you haven't done in the past. Dare I remind you of how many of our kind you've killed?" Roman's voice cool and calculated.

"It's not the same, and you know it." Dante's voice grows tight and constrained as he still tries to remain respectful of Roman's authority.

"Do I?" Roman's voice never changing its tone.

I shift closer and Roman counters my movements, all the while smiling and laughing. This is nothing more than a game to him. His eyes dance wildly before shoving Katarina out of the way and lunging. Pushing off, we collide midair, tangling and falling hard onto the ground with a thud that shakes the whole house. Snarling, fangs bared, spit flying, I shove his head hard into the ground. Again.

And again.

And again.

A quick flip and he laughswhile pinning me down.

Sinking his fangs into my neck, he pulls back with a satisfied look overtaking his face. "I can taste the power surging through me. Now I see why Dante wanted to keep you all to himself." Laughing continues, "Ahhh … I see you've found out. I was wondering how long it would take you." My blood drips from his mouth onto my forehead like a leaky faucet that won't turn off.

"She was in love with you, and you knew it." The hate spewing from my voice is uncontrollable. I hate him, and now he knows it.

"I didn't know until it was too late. Do not speak of things you know nothing of, little girl." Roman's hot breath on my face nauseates me.

"I'm speaking of things I have seen, Roman. From you, through your eyes, your memories. Don't tell me I know nothing of them. I know what I've seen. Your blood tells no lies. I know what you've done. I know what you did to all of them, including my grandfather. If I don't kill you, they will. Dante has some of my blood. He's already sent it to the Ancient Ones. They will see it all, Roman. Either way, you're dead."

A sadistic smile crosses my lips, and I see my chance. Turning his head to seek confirmation from Dante, I rip through his throat the way I saw him rip through Margaret's. Unfortunately, I'm not as skilled at it as he is, and I miss my mark. It's not a kill bit but it still could prove fatal to him.

Pulling away from me, he crawls over to the wall holding his wound, cowering like a wounded animal.

Laughing, he says, "Do you really think they will accept you, Alyssa? The only reason they tolerate Dante is because I tell them to. Tell them what you want, but then you will never find out what I have for you."

"You shouldn't cower, Roman. It's beneath you." My taunting him with his own words sends shivers down his spine. "I don't want anything from you except your blood pooling on the floor next to your lifeless body." I stagger closer, my own wound still seeping.

"Ah, ah, ah. I wouldn't if I were you. Trust me when I say you will want this." His voice gravelly from the gaping hole in his neck.

"Enough of these games, Roman." Dante moves away from Katarina's side. "What is she talking about? What have you done? What did you do to Alex?" Picking Roman up, Dante slams him up against the wall. All fear dissipated.

"Ah, Alex. You always did favor him didn't you?" Roman has to have something up his sleeve. I just can't figure out what. He knows he's in a losing situation so why is he playing all of these games? Whatever he has, he believes is a game changer. That, I highly doubt.

"He was the bloodline. It was my job to protect him," Dante growls.

"Is that all it is? Or perhaps is it that he took pity on you? A child left alone. Parents dead. To him, you were nothing more than a sniffling nose little brat who would do his bidding. That's it. If you think it ran any deeper, you're sorely mistaken." Roman sneers. Slamming him into the wall a few more times, Roman only laughs. "Yes, yes, yes. Get it all out. The truth hurts, doesn't it, Dante?"

With Roman's weakened state from my bite and Dante's raging fury from the words spewing from Roman's mouth, it didn't take much. With a quick snap, the chair leg breaks off, and Dante rams it through Roman's heart with one violent heave. "Have you seen my secret yet, Alyssa?" With those final words Roman is dead, his body turned to a pile of black ash lying on Katarina's kitchen floor.

Katarina lets go of me and says, "Dante, what have you done? They will kill you."

"Not if Alyssa is telling the truth and knows something, anything that can turn the tables on him. If he did kill Alex, that's more than enough. That's a death sentence in itself. I just did it for them."

Both pairs of eyes staring at me, I'm only focused on the pile of ash that was once Roman. Is that what we're reduced to in the end? A pile of ash? Is that all we are?

"Alyssa?" Katarina's voice doesn't even register with me.

"Alyssa? Tell me you were telling the truth." Dante's touch startles me.

"What?" I ask, snapping back to see a waving glass in front of me.

"You need blood to heal. Plus, you were hungry before you even came down the stairs. Here." Katarina thrusts the glass into my now trembling hands.

With my adrenalin winding down, I can feel the dizziness setting in. Sipping slowly, I lean against Dante as he leads me to the table.

"Tell me you were telling the truth about Roman and what you say you saw," Dante's voice is shaky and full of urgency.

"Yes. Roman told Miriam's father what my grandfather was. He even watched as they burned down the wooden shack, laughing the whole time." How could he doubt me? Why would I lie about that?

"How do you know? What else do you know?" he asks, pumping me for information with his eyes boring into mine, lips pressing into a hard line and his nails digging into his palms. He is a nervous mess.

"I bit him, Dante. I bit him when I was trying to escape. You know, when he was torturing me. I saw it all. He killed Margaret and other Ancient Ones. He tried to kill Monte." My voice rising. All the feelings of what I saw boiling over and the gaping wound on my neck make it impossible to control my emotions rising up.

"Monte is dead," Dante says, head cocked and shaking at me.

"No, he's not. Roman tried to kill him, but Monte got away. Don't you look at me like that, Dante. I know what I saw. Like I said to Roman, his blood tells no lies." Finishing the glass, Katarina quickly replaces it with another for me.

Wiping the incredulous look off his face, Dante scoots back from the table to join Katarina by the island. "Dante, this has to be made right. I cannot lose her, too." Katarina confides.

"They won't touch her. She did nothing wrong. She's one of them. Technically, she's the last of the true bloodline. Although I'm not sure how she can keep it pure with her being a mixed blood." Their whispers are anything but. I'm not sure if they think my wound is keeping me from hearing, but this, them, isn't helping.

"I can hear you two." Shaking my head, I don't even turn to look at them.

"Honey, Alyssa, I'm worried for you." Kat's soft voice is matched by her gentle hand stroking my hair.

"I know you are. I know, but I'm fine. My only concern now is figuring out what I'm supposed to do." Rubbing my forehead, I move down to my newly healed neck. "I have an idea, just ...shhhh."

Concentrating with all I have, I try to summon Monte. Closing my eyes and taking few deep breaths out of habit, I focus. Remembering his cerulean blue eyes, his silky chestnut hair and his soft sandalwood smell, I call his name in my mind.

'Monte. Monte, my name is Alyssa. I'm Alex's descendant. Please. Things are happening, and we need your help. I know what Roman did. I saw it all.' I can feel him. He's trying to fight it, but I feel him. *'Monte, please. Roman is dead.'*

'Leave me be.' His voice shaking.

'Please. Roman's killed almost all of the Ancient Ones. Now that he's dead there is only three. They need you. You and I are the only ones who were able to escape from him alive. If you do it for no other reason, do it for my grandfather. Alex.' I try to stay focused

and not let my emotions get the better of me. If I lose the connection with him now, I'm afraid I won't ever be able to get it back.

'I had no other choice but to run. The power he has, the power he holds, he was going to kill me. If it wasn't by his own hands, he would have convinced the others to do his bidding.'

He didn't need to convince me; I'd seen it all. I know the power Roman had. I know how he abused it. I know Monte's right. Either way, he would have been dead. *'I know. I've seen it, but he's dead now. Can you meet me here? In New York?'* I keep my hopes high, but I can't force him to do anything he doesn't want to do. After all he's been through, I don't know if I would trust anyone anymore, either.

'I'll meet you there. I can see where you are, but if you're lying to me, I will kill you.' His normal calm tone turns dark, and I believe his threat.

'I'm not lying to you. I promise.' And with that he was gone. "Monte's coming here."

The glass filled with crimson liquid drops from Dante's unshakable hands at my revelation of that information. "Why do you say that?" Dante asks anxiously.

"Because I just spoke to him. Well, in his head. You know what I mean. I told you he was alive. I'm really tired. I'm going to lie down." Dante and Katarina's eyes follow me as I retreat up the stairs back to my sanctuary of a room.

This has to work out. Justice has been served for the wicked Roman did, but was he right? Would the Ancient Ones not accept me? Do I care if they don't? I don't, but I know Dante does. And what secret did Roman think would stop me from killing him? It doesn't matter, it wouldn't have stopped me. Nothing would've. The atrocities he committed were more than enough to seal his fate. My body is exhausted, but my mind won't allow me to sleep. Even with all the evil I know Roman did, seeing him as nothing more than a mere pile of ash has left me shaken and my stomach in knots.

I can hear the soft murmurs of Kat and Dante talking, but I blur it out. I've had enough for one day. I've had enough for a lifetime. If that's what power can do to a person, I don't want anything to do with it. The want and need for power perverted Roman's senses. It overtook his thoughts and corrupted his mind. There was no coming back from that with Roman. I don't want to suffer the same fate.

My soft bed lures me to it, silently calling my name. I abide and wrap myself in the protection of the soft, silky sheets letting them slide across my body. Hugging my pillow, I close my eyes praying for an end to this horror of a day. At last, I slip silently into the sweet escape of my own dreams.

Chapter 25

The sun blazes high in the sky and pours in through my window. There's no escaping it. The crimson sheets can't block it out, not even my pillow can filter it out completely. Having no other choice, I relinquish. I roll out of bed, grumbling and stomping my feet all the way down the hall to the bathroom just to let the sun know how much of an annoyance it really is to me today.

The steaming water beads down my face and drips off to join the water swirling around my toes and down the drain. Smiling at the remembrance of the beautiful dream that visited me last night, I close my eyes hoping to relive it once more before it disappears into the oblivion of forgotten happiness.

Nick's face greets me. His eyes warm me as his smile excites me, that devilish upturned smirk of his gets me every time. His smell, although now faint in my memories, fills my nostrils awakening my every sense. His warm, strong hand caressing my face so tenderly as his other pulls me ever so close. His hot, sweet breath on my neck sends goosebumps up my arms, and the feel of his full lips pressed hard against my own sends pulses of electricity coursing through my body.

"Alyssa, you're finally up. Monte, he's here now. Are you going to be much longer?" Kat's voice is a little too chipper for me, especially considering she just ruined the best dream I've had in ages.

"I'll be out in a minute." My gruffness must have caught her off guard because she sneaks out without another word.

Thoughts of Nick have crossed my mind every day since the night his life was cut short by that scumbag of a human Alonzo. I'm still trying to figure out where I went wrong, what I missed in seeing inside Alonzo's demented little mind. There still are no answers to be found for those questions, and that only ticks me off more. Thoughts of what was and what could've been with Nick still invade my head and my heart. And then having my perfect dream ruined by Kat's interruption cutting my escape from reality short doesn't help matters.

The fogged handle is cool in my hand as I turn it off. The remainder of the water swirls around and disappears down the drain. Squeezing my hair, I watch as the water pours off before grabbing a towel and wrapping myself in it. My finger draws two dot eyes and a smiley mouth on the steamed up mirror which I quickly wipe away. Doing the ritual I have done many times before, I stare at the perfect looking monstrosity I have become. This is my reality. There is no going back now, only pressing on. Speaking of pressing on, Monte is downstairs waiting, and I have to meet him. He's the only one, besides myself, who's beaten Roman. Drying off, I throw on a pair of faded jeans and a white button-up shirt and head down.

"Here she is," Kat chirps.

"Alyssa, we have company." Dante's clenched jaw shows the tension he feels or is that me actually feeling his emotions again? Either way, he's under a tremendous amount of stress.

"I was told." Glancing at Kat, she shrugs innocently.

"So, you are the one I spoke to, I presume?" Monte's voice cool and calm, just as I remember it from Roman's memories.

"Yes. Thank you so much for coming. We really do have a lot to discuss." My voice becomes more refined and self-assured than even I, myself, have ever heard it sound.

A pleasing smile crosses his lips lighting up his soft, warm eyes. He looks somehow kinder than he did in Roman's memories. Gentler, more fragile, but the one thing I've learned in this new life of mine is to never underestimate anyone. Within each one of us is a dangerous killer. That predatory trait is never too far from the surface.

"So, you are the great Alexander's descendant?" There's no sarcasm behind his words, and I find great comfort in that.

"Yes. A few generations or so down, but yes."

We all gather and sit around the kitchen table as if by instinct. Our own private meeting, if you will. Kat, and all her mothering ways, brings glasses full of the red goodness to us as if she knew what we would want. As she sits them down, I catch a glimpse of an interchanging of smiles between her and Monte. He graciously stands and like a gentleman pulls her chair out for her. A sweet smile slides across her lips as she tucks her head down, but I know what that means. She finds him attractive and, even more so, appreciates the gesture long ago lost among men.

"You say he's dead. What do you propose we do now?" Monte asks while taking his own seat again.

"Well, I propose we go to the Ancient Ones. We tell them what a monster Roman was and how he killed my grandfather, tried to kill you, and did kill other Ancient Ones. He was out of control and they were clueless about it all. That, in itself, should make us practically heroes to them. We figured it out. We, well, should I say Dante, did what they should have done centuries ago. There will be no reason for punishments. Not to Dante for killing him, not to you for running, and not to me for well, all that I've done. Kat, she's never really committed any acts to be punished for except for turning me, so we're all in the clear." My blunt and matter-of-factness leaves everyone speechless. They do nothing more than nod and sip on their blood in unison. What else is there to say, really?

"I wouldn't mention they were clueless but other than that I believe you to be right. To the Ancient Ones then. Do you know how to reach them to call an assemblage?" His eyes dart between Dante and I.

"No. Not a clue." I shake my head.

"Roman did that. I had no right to talk to them according to him." Dante presses his lips firmly together.

"Well then, I see it's left to me to persuade them to come here. It shouldn't prove to be too hard. I am supposed to be dead, so hearing from me just may do the trick." An easy smile tugs at his lips, and a soft giggle escapes Katarina.

Hands folded on the table and looking blankly out the window past Dante, Monte seems frozen. I can't help but wonder if that's how I look when talking to someone in my head? Do I seem as spaced out as he does right now? I must because I remember Nick waving his hand in my face when Dante was talking to me in my head. There I go again. Nick. Dante's comforting hand gently squeezes my knee under the table. Placing my hand on his, I return the squeeze and interlace our fingers. Kat, focusing solely on Monte, is an easy read, and this time, she doesn't have to hide the fact she wants to get to know him. He's one of us. He is a very powerful one of us.

Ten minutes pass before Monte snaps out of it and rejoins us. Eager to know what was said, we wait staring in anticipation like a bunch of five-year-olds waiting for dessert. Twiddling his fingers nervously, he says, "They're on their way. Imagine their surprise hearing from me after all these years of believing I was dead."

"I can only imagine," Katarina says looking on in admiration of him. "Would you like a tour? Perhaps I can show you to a room so you may freshen up or relax and take a short nap. You must be exhausted."

"I am a bit," Monte admits.

Disappearing up the stairs whispering in soft murmurs, Dante and I are left alone for the first time in what feels like a lifetime. With our hands still intertwined, he shifts out of his chair pulling me up to him. His muscular arms wrap around me, and I relinquish to the strength of them. All the burdens I've been carrying slowly dissipate with the feel of his body pressed against my own. His heartbeat against my chest lulls me, and a sigh of relief escapes my lips.

"Is it really all over now?" My voice riddled with uncertainty as my tear soaked eyes look up at him for answers I'm not so sure I want to hear.

"I don't know. I hope so, but the one thing I do know is if it's not, we can beat anything that comes our way as long as we're together." Gently pushing the hair out of my face, his velvety kiss dispelled any and all thoughts running through my mind.

I needed that. I need the distraction, the peace of mind. I need him. Surrendering to his will, my kiss deepens and hardens with every second that passes. Dante's kisses wane as mine increase in passion. Tearing his lips from mine, he exhales a soft murmur of pleasure before delicately kissing my forehead.

Stunned, I'm unsure of what to do other than follow him as he ambles outside making himself comfortable on the front stairs. Taking a cue from the tug on my hand and the smile on his lips, I make myself comfortable in the space between his legs. The sound of his heart is a melodic beat that continues to keep the chaos in my head at bay. With all the harrowing situations I've managed to find myself in lately, it's nice to sit and be still for a change.

Seconds turn into minutes that turn into hours. The beautiful sunny day turns into a bustling night full of cars and people whizzing by in a hurry. Dante and I never moving once, we simply sit and enjoy the tranquility of it all. The soft pull of my hair being interwoven between his fingers relaxes me to a point of drowsiness.

"Are you ready to go inside?" His deep voice by my ear brings a sleepy smile to my face.

"Yeah. Let's see what Kat and Monte are up to. You know she likes him right?" I angle myself to face him and laugh at the dropped jaw I receive.

"No. What? How do you know that? Did she say something?" There was no hiding his protectiveness of her. Why was he so protective of her?

"No, she didn't say anything, but all you have to do is look at how she is around him. The smiles, giggles, and especially, the looks. It's quite obvious. Are you jealous?" I jest.

"No," he spits out quickly.

"I'm joking, Dante. Are you ready?" I say, standing and brushing myself off. I reach my hand out for him and pull him to his feet.

The house is aglow with candles, and the fireplace is alive with pops and crackles in the living room. This time, it's him following me as I glide down the hall. I hold back to allow the view to be seen by Dante's own eyes. Katarina snuggled in next to Monte, him quietly reading to her while she turns the pages for him. It was quite a scene; the fire in the background, them snuggling, the leather bound book and two wine glasses, that if not examined too closely, looks full of red wine. In fact, it's a perfect scene I secretly am extremely jealous of.

A few minutes pass before we're discovered. "What are you two doing standing there? Come, sit. Monte's reading Shakespeare." Kat pats the seat next to her for us.

"Okay." Sitting opposite of Monte, I lean into Dante laying my head on his shoulder.

Listening to the words of one of the greatest writers in history flow from Monte's mouth is a pleasure. The eloquent and sophisticated speech of the Capulet's and Montague's soothes my ears as he reads without hesitation, smooth and fluid as if it's his own natural speech.   Thinking back, I realize it probably is. Watching Kat's face, I can imagine her like this forever. If we get a forever, that is. It's a serene happiness. A completeness. The glow on her face isn't just from the roaring fire.

Hours of laughing and storytelling pass before I surrender to the sleepiness taking over me. With Dante's hand on the small of my back, he guides me up the stairs and an innocent, chaste kiss is given before I retreat to my room. I welcome the slumber I know is coming as I pray for another sweet dream about the one I loved. The one I lost. The one I failed. Nick.

Chapter 26

Bouncing my way down the stairs, I can't wait to start this day. I had yet another wonderful dream and woke with a renewed sense of hope. Things have to work out. There is no other outcome that can happen. Not after all we've been through. All I've been through.

Climbing over the obstacle of sleeping bodies that stayed up until who knows what hour of the night, I navigate my way to the kitchen and heat up a coffee mug of morning goodness. High stepping, twisting and turning, I'm able to make my way out of the house undetected where I can sit on the front stoop watching the morning commuters all hurriedly scurry by. Sipping slowly on the deliciousness, I wonder if that would've been me had I not been turned. Probably. I would have a job or, at least, be in college. I would like to believe I would've had a good balance of studying and having fun, although I must admit the studious side of me probably would've won out. Continuing my leisurely pace of sipping, they all continue on their hurried way to wherever it is they're heading.

Goosebumps line my arms as a knot grows in my stomach. Something's coming. I'm being watched. I can feel it in my bones. I thought the feeling would pass but it hasn't. It's only gotten stronger. Someone or something is watching us, and I have no clue as to why. With me being the youngest, I have no idea what's going on, but maybe the others will have an explanation.

"Dante." I don't even have to shake him. A simple call of his name suffices to wake him.

"What's wrong?" He shoots up, glancing around.

"Someone's watching us. I felt it before but didn't think too much about it. But now it's gotten stronger. I can feel it, Dante. Something's not right." Worry lines his face.

Stilling himself for a moment, he's concentrating, focusing to see if he can sense it as well. "You're right. I can feel it now, too. I don't know why I didn't notice it earlier. Monte. Monte, wake up." Monte's stirring wakes Kat also.

"They're here. The others are here." His eyes aren't even open before he answers Dante's unasked question.

As if on cue, there is a knock on the door. Eyes shifting around, Kat straightens herself before answering it. There are polite hellos and then Monte's name. "Yes. Yes. This way." Kat ushers them in.

A beautiful, tall woman of five feet ten with flowing raven hair enters first. Her soft blue eyes are offset by the flaming red streaks framing her porcelain face. The black lipstick and dark eyeliner only emphasize her paleness. She has the vampire, gothic look down pat.

Her counterparts enter right after her. The other female is a bit shorter at five feet eight and is her complete opposite. Her soft blonde hair and gray eyes look delicate without the use of any makeup. The male resembles the first woman. Short spiked raven hair with tips of fiery red, his deep-set emerald eyes watch all our movements carefully, and his clenched jaw shows he trusts no one in this room. He towers over both of them at what looks to be six feet four inches tall. His strong, athletic build only adds to his attractiveness.

"Monte, it's good to see you again. We've thought for many years you were lost to us." She pushes a red-streaked chunk of hair behind her ear.

"I'm sorry to have worried you, Noble, but as you can see, I'm fine. Roman tried unsuccessfully to eradicate me. I had no other choice. I'm not the first he has done that to, only the first to survive." Monte's soft-spoken tone is met with a smile from her.

"I apologize for being rude. Please, have a seat." Kat gestures for them all to sit. The two females do, but the male stands behind them, arms crossed over his wide chest guarding them against all possible dangers. Maybe he's their bodyguard. It makes sense.

"Thank you. My name is Noble, and this is Willow. He is my brother Eli." The dark haired woman, now known as Noble, waves her hand dismissively at the man behind her. Okay, apparently he's not their bodyguard.

"It's nice to meet you. I'm Alyssa, you know Monte, this is Kat, and I think you may already know Dante, as well," I say, pointing each person out.

"Yes. I've known Dante for many years." Noble cast a sideway smile at Dante. "I must admit we've been observing you all for a few days. We had to be sure this wasn't a trick or trap. We hope this isn't to offensive to you, but I'm sure you understand."

"Oh no, it is fine. We understand completely. We're just happy you're here. We hope there'll be no issues with what happened to Roman." Monte's concern is evident, but he isn't bowing to them either. I think I'm definitely going to like him.

"No. There are no issues regarding him. If what you say is true, which I have no doubt it is, he should have been dealt with long ago. I'm just ashamed we never saw through his facade. That must've been why he made and enforced his rule of no vampire biting another so strictly. He implemented it shortly after Margaret's death. Now I understand why. He would've been discovered. How did you find out, Monte?" Noble's eyes narrow.

"Alyssa." That's good old Monte, short, sweet, and to the point. All eyes turn on me. Thanks for throwing me under the bus there, buddy.

"And how did you find out, Alyssa?" Her tone is sweet, but there's something about the look in her eyes and the underline current of her words that clutches at my stomach.

"I bit him. Twice, actually. Once when I was trying to escape, he was holding me captive, and the second time when he was trying to kill me."

"I see. You must be very powerful to take on Roman." I'm not quite sure how to take that statement. Is it a compliment or an accusation from her?

"Well, you know what they say, desperate times and all." I try to avoid any answers she might be seeking. If I'm too humble, I'm perceived as weak. If I'm too boastful, I'll be considered another Roman. A rock and a hard spot is not a fun spot to be in.

"No. I don't know what they say," Noble says, shaking her head.

"Desperate times calls for desperate measures. When you're put into a bad situation it's fight or flight. To flight, I had to fight." This is becoming uncomfortable. I suck at explaining things, and now I look like an idiot in front of the Ancient Ones. I am putting my foot in my mouth in front of the highest of the vampires, and I can't seem to quit.

"Are you hungry? Kat has some bags of blood if you would like." Monte interjects.

"That would be perfect. Thank you." Willow's voice, silvery and smooth, is refreshing.

"That would be perfect. We're simply happy to have you back, Monte, and now we have a descendant of Alex's. This is a great cause for celebration. Welcome, Alyssa. I hope we will get to be great friends." Noble's sweet smile is laced with something I can't quite put my finger on, but I find myself nodding and smiling back. "Good," she says clapping her hands together, "let's have fun. Business can be dealt with later."

Everyone's smiling, the blood is flowing, and laughter fills the air. Noble is talking with Dante, Monte's holding Kat's hand while listening to Willow tell an elaborate story about a mutual friend of theirs, and Eli is holding up the wall. I know the feeling because I'm not fitting in to any conversation either. I decide to take the opportunity to introduce myself to him. Everyone else is having fun, he should be too. There's no danger here. None of us want to hurt them, so he can relax a little.

"Hi. I'm Alyssa." I smile, but a curt nod is all I receive. "Are you always this standoffish?"

"How would you like me to be?" His toneless question catches me off guard. He doesn't even look at me. He stays focused on the two Ancient Ones he came with.

"I don't know. I'm sorry. I just didn't want you to be left out. I guess that's the way you want it, so, I'll leave you alone."

Walking away, my skin heats and I know Eli's eyes are still on me. I tried to be nice. I tried to be polite. There's absolutely nothing more I can do. Everyone else is enjoying themselves. I can't include someone who doesn't want to be included. Catching Dante's eye, I sneak outside.

Standing on the front porch, I stare out at the setting sun. Orange, pink, blue, and lavender fill the sky as the red sun sinks down in between the buildings. I look back to see Dante standing behind me. I close my eyes taking in a deep breath. A calm takes over me because even though I know there are so many questions left unanswered, for right now, at this moment, our world is right.

As long as we all have each other, we have and can overcome anything that comes our way.

The Bloodline

The Ancient Ones Chronicles

Barbara Hinesley

Keep your eyes out for the next installment in The Ancient Ones Chronicles by Barbara Hinesley. Thank you all so much.

http://www.barbarahinesley.com

https://www.instagram.com/barbara_hinesley/

https://www.facebook.com/BarbaraHinesley01

https://twitter.com/barbarahinesley

www.ingramcontent.com/pod-product-compliance
Lightning Source LLC
Chambersburg PA
CBHW071433260626
47170CB00008B/2695